Beyond the Edge
of the Universe

Beyond the Edge of the Universe

Virgil Renzulli

Copyright © 2001 by Virgil Renzulli.

Library of Congress Number: 2001118217
ISBN #:   Hardcover   1-4010-2548-X
          Softcover   1-4010-2547-1

All rights reserved. No part of this book may be reproduced or transmitted in any form or by any means, electronic or mechanical, including photocopying, recording, or by any information storage and retrieval system, without permission in writing from the copyright owner.

This is a work of fiction. Names, characters, places and incidents either are the product of the author's imagination or are used fictitiously, and any resemblance to any actual persons, living or dead, events, or locales is entirely coincidental.

This book was printed in the United States of America.

Cover design: Patricia Childers.

To order additional copies of this book, contact:
Xlibris Corporation
1-888-7-XLIBRIS
www.Xlibris.com
Orders@Xlibris.com

For Vigi and Theresa

Special thanks to Patricia Childers, Robert Ashton, Danielle Bizzarro, Barbara Jester, Pamela Vu, and Linda Kettner.

Contents

1. Phantom Ship 9
2. Well of Life 26
3. The Outcome 44
4. The Android Bellycold 49
5. The Return of Julian Alfiri 66
6. A Hellish Night on Imrada 77
7. Unholy Allies 95
8. A Hard Offer 107
9. Into The Void 121
10. The Other Side 135
11. Strange Encounters 151
12. Back to Where He Had Never Been 165
13. Assault on The Nemesis 178
14. Nuzalu's Killer 193
15. Showdown 201

1 | Phantom Ship

A small, blue light appeared in the upper left corner of the radar display and slowly moved toward the center of the screen. But Kellan Blake did not notice. After two uneventful years on this military base, Kellan could not imagine that anything threatening, exciting, or even faintly interesting could happen here, especially now when his military obligation was virtually complete, and his ride home, a space freighter, was only 30 hours from blast-off. Instead of monitoring the array of computer screens and radar equipment surrounding him, Kellan was amusing himself during his last night on watch by playing a computer strategy game called Three-Dimensional Gambit Chess. The game was a tradition on the base, passed down from one bored group of Imperial Rangers to the next.

Despite Kellan's inattention to the visual warnings, he should have been alerted to the intrusion of the approaching space vessel by a computer-generated voice. But the audio system had been deactivated long ago, well before Kellan's tour of duty, by a Ranger who considered the voice unbearably annoying and completely unnecessary. This region of the galaxy was hardly a high-traffic area, and the few ships that did come to the desolate moon base that orbited the planet Gondar were scheduled many months in advance. No new arrival—not the occasional interstellar trader or the routine supply ship from home—was expected for weeks.

The blue light crossed one of the inner circumference lines on the radar screen and turned bright yellow.

"Your relief is here, Blake," announced Mike Fencik as he entered the control tower, a circular room lined with thick, triple-insulated windows.

Without moving his eyes from the computer screen, Kellan motioned for Fencik to join him at the console. "I want you to witness this," he said, his voice full of confidence.

Fencik shook his head. "You don't actually think you're gonna beat the computer, do you?"

Kellan, who had been a top student at the Academy and a good athlete, once believed he would be a great success in whatever career he decided to pursue, in science, business, or even politics. But here on this life cul de sac, his optimism had been dulled, and playing computer games had become the primary outlet for what remained of his competitive nature and perfectionist tendencies.

He rotated the 3-D computer display to show Fencik the complete state of the game and said, "I'm closing in on checkmate. If it's the last thing I do here—and it will be the last—I intend to win at this damn game."

"I still say you won't beat the machine."

Both Blake and Fencik were draftees who hated the regimentation of the military and the countless empty hours they spent on this isolated base. Kellan with his close-cropped hair, hard jaw line, and muscular body looked the part of an Imperial Ranger. And although he had what his friends called a "deep side," Kellan was also the base storyteller and one of its better comedians and pranksters.

Fencik, by contrast, was chubby and wore thick glasses, which combined to give him a soft appearance. He was one of the least aggressive and least physically competent of the Rangers stationed on the moon base, and therefore, often the butt of jokes.

Mike Fencik may have been a good sport, but he was a terrible three-dimensional chess player. That did not stop him now, however, from giving Kellan advice on how to complete his game. He leaned close to Kellan, whispering as though the computer might overhear what he was saying, and suggested that Blake advance his queen.

The blip on the radar display crossed another circumference line and turned red.

Ignoring Mike's advice, Kellan used his cursor to move his knight across the multi-layered game board into position against his opponent's king. The computer's queen flashed, then dropped down two vertical levels, and the machine announced "check" on Kellan's king. As he quickly assessed the situation, Kellan realized that he had been lured into a trap that left him only one move from being checkmated, a development that caused Mike Fencik to laugh heartily.

The intruder crossed the innermost line on the radar display, and the red light began to pulse frantically.

Mike slapped Kellan on the shoulder. "Maybe you should quit now."

"Maybe I should," said Kellan as he rotated the three-dimensional game board on the computer display looking for a way out of the trap.

At times Kellan became annoyed with himself for taking this game so seriously, but there was little else to do here. This moon had an unbreathable atmosphere, and its temperature never rose above minus 25 degrees. So the crew rarely left the base, where the only diversions were eating and sleeping; working out in the exercise room, which was why Kellan was more muscular now than when he left home two years before; and searching the Web for pictures of naked women.

The absence of women made life on moon base more difficult than it had to be. No woman had ever set foot here because the Holy Asturian Empire, still very much under the influence of the Church, severely limited the roles women could play in the military. In the earliest days of the Church, key members of the Patriarchy considered women temptresses at best and pure evil at worst. Modern theology was no longer so harsh in its view of women but was still suspicious of interactions between the sexes and almost intolerant of sexual intercourse, which, in its highest form, was supposed to be a joyless act performed solely for the procreation of children. It, therefore, followed that the body was evil, nakedness was shameful, and the sexes, to avoid the temptations of the species' base nature, were to be kept as separate as possible, as they were in school and in the military, even during religious services.

Kellan often thought that the forced separation of men and women fanned, rather than dampened, the fires of curiosity and passion. It was one of the many Church precepts and policies that he challenged, and when he was in one of his serious moods, he searched the Web for information that had not been available in the Church-affiliated schools that he had attended, information that often questioned and sometimes contradicted what he had wholeheartedly embraced as a youth.

The planet Asturias was the birthplace of the human race and the capital of the Holy Asturian Empire. It orbited the Poltare twin-star system, which was located near an enormous blackness on the edge of the galaxy, an entire portion of the sky that was starless, a region that had a firm hold on the imagination, religion, and science of the Asturians. On star maps, this blackness or The Void, as it was called, was shown as a black vertical line on the eastern edge of the galaxy where the number of stars diminished, then disappeared altogether. And this military base was in the last star system in the east, the outpost nearest the blackness, nearest in a literal sense to The Edge of the Universe. In the era before space travel, everyone believed this empty section of the sky was hell, The Void in which lost souls spent an eternity of damnation. Even today, some of the Patriarchy, as well as many of the steadfast members of the Asturian Church, still considered it the literal hell.

The Void, however, was actually a galactic cloud consisting of an unknown black matter and of immense proportions, as if a black curtain had been thrown over a part of the universe. The cloud could not be navigated by sight because there was nothing to see or by computer because the cloud was so magnetically charged and unstable that it rendered electronic devices erratic. The cloud was also dense enough to make traveling at anything remotely approaching light speed impossible. There would be too much resistance, too much friction. So even if it could have been navigated, The Void could only be traveled at speeds so slow that it would take an eternity to get anywhere. Nevertheless, more than a dozen robot probes had been sent to explore what was beyond The Edge of the Universe, but none was ever recovered.

The black cloud could not be crossed and was too enormous to go around, and so no one knew what, if anything, was on the other side.

Over the centuries the Holy Asturian Empire had moved out from the Poltare System from planet to planet and star to star away from The Edge of the Universe. The Empire eventually became too large to be effectively governed, and the decline in Imperial power began when a few of the most distant colonies rejected both the Empire and the Church, setting up their own government and abandoning religion almost entirely. The Federated Republics were formed, and in less than 50 years had come to occupy more of the galaxy than the Empire.

The Empire and the Republics were in perpetual competition and at times, outright enemies. It was on the frontier between the two that the bulk of the Empire's military bases were located. Although Kellen did not see how the Republicans could mount any real military threat in this part of the galaxy, it was always possible for them to smuggle in a small force on a neutral trading vessel such as the R'Tani freighter currently docked at this outpost, and so one isolated moon base, this one, was maintained at The Edge of the Universe to protect the Empire's "back door."

The base was small but as technologically advanced as anything in the Empire. It consisted of a single building with three levels: the control tower at the top, a large middle section that housed the crew, and a ground-level section that had four launch pads, one facing each of the cardinal compass points. On each launch pad was an Interceptor rocket, which could function both as a jet fighter and a short-range spacecraft. The Interceptors were somewhat larger than conventional military aircraft and similar in shape except they were sleeker and had more powerful engines. They had black pointy noses, chrome-colored, swept-back wings, and a crew area that could hold four. The only marking on the ships—other than a serial number—was the Imperial insignia: two pale blue stars, tall diamond-shaped stars with flares of blue light behind them. On the left was the star Poltare-Major, and on the right, a third smaller and deeper in the background, Poltare-Minor.

Kellan, stymied by the trap the computerized chess game had placed him in, turned away from the computer screen and glanced up at Mike Fencik, who was waiting for him to make his next and possibly final move. Kellan then examined the entire game board once more and tentatively started to make a move to uncheck his king and buy himself more time when Fencik said, "I think you should call it quits. You have no hope."

Kellan again looked up at Mike, intending to express his annoyance at the comment, and noticed a small, blinking red light reflected in Fencik's eyeglasses. Kellan froze for an instant, then whirled around in his chair toward the radar display. The light represented a space vessel. And it was in quadrant C-9, almost on top of the base.

"Good lord!" shouted Mike, when he too saw the blinking red light on the screen. "What do we do now?"

"Try to raise the ship on the radio," said Kellan, who always performed well under pressure—that is, during the pressure of drills. But this, of course, was different. It was potentially a life-and-death situation. While Fencik went to the communications console, Kellan flipped a switch on the radar computer that lit a display retracing the flight path of the intruder. A straight white line appeared showing that the ship had come from inside the black cloud, from beyond The Edge of the Universe. "That's impossible," Kellan whispered to himself.

"Do you think it could be one of ours?" asked Mike, who had not heard Kellan's comment.

"Probably," answered Kellan as matter-of-factly as he could. "I don't see how it could be Republican. They wouldn't attack with a single ship." Nor did it seem likely that a vessel had crossed The Void from some other universe on the other side into their own world. But whatever the case, Kellan knew that he had been too slow in discovering the intruder. "Get on that radio," he said to Fencik. "Give them a warning.

While Mike fitted the radio headset over his ears, Kellan hurried to the weapons control panel, where he armed one of the beta-laser satellites and instructed it to locate and track the vessel in quadrant C-9. After a seemingly interminable delay, the satellite indicated that it had found and locked onto the target.

Mike Fencik, turning up the volume on his microphone, asked the intruding vessel to identify itself, then repeated his request, and finally challenged the vessel to comply or face attack. He waited a few seconds for a response, but none came.

Kellan Blake hoped that this was not a hostile ship or a ship of any sort, as the radar display clearly indicated that it was, but rather an aberration of some kind, an oddly shaped meteor or a piece of space junk. In any case, the manual was clear about how to respond to situations such as this. Kellan shrugged his shoulders at Mike, then pushed the alarm button that put the base on alert by sounding a piercing buzzer and flashing red lights throughout the complex.

Gordon Stoney, a likeable if often sarcastic Ranger, was the first to reach the control tower and shouted over the buzzer, "What are you trying to do, Mickey, get everybody overexcited?" Stoney seemed as relaxed as a man who was telling a neighbor to turn down the music, reinforcing Kellan's hope that the situation was not as serious as the buzzer seemed to indicate.

Fencik pointed to the radar screen. "We've got an intruder. And don't call me Mickey. The name is Mike."

"Anything you say, Mick," said Stoney as he walked to the radar display for a closer look. "Are you tracking it with a laser satellite?"

"Yes," answered Kellan, glancing at the control console to make certain the beta laser was still active, "and Mike gave it three challenges, but no answer."

Stoney cracked a devilish smile. "Then blow it the fuck out of the sky."

Kellan and Mike looked at Stoney, then at each other. No one could be certain when to take Stoney seriously. "Blow it the fuck out of the sky," said Kellan in a reasonably good imitation of Stoney. "Ever read about the rookie Ranger on Cyrus 3 who misread a radar signature and blew up a passenger vessel transporting 50 monks and sisters on a holy retreat?"

"That's what I mean," said an unrepentant Stoney. "Blow it the fuck up."

Captain Zeitz, the base commander, was entering the tower. Zeitz, a middle-aged man of medium stature and mild demeanor, asked calmly, "Something interesting on the radar screen?" Kellan nodded yes as Zeitz turned off the alarm buzzer but left the blinking alarm lights on throughout the base. "A meteor?"

"It has the radar signature of a ship."

The Captain joined Kellan at the radar console. "So it does."

"I used the flight path tracer," said Kellan nervously, "and it indicated that ship appeared at the edge of the black cloud."

Both Fencik and Stoney were stunned to hear that the vessel might have come through The Void, but Zeitz said very calmly, "Impossible." Kellan then showed the Captain the radar trace, and Zeitz corrected himself, "I guess it's not impossible."

Stoney repeated his suggestion that they "blow it the fuck out of the sky," only this time he meant it.

Zeitz merely stared disapprovingly at Stoney, then ordered Kellan to retarget the beta laser, and Mike to again try to raise the approaching vessel by radio. The Captain, still displaying no sign of concern, went to the base central computer and instructed it to use its microwave imaging system to identify the ship. Usually a three-dimensional skeletal illustration along with basic information such as class, weaponry, and history appeared within seconds. But this time no image materialized, only the words, "interstellar vessel of unknown type and origin."

So much for Kellan's hope that the radar blip was space junk or a meteor.

"Well," said Zeitz nonchalantly, "our visitor does not fit the profile of any commercial or military vessel currently registered anywhere in the galaxy."

"It's a phantom ship," smiled Stoney, "come from hell to suck up lost souls, chubby little souls like yours, Mickey." Agitating Fencik helped Stoney relieve his own tension, unkind though it was.

Fencik, visibly shaken by the presence of the intruder, stared at Stoney but was unable to think of a comeback.

"Okay, gentlemen, you know what's next." All three Rangers looked at Captain Zeitz, dreading his next words. "You'd better go up and take a look at the intruder."

As several more Rangers entered the control tower to assist Captain Zeitz, the trio of Kellan Blake, Mike Fencik, and Gordon Stoney hurried to the locker room to don their spacesuits and arm themselves. The whole time Stoney chattered on about the "phantom ship," which he claimed appeared at 25-year intervals in different parts of the galaxy to lure onboard unsuspecting victims—victims like Mickey Fencik—then disappeared again to wander the universe with its cargo of "undead" captives.

"Give it a break, Stoney," said Kellan as much on his own behalf as Mike Fencik's. Kellan was just superstitious enough to believe that he could spend two crushingly boring years on this base only to run into a major problem during his last full day on active duty. He was beginning to believe that the best he could hope for, in the face of this mysterious ship, was an extended base alert and missing the next flight home. The worst that could happen? He tried to blot that from his mind.

By the door of the locker room was a copper relief depicting the Well of Life, the holiest of all Asturian places. There was a similar relief at every military installation in the Empire, and soldiers often had smaller versions inside their lockers or hung around their necks. When they were dressed and ready to leave, Mike Fencik touched the relief and then his head, a gesture meant to ensure that God would protect him from harm. Stoney left next; he too performed the ritual. But Kellan merely looked at the copper icon before following the others out.

The red alert lights were still flashing when they reached Launch Pad A, where Skip Romanchuk, their pilot, sat in his Interceptor, checking out the instruments. Jetpacks strapped to the backs of their spacesuits, and laser rifles hung over their shoulders, Kellan Blake and the other two Rangers took their seats in the Interceptor. Romanchuk then lowered the ship's clear plastic canopy and raised the roof of the launch pad.

While Stoney began to sing, off-key, a song about wandering down lonesome railroad tracks after losing his best girl and all his money, the pilot began the launch sequence and elevated the pad to its 45-degree firing angle. Romanchuk flipped the first ignition switch, and the booster rocket lit. "Ten seconds to lift off," he said as Stoney continued to sing. "Five, four, three, two, one." The pilot hit the second switch, and they blasted off the launch pad.

Kellan suffered from motion sickness, especially during launches of this sort. His head was throbbing, and he was in a cold sweat. The force of the thrust felt as though it would rip open his rib cage and split his skull, and as the ship began to vibrate, he struggled to keep from vomiting.

He wondered if he would survive this launch let alone their encounter with the phantom ship.

Sitting next to him, Mike Fencik was even more rattled by the blast-off and was reciting the Asturian Prayer of Safekeeping:

"Well of Life, Keeper of Souls, watch over me now, as I enter the jaws of darkness."

From the watchtower, Captain Zeitz followed the rocket's first few seconds of flight, a large fireball that quickly disappeared. Over the radio he could hear Stoney's singing and Fencik's praying, and he knew that Fencik must have been very scared because he stopped reciting the entire Prayer of Safekeeping, instead repeating only "Well of Life, Keeper of Souls" over and over.

On board, Romanchuk checked the flight time: 45 seconds. They would shortly break free of the moon's atmosphere. The force of acceleration began to ease. The Interceptor stopped shaking, and Kellan began to feel that he would survive this part of the flight.

"Anybody want to claim that their undershorts are still clean?" asked Stoney, still sounding completely undisturbed by the launch. Then turning to Fencik, who was seated behind him, he said sarcastically, "Hey, Mickey, did I hear you praying back there?"

Mike's mouth was dry, and he could not find his voice. So Kellan answered for him, "He was praying that you'd stop singing."

They were in space surrounded by tens of thousands of bright stars, except, of course, in the direction of The Void, when Captain Zeitz contacted them over the radio. "Romanchuk, put an optical on the target. I'll feed you the coordinates."

Romanchuk activated the Interceptor's television camera. They all watched the cockpit screen with great interest but saw nothing. Romanchuk gradually increased the magnification until they noticed the faintest black outline against the black sky, still nothing they could recognize or would even have found without the help of radar.

"I told you it was the ghost ship," said Stoney.

"Damn," said Romanchuk, "you might be right."

During the next few minutes, Romanchuk took their Interceptor in a wide arc around the intruder so that they were running parallel and behind it and gaining rapidly. At last, they could make it out clearly. The ship had an odd shape, like a bullet, and was powered by a set of double thrusters on either side. Its black color appeared to be from friction scorching. There were no navigational lights or any other signs that the vessel had power. As they pulled along side it, all four Rangers knew they were viewing a death ship. Stoney had not been that far off.

The canopy on the Interceptor lifted up and back. Stoney trained his laser rifle on the strange vessel. Kellan, his rifle slung around his neck, stood and walked onto the wing of the Interceptor. His boots as well as his gloves were magnetic, and by pushing down with his feet or squeezing his hands, he could increase the power of the magnetic pull. With practice, he had learned to move around in weightlessness with little difficulty. He reached back and under his jetpack, where the control arm was folded and stored, and swung it open and around so that it was in front of him. He hesitated while estimating the distance to the other ship, which was about 75 yards, relaxed the pressure of his feet against the interior of his magnetic boots, and blasted gently into space and toward the mystery vessel. He floated on a straight line, and giving several more short blasts on his jetpack, he closed in slowly on the black ship until he was able to reach out and secure himself to its hull with his magnetic gloves.

Mike Fencik was up next. He walked out onto the wing with difficulty and unfolded his jetpack controls. Mike took a deep breath, said a prayer, and gave several blasts on his jetpack but did not move an inch. Mike was so tense that he had locked himself to the Interceptor with his magnetic boots. He worked the jetpack control again without success and finally opened the throttle completely. Fencik's boots let go, and he shot out into space. Before he realized what he had done, Mike was almost half way to the black ship and closing quickly. Kellan turned to see him coming in much too fast. "Brake, Mike, brake. Reverse your thrust." But Fencik was afraid that if he did anything now, he would miss the ship entirely and fly off into space to be lost forever. As he came within a few yards of the black ship, he held out his arms and tried to brace himself for the impact.

Had they not been in the vacuum of space, Mike's crash landing would have made a loud thud. As it was, Kellan saw him silently plaster himself against the ship's hull; then they all heard Mike's moaning and groaning over their radios. Both Romanchuk and Captain Zeitz inquired about the strange sounds but were immediately put at ease by Kellan, who said, "Mike Fencik decided to test the structural integrity of the intruder and found that it is actually quite solid. Isn't that right, Mike?"

"Right," answered an exasperated Fencik as Kellan worked his way across and made certain that Mike's magnetic gloves and boots were attached to the ship's hull.

"Are you okay?" asked Kellan. Fencik, the visor to his helmet fogged by his heavy breathing, nodded that he was all right. "You're lucky you didn't break every bone in your body."

"I may have broken half of them," Mike answered, making a brave attempt at humor.

After Stoney jetted across from the Interceptor, he and Kellan waited a few minutes while Mike Fencik continued to gather himself together. Then the trio edged their way across the phantom ship's hull to the hatch. The hatch door, which must have been struck by a small meteorite, was dented and not perfectly seated in its frame. Stoney found the manual door control in a recess next to the frame and pulled it. The hatch, stiff and cranky, opened most of way, then stuck, and would budge no farther. Kellan turned on the floodlight at the top of his helmet, unslung his laser rifle, and looked into the hatch opening while poking his rifle barrel inside at the same time. He moved the light beam all around the darkness, but there was nothing to see except the gray bulkhead of the airlock.

Kellan would have preferred to simply declare the ship a derelict and return to base, but he knew Zeitz expected a thorough inspection of the vessel's interior. The sooner it was done, he told himself, the sooner he could return to base and prepare to go home. "I'm going in," said Kellan over his helmet radio, and he squeezed inside the airlock.

Mike Fencik, helmet light on, laser in hand, followed as Stoney found a barely legible serial number on the ship's hull and radioed it back to Captain Zeitz.

As soon as Mike was inside the airlock, Kellan pulled the lever to open the door to the ship's interior. As it slowly slid up, he waited to feel the rush of air escaping into space. There was none. Whoever or whatever was on this ship was dead. That had been suggested by the exterior of the vessel; now he was certain of it. With Mike following him and breathing heavily into his helmet microphone, Kellan walked down a dark, narrow passageway toward the nose of the ship to where the bridge must be. The corridor opened onto the ship's command center, where his helmet light fell across the backs of two figures in spacesuits; one slouched back with his head tilted up, his arms drifting at his side in the weightlessness; the other bent over forward.

From the corner of his eye Kellan spotted something just above him and to the left. He turned to see a figure in a spacesuit floating like a lost balloon. Kellan let out a gasp of surprise, then when he saw, through the dead man's frosted helmet visor, the decomposing human face, he yelled and pushed the floating figure away from him with his rifle butt.

Fencik panicked and fired a laser blast at the floating corpse but missed. Stoney, who was just approaching the bridge, started shouting, first asking what was happening, then trying to calm Mike Fencik before he fired another wild shot. And both Romanchuk in the Interceptor and Captain Zeitz back at the base were on the radio asking what was happening.

It was Stoney who rose to the occasion. He got Fencik to lower his rifle, then he secured the floating body to a service ladder built into the bulkhead, while reporting to base that everything was under control. Kellan, however, had been profoundly shaken by his encounter with the corpse and was not sure why. It was an experience that would frighten most people, but he had seen dead people before without feeling shaken to the bone marrow as he was now. He stood perfectly still, eyes closed, sweat running down his forehead. He wanted to get off the ship and considered going directly back to the Interceptor. But he knew they would have to finish their search of the vessel, and that if he showed another sign of weakness, he would disgrace himself with the other Rangers.

Captain Zeitz was on the radio with instructions. In the excitement, no one had bothered to check the course of the derelict ship. It was heading very close to Gondar, the planet their base orbited, and would likely crash into it. Zeitz told them they had to try to re-power the ship and alter its course. If they failed, they would have to evacuate the ship in less than 30 minutes or risk going down with it.

"You two try to power it up," said Stoney. "I'll search the back compartments."

Kellan and Mike did not want to imagine what other gruesome sights Stoney might encounter in the rear of the vessel and were grateful that he volunteered to do the dirty work. This was the kind of demonstration of courage that Stoney had felt compelled to make his whole life because his grandfather had been an Asturian general, and his father, a lieutenant colonel. His family always had high expectations for him as far back as he could remember, back certainly to the age of 11, when his father took him hunting on one of the last remaining Asturian game reserves to "bag his first giant boar," a family rite of passage. Stoney was still troubled by memories of that hunt, still did not know what bothered him more: the fear of being impaled on a tusk or hearing the animal squeal when he put a fatal bullet into its belly. And even now he was still trying to please "The Colonel," as his father was still trying to please his grandfather, who, in his 70s, remained the family patriarch.

Stoney would soon be discharged from the Ranger Corps without having been promoted, without having distinguished himself in any way. Despite that disappointment, he was supposed to attend law school next and eventually join his father's private legal practice and become a great lawyer. Expectations of this kind were the family curse, his mother claimed. They were what made the Stoney men eager to take risks, she said, and the reason that her husband was a drunk and her son was becoming one.

While Stoney went to the rear compartment, Kellan, feeling that he had to redeem himself, began to move one of the two corpses seated before the control panel. He approached the spacesuited figure in the pilot's chair from behind, reached around to the front of the seat to release the latch on the safety belt, and gently pushed the corpse up and away from the control console to a corner of the bridge.

Fencik followed Kellan's example in removing the second corpse from the co-pilot's chair, and the two Rangers sat at the control panel.

Neither man had any flight training, and they randomly tinkered with every button, switch, and lever on the panel. Nothing worked. The ship had been without power for years, perhaps decades, and it was unlikely that anything they could do would revive it.

They were interrupted by a radio call from Captain Zeitz. He had run a check on the derelict ship's serial number. It fit the sequencing of the Imperial space fleet, but there was absolutely no record of it, which added to the mystery of what this ship was, where it had been, and what misfortune had befallen it.

A second interruption followed Zeitz's message. It was from Stoney. A call for help.

Moving as fast as they could in zero gravity and dressed in bulky spacesuits, Kellan and Fencik got out of their seats and rushed to Stoney's aid with their lasers ready. They found him in a rear compartment, standing rigid, his head tilted up, his rifle raised to a firing position. When he entered the chamber, Kellan saw what had prompted Stoney's reaction. Standing in a corner of the compartment was a gigantic robot, human in shape and facial appearance, standing as lifeless as a store mannequin.

"Do you suppose the robot killed the others?" asked Stoney, keeping the strange figure square in the sights of his rifle.

"No, robots rarely run amuck," whispered Kellan, somewhat in awe of the size of the robot and its human appearance. "Besides, there seemed to be no marks on the bodies, and the ship itself is damaged and without power. The crew probably died from suffocation or starvation or maybe old age."

"I wouldn't be so certain," warned Fencik, who also trained his laser on the robot. "Everything about this ship is weird. I wouldn't dismiss any possibility."

Kellan took a closer look at the robot's silver-colored but otherwise perfectly human-like face as though it might hold a clue as to whether it was malevolent. The robot's eyes suddenly lit up with a yellow light. It was alive!

Kellan raised his rifle to eye level and pointed his laser at the robot's head. The silver-faced robot looked first at Kellan, then at Stoney and Mike. It extended a hand in Stoney's direction and started to step forward. Stoney, hesitant to destroy the android, fired a blast that came within inches of its shoulder. The robot turned its head to see a smoldering hole in the bulkhead, then fell to his knees, and clasped his hands.

"What the hell is it doing?" asked Stoney.

Kellan lowered his rifle. "I think it's praying."

2 | Well of Life

While the phantom ship remained on its collision path with the planet Gondar, Kellan and Mike Fencik used bunk sheets to cover the three dead crewmembers. Stoney, meanwhile, kept guard on the large but apparently harmless robot, which had to shut down for lack of energy. Because they were unable to re-power and save the derelict ship, Captain Zeitz ordered them to return the robot to base for a debriefing or a download of his databank. Zeitz also wanted to recover, for autopsy and eventual burial, all the bodies, which he believed were probably Imperial astronauts and Rangers, and he dispatched two more four-passenger Interceptors to provide the necessary transportation.

The evacuation of the ship was accomplished in three parts. First, Stoney, towing the robot behind him on a long tether line, jetted back to the Interceptor. With Romanchuk's help, he stored the large android across the two rear seats, and then they headed back to base. The second Interceptor was for Mike Fencik. Because of Mike's misadventure during his jetpack ride to the ship, Kellan offered to let Mike go next. If Fencik overshot the Interceptor, Kellan could go after him. Mike stepped out of the airlock hatch and carefully blasted off. Tethered behind him was the eerie figure of a dead crewman, the upper part of his lifeless body wrapped in a white sheet.

That left Kellan behind in the airlock of the phantom ship tied to two more weightless corpses wrapped in sheets. His eyes momentarily left Mike Fencik, who was making slow progress toward the Interceptor, to glance at his macabre company. How did he get here? he asked himself. And why was he so shaken by the sight of a dead man? Because he no longer had a shield against death. When he looked at that decaying face, he knew he was looking at his own face years in the future, and it suddenly struck him that death cast a perpetual shadow over life. That fear, he believed, would be constantly and forever on his mind. As a faithful young member of the Asturian Church, he had believed that death led to an eternal spiritual life. But when he rejected the Church, he had lost his psychological protection against death and had given no serious thought to the issue until he encountered the corpse. Now his metaphysical view was as dark and empty as the space he would have to cross to reach his Interceptor.

It was a strange and unhappy path he had taken to be at this place at this time, and in reviewing the chain of events that had led him here, he thought back to the day his family celebrated his graduation from the Academy. He remembered that day well. It was one of the high points of his life, and as he sat on the death ship, waiting for his turn to leave, his thoughts returned to Capital City and his graduation party.

* * *

Kellan was on the front porch of his parent's modest house, his best friend, Miles, a tall, thin youth, sitting next to him sipping a beer. The graduation party was winding down, and most of the guests, except for a few of his mother's friends, were gone. Kellan, his long, dark hair curling over the back of his collar, had drunk several beers and felt relaxed despite the fact that the Asturian Church imposed rituals and religious concerns on the happiest of occasions: births, weddings, even school graduations. He, like all Asturian youths, had taken a pledge in high school not to drink alcohol until he was a full-fledged adult and then only to drink in moderation. That idea he now considered old-fashioned and overly restrictive, and it did not much concern Kellan, as it once might have, that he was nearly drunk and that he had also committed the sin of gluttony by eating enough at the party to be suffering slight indigestion now.

No, these small transgressions did not bother him at the moment nor did the fact that his future was unsettled. He was in high spirits, and as he glanced over at his friend, he pointed to the beer foam on Miles' anemic blond mustache. "Looks good, augments the natural growth. I think you should keep it."

Miles smiled as he wiped his upper lip with the back of his hand and suggested that they stop by Auburn's house—a casual remark that sent a jolt through Kellan. Auburn was Kellan's first serious love. She was the most beautiful and most popular girl that he or any of his acquaintances knew. He had been out with Auburn a handful of times in the last year. Their dates were magical for him, and she seemed to enjoy them too. The trouble was her popularity. Her social calendar was often filled a month or two in advance, and sometimes simply getting a phone call through to her was impossible. The idea of dropping in on her was unthinkable, especially because her "busy schedule" might be her way of avoiding seeing him with any regularity. It was a possibility that he hated to consider but could not dismiss.

This had been such a good day that Kellan did not want to spoil it with another rejection from Auburn, and he gave Miles' suggestion a one-word response, "Nah." His friend then came up with a more palatable idea, hopping a streetcar and going down to the old amusement park. Kellan agreed, and soon they were aboard a clanking, old, green-and-white Capital City trolley.

The planet Asturias, in general, and Capital City, in particular, were considerably less technologically advanced than other parts of the Empire, and there were several reasons for it. On the practical side, the economy on this planet was old and declining as was the population itself. The revitalization plan that resurfaced periodically was to use the age of the planet's infrastructure to its advantage, to turn Capital City into a living museum of Asturian history and make it a major tourist destination. While that plan never had quite enough strength to be implemented, it always had sufficient support to block other kinds of proposed projects. Another and perhaps more important reason that Asturias was backwards in so many ways was that the Church wished it to be. The antiquated nature of the planet evoked the ancient Age of Revelations and spoke of the immutability of the Church, which remained a rock of stability in a sea of change. Asturias might not have become a magnet for vacationers, but it was still the place where pilgrims came.

Like much of Capital City, the amusement park was shabby and underused. The iron arch at the main entrance was rusted, and the faded likeness of a clown at its top needed paint. Some of the rides for younger children were closed for repairs; others required their attendants to run onto tracks periodically to give the little trains and toy airplanes a push to get them going again. Other than nostalgia for their early teen years, there was not much here for Kellan and Miles—a few games of chance and skill, several snack bars, and the possibility of bumping into old friends.

As they walked down a gravel path by the empty merry-go-round, Miles grabbed Kellan's arm and pointed to one of the game booths. There was Auburn, standing near shelves lined with stuffed animals waiting to be won by anyone who could knock down three stacked metal milk bottles with a single throw of a ball.

Auburn had long blond hair that fell over her shoulders, a few dozen strands from each side pulled back from the temples and twisted in a loose braid at the back of her neck. She had the high cheekbones of a model and skin so fair it gave off a glow. Her eyes were light blue, her teeth perfect, her full lips puffy in a very appealing way. She always dressed, as all good Asturian girls did, to hide, rather than to flatter, her shape, and the loose white silk dress she wore might have been concealing had it not been tied at the waist tightly by a belt. It was the most revealing outfit Kellan had ever seen her wear, and her breasts and her buttocks were larger and shapelier than he had realized. If Auburn's appearance was not already tormenting enough, when her companion at the game booth, Aldo Peyton, cocked his arm and tossed a ball wildly, she lifted her blue eyes skyward in a manner that Kellan found most alluring.

When Auburn saw Kellan approaching with Miles, she smiled warmly and waved. Kellan waved back and walked up beside her. "Your date seems to be ignoring you," he said loud enough for Aldo to hear. Aldo, a classmate of Kellan's at the Academy, dated a number of attractive women but was not in love with Auburn. If he had been as crazy about Auburn as Kellan was, Aldo would not have been so absorbed in trying to knock down the metal milk bottles.

Aldo missed with another throw. "At this rate," smiled Auburn, "we'll be here forever."

Kellan found himself standing so close to Auburn that their shoulders and the upper portions of their arms were touching. He was in a daring mood and impulsively decided to pull a prank on Aldo. Taking Auburn by the hand, Kellan started to lead her away.

"What are you doing?" she giggled, glancing at him from the corner of her eye.

He leaned next to her ear and whispered, "I'm kidnapping you." She giggled again but did not resist. Kellan turned back toward the game booth. "Aldo," he shouted, "I'm kidnapping your date."

As he reached for yet another ball, Aldo yelled back at them, "Better not be gone long."

The farther they walked, the less concerned he became about Aldo, and the more determined Kellan became to find a way to prolong his time with Auburn. A short distance ahead was the entrance to a miniature streetcar ride. If Kellan could not be with her for hours, he would settle for the duration of the ride. He slipped his arm around her waist and led her toward the ride's entrance. She did not complain. Nor did she object when he paid the attendant for two tickets.

The park was nearly deserted, and the streetcars, each with the almost life-size metal figure of a conductor at the front, were running empty along their track, disappearing one by one behind a high, green, wooden fence. Kellan and Auburn got into the first available car. The seats were small, and they sat with hips and thighs touching. He kept his arm around her, and she seemed to be snuggling against him, although he could not be certain it was not just the narrowness of the seat that brought her so close.

The car moved into an area where the tracks twisted and turned and were fenced in by high walls on both sides. The mechanical conductor at the front of the car turned his upper body around 180 degrees on his hips to face the passenger compartment. The conductor had an old man's face with hollow cheeks and a long nose. His uniform was dark blue with silver buttons, and his blue hat had a large chip of paint missing from the top, revealing the bare metal underneath. With his lips moving and his large white eyebrows flapping like wings, he said, "Welcome aboard. I hope you will enjoy your ride."

Auburn had been on this ride before but not in several years, and she laughed at the way the conductor's eyebrows moved. The mechanical man opened his metal mouth again. "We're coming to a low bridge," he announced. "Better duck your heads." Although there was plenty of clearance, they played along, lowering their heads as they went through a small tunnel and began to climb a hill. "This incline is steep," warned the conductor. "Better hold on tight."

The head of the mechanical conductor suddenly disappeared down a hole that opened between his shoulders and was replaced by a less benevolent-looking face, the classic Asturian representation of the devil, a face with black, furrowed cheeks, a large hook nose, red eyes, and ram's horns that circled around pointy ears. Auburn screamed when she saw it; then covered her mouth with her hands and laughed, "I forgot about this part."

"You're mine now," said the mechanical devil as a metal bar lifted out of the floor to close them in. The car continued its climb to the top of the hill, then dropped sharply down the other side.

The little car continued to strain up inclines and roll down drops at great speed, and when the tracks finally leveled out again, the devil vanished, and the conductor reappeared. As the streetcar rounded a last curve and moved toward the exit, Kellan made his move, leaning over and kissing Auburn on the lips. He pulled back to look at her; she remained motionless, whether from passion or merely surprise, he could not tell. He leaned over and kissed her a second time, harder.

"We're arriving at the station now," said the conductor. "Hope you'll ride with us again."

Auburn glanced at the station platform, and seeing Aldo and Miles waiting, she sat up. While Kellan withdrew his arm, she straightened her dress and rubbed her chin and cheeks to clear them of any smeared lipstick. Then she leaned toward Kellan and whispered, "Call me."

Convinced that he had finally achieved a breakthrough with Auburn, Kellan was euphoric, and later that day, when he tried to sleep, he had waking dreams about her, remembering how she looked in that revealing white dress, how she laughed when the conductor turned into a devil, but most of all, he remembered the kisses and her parting words, "Call me." And he did call her over a period of days, dozens of times when her line was busy and several more times when he managed to get through only to find that she was not home. That was when he decided to take the Journey to the Well of Life.

In the Asturian Church, sacrifice was the key to obtaining desired outcomes, usually a ritual sacrifice as opposed to a practical one like working hard to hone a skill or to achieve a good grade in a test. Kellan thought his relationship with Auburn was at a critical point. Indeed, his life was at a critical point. Now that he had graduated from the Academy, he faced a two-year military assignment. He had requested to stay on Asturias but could be sent anywhere. His entire future was at stake. In recent years he had not been the staunch churchgoer that he had been as a youth, and in fact, he had become skeptical about certain religious practices and beliefs. This was the time to pull himself back together, he decided, to make the traditional sacrificial journey to the Dark Side.

* * *

Asturias was an unusual planet. At some point in the development of the Poltare system, Asturias was knocked over by some other astral object. While all the other major planets spun around their vertical axes, Asturias orbited its twin suns while rolling on its equator, presenting one hemisphere always to the light and the other always to the darkness. Asturias was a world in which one half was in perpetual day and the other perpetual night, a metaphor, said the Church, for good and evil, enlightenment and ignorance, salvation and damnation. And there was no compromise between the two extremes.

The lack of a day-night cycle turned out to be an advantage when the age of space exploration began. Asturians kept time by the natural 25-hour rhythm of their bodies, and that was how they measured time aboard ship during long space flights and on every planet, moon, and space station where it made sense to impose Asturian Standard Time or AST. Many areas of the galaxy, particularly in the Republics, had a local measure of time, but minutes and hours were always AST, and days, months, and years always had an AST conversion number.

The Dark Side was almost entirely uninhabited now. During the last century, Asturians had been migrating farther and farther into space to planets and moons where there were natural resources to be developed and good jobs to be had. For those relative few who stayed behind on the mother planet, there was no reason to live in constant night when they could live in constant day. As a result of this and years of Church indoctrination, the Dark Side remained foreboding, and the average Asturian avoided it altogether unless he or she was taking the Journey to the Well of Life.

In preparation for his journey, Kellan, with dozens of other pilgrims, spent several days at a monastery near the Dark Side, where they endured a long fast and short sleep periods. On the day he was to actually begin his pilgrimage, he walked on slightly shaky legs past the monastery's cafeteria and paused at the door to look inside. Another group of pilgrims, all women, had just returned from the Well of Life and were in the monastery's cafeteria, gorging themselves after their long walk and even longer fast. Kellan surveyed the faces in the crowd, wishing that he too had already completed his challenge and could at this moment be enjoying a hot meal.

Then he noticed a girl. She was in her late teens, perhaps even younger, and she sat alone at a table, hunched down in her seat, her head covered with a scarf, never looking up, and nibbling at her meal with little enthusiasm. The girl was small and thin, and had a long slender neck and a pretty face with delicate features. Kellan noticed that under her scarf her head appeared to be shaved, the traditional punishment for having premarital sex, a major sin in the Asturian Church. Sex was natural, even good, Kellan thought. Someday he hoped to have intercourse with Auburn, but if they had sex before marriage and were found out, Auburn, like this young woman, might bear the mark of shame for life. It seemed too harsh a punishment to Kellan.

Another pilgrim, a young man with a beak-like nose, hollow cheeks, and a playful look in his eye, a man who could have been the model for the mechanical devil on the miniature streetcar ride at the amusement park, came up behind Kellan. He could see that Kellan was looking at the young woman. "Hope she hasn't become too pure," the man said in a voice that was much too loud for the circumstances. "I'd like to get into her pants when this bullshit is over."

Kellan, who was far from being a purist, was nonetheless shocked by the man's open irreverence, particularly the use of the word "bullshit" in reference to the sacred journey. The peculiar man must have been able to read the unasked question in Kellan's puzzled expression because he answered it. "I'm here for committing blasphemy," he announced with inexplicable pride. "I teach in a Church school and was disrespectful to God and Church—and during religion class." He finally lowered his voice. "So it was either cleanse myself or lose my job." His voice went up again, "And wind up in the fucking army."

Kellan held a finger to his lips. "Someone may hear you," he whispered.

The teacher dismissed Kellan with a wave of his hand. "I don't cower in chapel any more the way I did when I was a little boy."

"At least act respectfully while you're here," Kellan insisted.

"I lost my respect, m'boy," said the teacher, "when I started studying Church history. Ever study it?" Kellan nodded that he had, and the teacher smiled a devilish grin. "Yes, but only the Church history taught in Church schools." Kellan started to walk away, to the monastery's front door, where they were supposed to board a horse-drawn wagon to be taken to the Dark Side, but the man followed. "Ever hear of Octaves Orne, Bishop Octaves Orne?"

"Yes," answered Kellan without looking back at the man. "He was one of the first missionaries sent to the colonies."

"There! See what I mean?" the teacher laughed. "To the Republicans he was known as the Bloody Bishop because he executed more than 100 heretics—men, women, and children—in a single afternoon."

Kellan stopped walking and looked the man in the eye. "That's what you say."

"That's what the Republican chroniclers of the time said, m'boy. I'll give some references; you can look it up yourself."

As they walked down the long corridor and outside into the courtyard, the teacher continued to harangue Kellan. Mostly he talked about the Colonial Worlds Charter, a 175-year-old agreement between the ruling civil authorities of the era and the Church Patriarchy that made the Asturian Church the state religion. Kellan had heard of this document but knew little about it. According to the teacher, in return for government support, the Church agreed to make obedience to the civil authorities a matter of moral obligation, which meant that any opposition to the civil authority was a sin, and therefore, that liberal movements had to be anti-Church as well anti-government.

"Standard history," continued the teacher, "doesn't describe the Empire's habit of stripping colonies of their natural wealth to the detriment of the colonists, or make any mention of the brutal measures or brutal people like Bishop Orne that were used in the earliest days of the Empire to suppress rebellions and heresies. But the Church, regardless of the sins it has committed, is still the ultimate moral authority. And why? Because the Church says so, and as the ultimate moral authority, it can't be wrong." The teacher laughed. "Talk about a tautology!"

The teacher took out pen and paper, and began to write down the names of digital libraries containing information that he claimed had been suppressed or at least, largely ignored by the Church. And he described ways of circumventing the limitations imposed on Asturian Web search programs, programs, he said, that were intended to keep the faithful stupid and loyal. But Kellan did not want to hear any more and refused to take the paper the teacher was trying to hand him. The man's comments were impure and heretical, and if Kellan did not blot them from his mind, he would ruin the purity of his sacrifice. Fortunately there was a monk in the courtyard, and the sight of him caused the teacher to grow quiet. Kellan then gathered himself and silently repeated the Prayer of Safekeeping.

Kellan had never been in space and had never experienced night. It was silly to be anxious about a journey through darkness, but he was. People usually had a similar reaction when they entered the House of Fright at the old amusement park. Although they knew the dangers were not real, that did not stop their hearts from beating faster and their breathing from becoming more labored when they were about to enter it.

The time had finally come. Kellan, the teacher, and two dozen other penitents and petitioners climbed into the back of an open-top, horse-drawn wagon. The driver whistled and cracked the reins, and they began to move. For miles, as they rode toward the Dark Side, Kellan listened to the steady clip-clop of the two brown-and-tan horses and found the sound pleasing. Then with twilight's approach, their hoof beats took on a disturbing rhythm, like the ticking of a great clock moving relentlessly toward a climax.

The sky had grown dark, the small hills in the distance less distinct, and although he was dressed warmly, he began to feel the dropping temperature. The terrain grew more rugged, causing the wagon to rock from side to side and its rusted springs to squeak. The handsome, prematurely bald monk who sat next to the wagon's driver turned back toward the passengers. "You should prepare yourselves now; ask God to help you make a worthy sacrifice." The monk bowed his head, the others following his lead, and he led them in a prayer, which they fervently whispered along with him.

As they prayed, Kellan's attention wandered. First, he visualized the girl in the scarf back at the monastery, then Auburn at the amusement park, but his train of thought was broken when a hand was laid on his shoulder. It was the teacher again. "Hey," he whispered. "I never asked you why you're here." Kellan shook his head, meaning that they should not be speaking. "Bet it's a woman," the teacher guessed with a mocking grin. "No woman is worth this. They're all the same in the most fundamental way, if you know what I mean."

"Shsss!" The monk next to the driver, now only a black shadow against a near-black sky, turned toward the back of the wagon. "You are about to make the most important sacrifice of your lives." The monk was angry. "If you cannot hold your tongues and prepare your minds and spirits for your journey, you should not be here."

The strange teacher remained silent, and Kellan cleared his mind by listening to the groaning of the wagon's springs beneath them. The sky and the surrounding terrain had turned completely black; the pilgrims had entered the endless night of Asturias. A short time later, one of the horses whinnied, and the wagon rocked back to front. They had stopped.

"Kellan Blake," called out the monk, illuminating his clipboard with a penlight.

Kellan was first, and as he started to stand, the teacher grabbed him by the sleeve, "Don't worry, m'boy. Nothing to it." The man was so close that Kellan could feel his warm breath against his ear. "It's all theater."

Kellan walked down the narrow aisle at the center of the wagon and descended three wooden steps to the ground. The monk, who was waiting for him, put a hand on his shoulder and said, "God bless and watch over you."

Then the monk climbed back aboard the wagon, leaving Kellan standing on the side of the dirt road, his shoulders hunched against the cold, and his hands dug deep into his pockets. The reins snapped over the team of horses, and the wagon wheels turned. Kellan stepped onto the road behind the departing wagon and remained there listening to the horses' hooves as they moved farther and farther away.

Kellan knew what to do next; every Asturian child of seven knew. Look for the light. He slowly turned a full 360 degrees carefully searching for the flame but saw nothing. He turned a second revolution more slowly but still nothing. On the third try he finally saw the light, a flare in the distance shooting skyward. He squared his body to the light source and tried to fix its location in his mind until it disappeared. He then began his trek, moving slowly, his eyes unaccustomed to the dark, holding one arm extended before him as though he were feeling his way. Maintain your orientation, he reminded himself, and remember that a right-legged person will eventually drift left. So compensate.

He expected the light to make another appearance. It did not. Several times in the pitch darkness he stepped in a hole or bumped his foot against an obstruction, once hitting his right foot on a good size rock with enough force to cause him to cry out and to step gingerly until the pain subsided. When he thought he had covered about half the distance to the light, the first of 10 locations he would have to visit, Kellan, as instructed, paused and looked in all directions for the elusive light. Eventually he saw it again, almost a full 90 degrees to the right of where he thought it was and still a good 1,000 yards off.

When he finally reached the light, he saw that it came from a small fire burning from the hollow top of a metal tube. It was timed to flare intermittently to guide pilgrims from a distance but always provided a modest amount of light in the immediate vicinity. Next to the flame was a post with a wooden tablet nailed to it containing one of the basic precepts of the Church: "Man must strive constantly to overcome temptation and avoid sin, to atone for his past offenses, to resolve to countenance no future transgressions."

Kellan knelt and prayed: "Well of Life, Keeper of Souls, watch over me now, as I enter the jaws of darkness."

He stood up, looked for the next light, and found it immediately, just a speck in the distance. "One down," he said aloud. "Nine to go."

After a long walk he reached the second location, then the third. He was hungry and tired—more from lack of sleep than the exertion of his trek—and the cold air was beginning to give him a bad chill. But the journey went well until he heard a strange whooshing sound just above and behind him. Something flew by his head close enough for him to feel the wind against his face. His first thought was that the demons of the Dark Side were real. He spun around right to left, then back left to right but saw nothing. A bat, he thought, it must be a bat. He started to walk quickly and nearly stumbled, constantly checking behind him and up at the black sky but seeing nothing. Then he heard the flapping of wings coming straight at him, and he ducked as the creature grazed the top of his head.

Kellan quickly unbuttoned his coat so that he could pull the top of it over his head to protect himself, and he began to run. He had put some distance between himself and the bat when he stumbled over a ledge and rolled head over heels down a steep hill. He came to rest at the bottom of a ditch, bruised and covered with dirt, but otherwise okay. He decided to stay there a moment to catch his breath and regain his composure.

When he finally began to climb back up the incline, he heard another whooshing sound but not that of bat wings. It was the sound of a gas-fed fire, and as he reached the top of the ditch, he saw the light of a prayer station not 50 yards away. Kellan walked to the flame, intending to say his prayer and rest under the light for a few minutes, but when he reached the wooden prayer marker, he saw that he was at marker 5, not 4. He had gotten lost and skipped a station. For an instant and only an instant, he considered continuing on, forgetting the light he had missed and taking the shortest route to the Well of Life and to safety and comfort. But there was no point whatsoever in taking the Journey if he cheated during it. He would have to go back, probably to the area where he encountered the bat, and look for the fourth light.

Eventually he lost all sense of time. Hours passed, perhaps days before he reached the final station, starving and exhausted and even a little delusional. Two dozen pilgrims, among them the eccentric teacher, had already reached the Well of Life, a large pond fed by an underground thermal spring. They were sprawled across a wooden deck by the waterline like so many people at an accident scene, trying to warm themselves by bonfires that burned in great metal bowls placed all around them. Kellan staggered in and was met by a monk, who led him to one of the fires. Grateful for the opportunity to sit and feel the warmth of the flame, he was the last pilgrim to arrive.

One of the monks, an older man, perhaps the one in charge, climbed to an unadorned lectern by the water's edge. "My children," he began in a loud voice, "awaken, my children." The other monks moved about gently waking the pilgrims who were asleep. The old monk began a sermon, at least Kellan thought it was a sermon; he was too weak and disoriented to pay much attention to it until the monk said after a few minutes, "My children, your trial is almost finished. If you have properly completed your sacrifice and have a pure heart, you may enter the Well of Life."

"You don't have to ask me twice." Kellan recognized the voice. The eccentric teacher was sitting a short distance away. "I can use a warm swim," he announced as he stood and stripped down to his bathing attire. Nudity was forbidden even when Asturians were baring their souls. "Coming along, m'boy?" he asked Kellan, but Kellan was too tired to move or even respond. The teacher shrugged his shoulders, "Suit yourself. But there's really no sense in waiting."

The teacher made his way past the other pilgrims to the edge of the well. Without hesitation, he waded in, first waist deep, then shoulder deep as the water rippled around him. The hot water was refreshing, and he occasionally ducked his head beneath the surface to warm his face. He reached the center of the Well of Life, where there was a wooden platform reached by means of five wooden steps that ran down to the surface of the water. The teacher lifted himself onto the first step and while still on his knees, turned and gave a victory wave to the others, a gesture considered inappropriate by monks and pilgrims alike. He raised himself to his feet and began to climb the remaining stairs, supporting part of his weight on a handrail.

The handrail gave way. The teacher lost his balance and fell forward, striking his head on the platform edge and dropping into the water. It happened so suddenly that few of the onlookers immediately comprehended what had happened. Kellan stared at the section of missing rail, the bloodstain on the side of the platform, the ripples in the water. Then he saw the monks, hampered by their heavy robes, hurry out to the center of the pond. While the shocked and frightened pilgrims watched, the monks searched for the teacher and failed to find him. Finally one of the monks ducked under the platform itself and returned pulling the teacher's lifeless body behind him.

Every pilgrim was convinced that God had punished the man for his irreverence.

After the initial shock, a few of the pilgrims began to sob, all of them prayed, and none of them now felt worthy enough to enter the Well of Life. The monks were some time attending to the teacher's body, and when their attention returned to the other pilgrims, several of them moved among the people, encouraging them to enter the water. No one would budge.

A monk knelt by Kellan; it was the young one from the wagon. "Please go into the water," he urged. "The others will follow. You had the hardest journey and were last to arrive. If you go, they will all know they can do it too."

Kellan shook his head. "I am not worthy," he protested.

"You are not unworthy," the monk insisted. "What you saw was an accident. The wood gave way. God permits such accidents, but it was not an act of God, not punishment for behavior that was more childish than blasphemous. You will be more careful." Kellan did not answer but merely looked the monk in the eye. "After you have come this far, you cannot turn back now."

This was true. He had come very far. And there was no turning back. With the monk's help, Kellan stood, removed all his clothing except his bathing suit, and walked to the edge of the water. There he hesitated, looking back to see that all eyes were focused on him. "Go on," said the monk, who was directly behind him. "It will renew you."

Kellan stepped in, just knee deep at first. The warm water did feel like a blessing that would renew him, that would take away the chill that had been with him ever since he had entered the Dark Side. His courage increasing, he slowly walked farther until he was chest-deep; then he paused to raise several handfuls of water to his face. He kept going until he reached the platform at the pond's center, where he hoisted himself up onto the first step on his knees as the teacher had done before him. Instead of standing upright, however, he crawled up the remaining steps on all fours, drops of water falling from him and soaking the wooden stairs.

He did it, reached the top. The weight had been lifted. Despite his tiredness and hunger, he was invigorated, and he prayed in thanksgiving.

The others still hesitated. A young man moved forward to the water's edge but could not take the first step. Kellan slipped back into the pond, waded across to him, and led him into the water by the arm. The other pilgrims, first individually, then in groups of twos and threes, followed them into the Well of Life.

3 | The Outcome

Kellan sat in the open back compartment of the green-and-white streetcar, feeling the warmth of the twin Poltare suns on his face and enjoying familiar sounds: the click-clack of the trolley wheels, the clanging of the streetcar's bell every time it left a stop, the occasional clamor of children playing along the sidewalks. He was glad to be home, but his thoughts often wandered back to the Dark Side. Indeed, he reveled in remembering the hardships he had overcome there and his courage in being the first to enter the Well of Life after the irreverent teacher drowned. He was a new man, a far more confident and mature man.

The streetcar stopped just across the street from Kellan's house. He threw his duffel bag over his shoulder and hopped off. His mother, as he imagined that she must have done frequently while he was away, was looking out the parlor window. He crossed the street, and by the time he reached the front door, a reception committee had formed. Kellan kissed his mother and younger brother and hugged his father. All three were speaking at once. His mother said she had dinner ready; his father had something to show him; his brother wanted to know if he had seen any real devils on the Dark Side. Kellan put them off by saying there was something he had to do first. Dropping his bag just inside the front door, he climbed the stairs two at time to his bedroom, closed the door, and sat on his bed by the phone. He dialed Auburn's number, and after two rings, a woman's voice answered.

It was Auburn, and she sounded happy to hear from him. Kellan could hardly contain himself. "I have something to tell you," he blurted out.

"And I have something to tell you," she answered. And he insisted that she tell her news first.

What she had to say was just about the last thing he expected to hear. Auburn and her entire family were moving to another star system, a distant one that was completely unfamiliar to him. But it was more than the news itself that upset him. He was also disturbed by how she delivered it. She was happy about the move. Indeed she seemed to be thrilled about it. And she said nothing about missing him or wanting him to visit. When he was finally able to find his voice and ask if he could see her before she left, she answered that she might not have the time. Kellan was shocked.

"But you haven't told me your news yet," she said.

This was not the outcome Kellan had expected from the Journey. He was confused and in no mood to talk about it. He wanted to hang up, and the only thing that kept him on the line was the thought that this could be the last conversation they ever had. Auburn kept pressing him for his news. He had to say something, and so he said completely without enthusiasm, "I've just come back from the Dark Side, from the Journey to the Well of Life."

Auburn was breathlessly excited for him—a reaction that Kellan found annoying, considering how things had turned out. She wanted details and coaxed him into telling the whole story, from the time he stepped off the horse-drawn wagon to the point when he reached the platform at the center of the Well of Life.

It was during the story that a last hopeful thought crossed Kellan's mind. His military assignment might also be on the frontier in the same star system, maybe on the same planet where Auburn would be living. Perhaps it would be there, rather than home on Asturias, where Auburn would finally fall in love with him. It was a possibility but an unlikely one.

They talked for a time longer, until Kellan's mother came to tell him that dinner was on the table. He said goodbye to Auburn and went downstairs to the kitchen, where his friend Miles had joined the family for a celebratory dinner.

As Kellan sat down at the table, his father reached for a letter that was beside his plate. When his mother noticed what her husband was about to do, she elbowed him. "Put that away until after supper," she whispered.

"Why?" He was annoyed. "It's important. A government letter."

Kellan, who had no appetite, extended his hand. "I may as well look at it now."

His father handed it over. "It's from the Space Ministry."

"It could have waited until he had something to eat," his mother said angrily.

Kellan opened the envelope, feeling certain that, the way his luck was running today, it would be bad news. It was. He quickly scanned the letter, then dropped it to the table. Auburn was going one way, and he to the opposite side of the universe.

He had drawn just about the worst duty in the Space Service, an assignment on the Ranger base at The Edge of the Universe, on a moon base orbiting the planet Gondar, which was as far as he could get from Auburn's new home and still be in the Holy Asturian Empire. It was official, he thought, the great sacrificial Journey to the Dark Side was a complete and utter failure.

Auburn was his first real love, but now the whole thing appeared to be one big tease. It seemed that every time he thought he had no chance with her, she would give him hope. And every time she gave him hope, it would soon become apparent that he had no real chance. Now it was completely over, and it was impossible for him to imagine that he would ever love anyone else. In this respect he felt that his life had already ended.

But more than that, now that he had nothing else to lose, he could admit that the Journey to the Well of Life made no sense. There were dozens of young men in love with Auburn. What if all of them had taken the Journey for the same reason? Only one prayer—at most—could be answered. And what if Auburn wanted none of them? What about her desires and her sacrifices? She seemed perfectly happy to be leaving Asturias and all of her suitors here. Perhaps that was what she had prayed for.

Even the monk at the Well of Life had said that the death of the impious teacher was not an act of God. But if God did not punish the unworthy and reward those who made a good sacrifice, why take the Journey at all?

Other issues that had long troubled him but that he had been reluctant to confront suddenly became more prominent in his consciousness: the intolerance that the Church had for nonbelievers; how it dismissed any information that challenged its own doctrines; the claim of an unbroken chain of moral authority back to the first prophets even though the Church had gone through its Gray Period, decades when the Patriarchy was rife with political tampering and corruption. The comments the eccentric teacher had made to him on the Dark Side were also clear in his mind.

Kellan noticed that his mother had picked up his induction letter and was reading it. But she had been too upset by his reaction to make any sense of it. Miles, always the loyal friend, glanced over her shoulder and said, "That's a great assignment."

Realizing that he would have to put on an act for his mother, Kellan smiled, "You wanted me safely away from the Republican frontier. I couldn't be any safer than this."

His mother looked from Kellan to Miles, who nodded in agreement. "I guess that's the most important thing," she said.

"Yes," said Kellan, trying to hide his bitterness, "that's the most important thing." He took the letter from his mother, folded it, and put it into the back pocket of his trousers, where his fingers touched another piece of paper he did not remembering putting there. Kellan pulled out a small, crumpled notebook page and saw that it contained a handful of database locations and access codes. This was the piece of paper the teacher had tried to hand him at the monastery. He must have slipped it into Kellan's trousers during the wagon ride. As soon as this meal was over, Kellan planned to go to his computer and use these databases to learn as much as he could about the Colonial Worlds Charter and Bishop Octaves Orne.

4 | The Android Bellycold

The third and final Interceptor moved into position a short distance from the derelict vessel. Kellan walked to the airlock's external hatch, which had been blasted completely open to accommodate the large android when it was taken from the ship. He stepped out into space, and when he had drifted in the weightlessness a few yards away from the hatch, Kellan tugged on the rope tethered to his spacesuit and pulled the remaining two corpses from the spacecraft. He then turned toward the Interceptor and gave a short blast of his jetpack. He covered the distance between the two ships in little more than a minute, and when he reached the Interceptor, the pilot helped him secure the two bodies in the rear seats. They then headed back to base.

The mystery ship continued drifting in space, only an hour or so away from a collision with the planet Gondar.

Once he was back on moon base, Kellan, thinking he was off-duty, joined Stoney and Fencik in the crew's quarters and began to take a regular turn on the bottle of liquor, or "hooch" as Stoney called it, that was being passed around. The encounter with the derelict ship had been a bad experience for all of them. Each intended to get drunk as quickly as possible, and Stoney, who was taking long swallows compared to their sips, was doing the best job of it. Their party was soon interrupted, however, when Captain Zeitz sent for them. The android had been recharged, and Zeitz wanted the three of them, the only Rangers who had been on the derelict vessel, present for the robot's interrogation. The trio, Stoney, watery-eyed and Kellan, looking disheveled with his uniform shirt unbuttoned at the top and his hair wild, assembled in the Captain's office, where Zeitz uncharacteristically had music playing and playing rather loudly. They took chairs at the back of the room while Zeitz sat at his desk and asked, over his desk communicator, to have the robot brought in. Smelling the liquor on the breath of his three crewmen, Zeitz hit the communicator a second time and ordered four black coffees.

It annoyed the Captain to have to speak over the music, but it was always safe to assume that Church spies or listening devices were everywhere. This was one conversation that he did not want overheard, and although the music itself would not afford sufficient cover, the static imbedded in the music, which was inaudible to the human ear, provided an "accidental" way to defeat electronic listening devices.

The android entered the room. The robot was remarkable looking, resembling a superhero from a children's comic book. He was big, about six-foot six-inches tall, with broad shoulders and a thick chest. His synthetic hair was blue-black, and his handsome face silver. Zeitz pointed to the chair across from the desk, and as the robot sat down, he said, "Bellycold's the name."

"What the hell kind of name is Bellycold?" asked Stoney, who was drunk enough to ignore military decorum.

"I'll tell you what kind of name it is," answered the robot with an equal amount of sarcasm. "Feel this," he said, pointing to his belly. "Go ahead, feel it. You're not afraid, are you?" Stoney reluctantly stood up, approached the robot, and extended his hand. Bellycold blew a perfect smoke ring into Stoney's face, startling the Ranger.

"What are you some kind of clown?" said Stoney angrily, waving the smoke away from his eyes.

"What are you some kind of clown?" The robot had recorded Stoney's comment and played it back to him.

Despite his morose disposition, Kellan smiled at this exchange and hoped that the android would provide even greater distractions.

Zeitz also seemed amused. "That's exactly what he is, a clown." The Captain leaned back in his chair and clasped his hands behind his head. "You three are too young to remember, but the Empire used to build very lifelike androids, lifelike not only in appearance but also in their capacity to react to situations and to react with a fairly sizeable repertoire of verbal responses and actions. Of course," continued Zeitz with an unusual amount of candor for a man of his rank, "that upset some of the more conservative members of the Church who considered androids that were too humanlike a sacrilege. Mimicking the work of the Creator. Questions about whether robots have souls. That sort of thing." Kellan, who was hunched down in his chair, was following the Captain's remarks but kept visualizing the three corpses wrapped in white sheets. "To avoid having the Church shut down their businesses altogether, the manufacturers of sophisticated robots like our friend Bellycold. . ." The robot gave a slight bow in appreciation of Zeitz's comment. "The manufacturers," continued Zeitz, "began turning out entertainment androids of all sorts instead of robots for more serious use. The fact that entertainment robots often acted in a silly manner concealed their incredible complexity."

Bellycold turned to the Rangers sitting behind him. "Listen to the Captain," he said, pointing a finger at Stoney. "The man knows what he's talking about. It takes brains to play the fool."

Zeitz suddenly turned serious. "Had a lot of trouble on this trip, didn't you?" If he hoped to catch the android off-guard, he was unsuccessful.

"Trouble is putting it mildly." Bellycold had a loud voice and a presence that commanded attention. "We were lost forever, so long that my batteries ran down, and I lost track of time."

"Too bad," said Zeitz, "because we can't find any record of your ship or your mission."

Bellycold looked back at Stoney. Many of the android's comedy programs involved picking on an audience member, and Stoney was the one he selected as his foil. Bellycold leaned toward Zeitz and pretended to whisper so that Stoney could not hear, "We were on a diplomatic mission for Julian Alfiri, himself, you know, the Commander-in-Chief of the Space Fleet." This reinforced Zeitz's belief that the android had been on a very important and potentially explosive mission.

"Who would send you on a diplomatic mission?" asked Stoney, who heard the comment and was still miffed at having the smoke ring blown in his face.

"That boy just doesn't get it," said Bellycold, motioning at Stoney over his shoulder with his large metal thumb. "Most people don't take a guy like me seriously. So who better to serve cocktails at a diplomatic party? To mingle with the guests, the important ones? You'd be surprised at the information I am able to pick up."

"I'm sure," said Zeitz matter-of-factly. "So why don't you tell us about your mission?"

"Say, do you think you could turn down the music?" Bellycold pointed to the speaker mounted in the corner of the office. "The buzz is giving me a headache."

The robot apparently could sense the jamming device, but Zeitz could not be concerned about that. "I'll turn it down as soon as you tell us about your mission."

Bellycold shook his head. "Nope, can't do it. Top secret. Just contact Julian Alfiri. Tell him Bellycold is back—in the flesh." Kellan was the only one to smile at the android's joke.

"We can download the information from your databank if we have to."

"No, you can't." Bellycold pointed to his head. "Tamper proof. Julian did it himself. You might as well just blast me with a laser rifle," the robot pointed at Stoney, "like this nervous one almost did back on the ship. But blast me and what do you say to Julian

Alfiri about his precious android and his even more precious data?"

"First," said Zeitz, "an unidentified vessel suddenly appears from nowhere. It's on a collision course with Gondar, and so we won't be able to learn anything from it or its computers. Then we find three dead crewmen and won't learn anything from them either. And now we have an uncooperative clown robot with a cock-and-bull story. That's not the kind of report I intend to send to Capital City. I need some answers."

Bellycold looked to the three Rangers for help; none was forthcoming. "Remember if you tamper with me, my poor little mind will be fried, and all that good information will be lost."

A Ranger arrived carrying coffee, an interruption which gave Zeitz time to consider playing a trump card. But first he had to clear the others from the room. The information he extracted from the android might prove dangerous to anyone who possessed it. "Why don't the three of you take your coffee and wait in the hall outside my office while Bellycold and I have a private conversation."

"You sure you'll be safe, Captain?" asked Stoney, standing to leave.

"I'm sure," answered Zeitz as he took a mug from the serving tray. When the three Rangers had left the room and shut the door behind them, the Captain turned toward the android and said casually, "Julian Alfiri is no longer Commander-in-Chief of the Space Fleet."

The robot paused for a moment. "Is that true?" he asked, apparently trying to read Zeitz's expression. "Then he must be one of The Triumvirate. Even better."

"He's retired," said Zeitz, taking a sip of coffee. "He lost out on The Triumvirate seat. Any obligation you have to report only to him has ended. So let's start from the beginning. You say you were on a mission for Julian, a diplomatic mission?" The robot nodded yes. "But you ended up in The Void?" Bellycold nodded again. "And the friction burns on the hull, they happened when you entered the black cloud?"

Bellycold held up one of his large hands. "No, that happened near the end—the end in terms of distance but not in terms of time. And don't ask me to explain because I have a program that absolutely prevents me from doing it."

Zeitz leaned forward, and his expression became more serious. "How did the crew die?"

"Meteor storm," answered the robot without hesitation. "It didn't seem like much of a storm, didn't seem to do much damage. However, what we didn't know at first was that the hull had been breached, and we started to slowly lose air, which is why the human members of the crew put on their spacesuits. It bought them a few more hours, that's all. And the power system must have been damaged too because eventually everything shut down, and we drifted for who knows how long." The robot suddenly stood up, which put Zeitz on alert. "That's it. That's the whole story. I'll be leaving now. Please let Julian know that I'm back. I have to report on my mission even if he is no longer Commander-in-Chief."

Zeitz pointed to a chair. "Sit down," he said forcefully, and the robot sat back down. "Your story is incomplete at best and a total fabrication at worst." Bellycold opened his mouth to speak but stopped when the Captain held a finger in his face. "I'm willing to risk downloading the information," Zeitz said convincingly.

Bellycold clapped his hands together. "Hey, have you ever seen my imitation of Bishop Carmello?" The robot pretended to clear his throat. "My children," he said in a deep and raspy voice. "Temptation is all about us. Be constantly on guard lest you fall into the abyss of sin and suffer eternal damnation."

The Captain shook his head. "Very good, but it won't work." Zeitz began tapping his pen against the top of his desk. "I was a protégé of Julian Alfiri and have a great deal of admiration and respect for him. I don't doubt you when you say that Julian built in a tamper-proof system to protect the information you are carrying. But I also believe that he built a self-preservation program into your operating system, a program that will allow you to reveal as much of your confidential information as you need to keep from having all of it lost. You are not telling me the truth, at least not the whole truth, and until I am convinced that I know what actually happened on that flight, you will get nowhere near Julian Alfiri. You must realize that I may be the only ally you have—other than Julian. What do you think would happen if a member of the Patriarchy, someone like Bishop Baggio, got a hold of you?"

Bellycold hesitated before answering, "You win."

Out in the corridor, Kellan and his two companions waited anxiously. One of them would occasionally place his ear against the door in an attempt to learn whether the robot was physically attacking Captain Zeitz, but they could hear nothing. A half-hour later, when the conversation in the Captain's office was finally finished, it was Bellycold who came to the door. "Which one is Blake?" he asked in a loud voice. And Kellan took a step forward. "He wants to see you next."

Kellan entered Zeitz's office not certain in what condition he would find the Captain. But Zeitz was okay. He smiled at Kellan, asked him to close the door, and motioned for him to take a seat. The Captain had a favor to ask of Kellan. Since Kellan was about to be discharged from the Ranger Corps in the morning and would be taking a spacefreighter back to Asturias later in the day, he wanted Kellan, as a civilian, to volunteer to escort Bellycold back to Julian Alfiri. It was important that the android report on his mission, said Zeitz without explaining why, and a robot could run into trouble travelling alone. Kellan trusted Captain Zeitz, and Julian Alfiri was the greatest living hero of the Holy Asturian Empire. It was an easy decision to volunteer. Besides, the most important thing to Kellan was that he would be returning home to Capital City, where he hoped the bright twin suns of Asturias would burn away from him this sense of death that was clinging to him like a bad odor.

Zeitz thanked Kellan and shook his hand, then told him he would make a similar request of Stoney, granting him an early discharge from the military if he agreed.

* * *

He was walking down a dark corridor. Exactly where, he was not certain, but he felt that he had been here before and knew this was a dangerous place to be. He was worried that something was going to spring out at him. It would come at him from behind and above, and he turned back, frightened of what he might see. It was there! A dead man with a grotesquely distorted face was floating behind him and just above his head. He backed away several steps, but the corpse remained in the same proximity, only a foot or two from him, as though attached to him by a rope. He tried to turn and run, but now he found that he could no longer control his body. He wanted to scream but had no voice.

Kellan awoke from his dream in a cold sweat. He had been suffering from insomnia since his experience on the death ship, and after lying in the dark for hours unable to sleep, he had finally dozed off only to be awakened by a nightmare. The room was as dark as a tomb, and it took him a moment to remember where he was, on an R'Tani spacefreighter docked at a cargo transfer station on his way back to Asturias. Stoney was asleep in the other bed, and Bellycold was powered down, standing somewhere in the darkness.

The image of the corpse faded, but he still sensed an eerie presence in the room. Now he heard a noise. It was the sound of footsteps, not a dream or his imagination. Something was in the room; someone was moving across the floor. Stoney, who had a lot to drink before he went to sleep, was still snoring in his bed, and the footsteps were too soft to be the heavy-footed android. From the corner of his eye, Kellan noticed a shadow moving toward the far end of the room. The door to the cabin opened and quickly closed again.

Kellan sprang out of bed. "Wake up, Stoney," he shouted as he fumbled for the light switch, then reached for his laser pistol. Bellycold's yellow eyes brightened as Kellan rushed to the door, opened it, and looked in the corridor. Whoever or whatever it was, it was already gone.

"What's going on?" groused Stoney, shielding his eyes from the light with his forearm. "Are you having another nightmare?"

"No, someone was in here, probably a thief," said Kellan. "But considering the situation with Bellycold, we don't need to call extra attention to ourselves by chasing after him."

"Impossible. You were having a dream." Stoney covered his face with his pillow. "This is an R'Tani freighter. They're neutral, and they're safe, or they wouldn't be able to stay in business."

"I saw him," Kellan insisted as he walked to the center of the cabin and looked around the room to see if anything had been disturbed. "We're docked at a freight transfer station. Someone could have sneaked aboard our ship."

"He's right," said Bellycold. The android was completely powered up, and he, like Kellan, began to scan the room with his eyes.

Nothing was out of place. The closet was still closed. Nothing had been moved on the nightstand or on the top of the small bureau that Kellan and Stoney shared. Kellan walked to where his trousers were draped haphazardly over the back of a chair and searched for his wallet. It was where he left it and apparently untouched. He was about to admit that his imagination might have gotten away from him when his eyes fell on something strange. There on the small table at the center of the room was a domed-shaped object about six inches in diameter. The top portion was crossed by thin metal slats, which held in place the four wedged-shaped pieces that made up the upper portion of the dome. Kellan pointed to the object. "I don't remember that being there before."

His remark caused Stoney to pull the pillow from over his face and sit up. Both he and Bellycold took a long look at the object. "It wasn't there before," said Stoney, his eyes locked on the strange device. "In fact, I can't even guess what the fuck it is."

"I can," said Bellycold, without his characteristic sarcasm and attempts at humor. "It's transmitting a radio signal."

"A bomb!" shouted Stoney as he leapt up from his bed. "We'd better get it out an airlock."

Kellan grabbed Stoney's arm as he reached for the domed-shaped object. "Don't touch it. It may be booby-trapped. We'd better get out of here before it goes off."

Stoney was frantic. "What if it blows up the whole ship?"

While Stoney's words still hung in the air, Bellycold's large metal fist came down on the object and smashed it to bits. Kellan and Stoney stood motionless and breathless, staring at the crushed device and the pieces that were scattered across the tabletop and on the floor. Stoney shouted at the robot, "You idiot! You could have blown us into a million pieces."

Bellycold shook his head. "It isn't a bomb, at least not the kind you are thinking of. It's an LEDD, a Localized Electronic Disruption Device. It's a technology that is little known outside the Imperial Intelligence Service," the robot continued in a matter-of-fact tone of voice. "LEDDs are meant to disrupt computer systems by exploding with a very brief but very intense electrical discharge within a very localized area. Sort of like hitting the old central server with a mini lightning bolt."

Kellan, like Stoney, was slowly regaining his composure. "Lucky for you," he said, "that you figured out what it was."

"Lucky for me! What do you think that little baby would have done to your brain?" said Bellycold, pointing to Kellan's head. "Ever hear of electric shock therapy? In the early days of psychiatry they used to run some voltage through the skulls of mental patients. That thing," said the android, now pointing to the wrecked device, "would have given the two of you bloodless lobotomies. Somebody is trying to prevent me from getting back to Julian Alfiri, and that somebody doesn't care if they take the two of you down with me."

"Worse than that," said Kellan, suddenly aware of a gnawing sensation in his stomach. "They may think that Stoney and I also know too much."

The android Bellycold quickly enumerated the possible reasons behind what he called "the attempted assassinations." Although Captain Zeitz planned to delay his report about Bellycold's mission to give them time to reach Julian Alfiri, somehow word could have reached Asturias about the ship that had entered and returned from The Void. The more reactionary members of the Asturian Church, said Bellycold, might not want the faithful to learn about the true nature of The Void. There had been enough trouble centuries before when science had shown that there was a natural, rather than metaphysical, explanation for why perpetual day existed on half of Asturias and perpetual night on the other half.

Or Julian Alfiri's personal enemies might have been behind the attack. No one could have accomplished what Alfiri achieved without making enemies. Bishop Baggio, said the android repeating what Captain Zeitz had told him, prevented Julian from getting a seat on The Triumvirate and helped send him into premature retirement. Certainly the Bishop had no desire to see an old rival return to the political stage to new glory.

Finally, Bellycold concluded, since the information he carried in his data bank might change the balance of power in the galaxy, they could not discount the involvement of Republican agents.

"We'll be lucky if they don't get all three of us during the remainder of our journey to Asturias," he said. "They'll be less subtle next time. And," he continued with greater emphasis, "if we do get back, all three of us may well be arrested the instant we set foot on Asturias. Believe me, I've seen this kind of stuff before."

"After two years of being on that desolate moon base," said Kellan, his voice shaking with a combination of fear and anger, "I have no intention of being thrown into an Imperial prison, especially since I've done nothing wrong. And I don't intend to be lobotomized, bloodlessly or any other way. The best thing to do is to find someplace else to go, another planet or space base, and to do it as soon as possible."

Stoney nodded in agreement. What he feared most, other than being killed, was having to face his father if he returned to Asturias in disgrace. Better to disappear for a while, he thought.

They had to move before the assassin learned that his first attempt had failed. After some discussion, they agreed that they could not escape on their own and had to risk taking the Captain of the R'Tani vessel into their confidence. Kellan went ahead to arrange a meeting, and a short time later they found themselves in the Captain's private cabin.

The R'Tani, Captain T'Mana, like most of his race, was diminutive and milk white, having descended from a long line of space merchantmen. His cabin, the only home he had, was richly furnished with upholstered chairs and reproductions of antique statues and paintings. It was paneled in rare blue oak and contained a large aquarium with an assortment of species from most of the water worlds. The congenial man with the pale green eyes invited them to sit in the soft armchairs arranged in the center of the cabin. He seemed genuinely concerned when he learned that there had been a security problem on his ship. "The R'Tanis aboard this vessel, like all R'Tanis, if I may say so, are completely beyond intrigues of this sort," he said slowly and very deliberately. "And I can, with some certainty, vouch for the non-R'Tani contract crew on my ship. Therefore, I would agree with Mr. Bellycold's conjecture," he said, nodding toward the android, "that someone has sneaked on board from elsewhere on this transfer station. There are indeed five other vessels currently docked here." T'Mana appeared upset by what he was about to say next. "Having admitted this much, I cannot, unfortunately, guarantee that the intruder is not still aboard, and therefore, cannot guarantee your safety. I will, however, extend you any assistance that is in my power to grant."

"My escape is easy enough to arrange," said Bellycold, whose voice seemed especially loud in comparison to the gentle R'Tani's. "I'm not biological. I can be disassembled—arms, legs, and head. Even the torso can be unbolted into upper and lower portions. Pack me in separate cartons and ship me to Harlan Knorr, an aide to Julian Alfiri."

"Another advantage to being non-biological," Kellan thought aloud.

And the R'Tani seized on his comment. "Even so, perhaps a similar arrangement can be made for you and Mr. Stoney. We could conceal you in crates with food, water, and oxygen canisters."

"You mean be buried alive," said Stoney. "No thanks."

T'Mana nodded politely. "But as I'm sure you know, Mr. Stoney, space travel is expensive. Considering the difficulty that you ran into on this ship," he continued in a more sympathetic voice, "I am authorized to give you each a voucher to cover a voyage anywhere you wish to go that is equal in length to the remaining distance back to Asturias. But that, of course, will not get you to where you need to go."

Glancing at Stoney, Kellan answered for the two them. "Neither alternative is very good. We'll have to think of something else, but let's tend to Bellycold first."

The R'Tani Captain escorted them to a workshop, where they were met by two of the ship's mechanical engineers. Bellycold, despite all the intelligence and personality he projected, was only a computerized machine. He powered down and within only a few minutes, the two engineers reduced the giant robot to seven pieces, which they then carefully packed into seven separate crates, all addressed to Harlan Knorr. Captain T'Mana took the smallest package, the one containing the head. "This must house the central processor and data chips," he said. "With your permission, I will store this package in the safe in my cabin."

Watching the robot being disassembled and crated, and wondering if the pieces would ever be reassembled, Kellan was now certain that he could not allow himself to be sealed in a box with only a water bottle and an oxygen canister as life lines. So he and Stoney returned to the Captain's cabin to see if they could arrange transportation to someplace other than Asturias, even though it meant further delaying their long-awaited return home.

After storing the parcel containing the android's head in his safe, T'Mana sat at his personal computer and with the light of the screen illuminating his pale face, he began to scan the freight exchange station's flight schedule. Kellan watched anxiously, then finally allowed himself to feel a tinge of hope when the Captain smiled. "This should do nicely," the Captain said as he continued to call up details to his computer screen. "I've heard good things about Imrada. A chance to make a fortune." Make a fortune? The remark puzzled Kellan, but he soon understood as the R'Tani continued, "There is a vessel leaving here shortly that will stop next at yet another cargo hub. There you can take another vessel to where survey teams are forming to start a mining operation on Imrada." Kellan still did not grasp the full implication of what the Captain was telling him in so casual a manner. "SED-Corp will pay full transportation and offers a generous bounty to anyone finding a strike worth mining." T'Mana turned toward Kellan and smiled. "It's a short contract as well. Only a year."

Now Kellan understood. They would have to sign away another year of their lives to pay for their transportation, another year away from home.

Stoney tapped him on the arm. "Better than a year or longer in jail," he said. Kellan halfheartedly nodded in agreement. "And hell, you're a geologist. They'll be glad to have you."

"Very true," said T'Mana. "Survey team captains get double shares. You may return to Asturias a rich man."

Kellan sighed in resignation. "Well, this place, whatever its name is..."

"Imrada," said T'Mana helpfully.

"Imrada," repeated Kellan. "Imrada can't possibly be as bad as where we spent the last two years."

"Ain't that the truth," added Stoney.

* * *

Kellan was napping in his window seat aboard the small shuttlecraft when Stoney elbowed him. "That's it," said Stoney, pointing out the porthole, "the ship that will finally take us to Imrada."

It had been a long and uncomfortable voyage to this point, and Kellan had not slept well. In fact, these little naps that he occasionally managed to take during their wake periods were the best rest he was able to get, and he was annoyed that Stoney had bothered him while he was enjoying a little of the deep sleep he found so difficult to come by. He opened an eye and glanced out at the vessel they were approaching. "I hope," he said with a yawn, "there are bigger crew cabins on this ship. And instead of a little cot, I'd love a good firm mattress on a bed large enough to stretch out on." And with that, he gradually fell back into unconsciousness.

Space travel could disorient the biological system under the best of circumstances, and this voyage, Kellan calculated, would take at least 20 times longer than his longest previous journey, the trip from home to moon base. Most of their voyage had been aboard the vessel they just left, an aging and cramped spacefreighter on which the gym and recreation rooms had been turned into barracks-like sleeping quarters to accommodate extra passengers. It was an uncomfortable ship with little space for privacy. The long periods of inactivity and the irregularity of meals and rest periods coupled with his continuing insomnia had left Kellan in what he called "a state of terminal spacelag."

At least this next ship, the one that would carry them on the last leg of their long journey, was a legitimate personnel transport vessel and should have the standard conveniences.

Kellan slept for the rest of the shuttle flight, even through the jolt of docking. And when it came time to stand up and walk off the shuttlecraft, Stoney had to shake him roughly by the shoulder to wake him. Kellan stood and threw his duffel bag over his right shoulder. Making no attempt to fix his hair, which was flat on the side he had been sleeping on, or to straighten the wrinkles in his tan jump suit, which he had been "living in" for most of the journey, he fell in line behind his friend, and they followed the other passengers to the bay of the larger ship.

At the end of a long, metal corridor in the reception area stood a woman who was studying the faces of the new arrivals as though she were there to greet someone. She was an attractive woman with a pretty mouth and short, light brown hair. She was tall and slender and had long legs that Kellan found especially sexy.

Kellan finally became fully alert. With his free hand he quickly raked his disorderly hair, then tried unsuccessfully to smooth the wrinkles in his jumpsuit. "Do you have any more of those mints?" he asked Stoney.

Stoney reached into his pocket and produced a foil-wrapped piece of candy. "Last one."

"I'll owe you," said Kellan as he grabbed the mint. The woman was looking straight at them. "Damn," he mumbled as he unwrapped the candy and slipped it into his mouth, "I haven't even shaved for days."

The woman smiled as she stood before them. "From the descriptions I received, I would guess that you two are Gordon Stoney and Kellan Blake."

"The real Stoney and Blake are much better looking," said Kellan. "We're poor holographic displays that have been living out of duffel bags for as long as we can remember. I'm Blake," he said, tapping his chest. "And that's Stoney."

"I'm Caitlin Cormack," she said, first shaking Kellan's hand, then Stoney's. "I'll be your base commander on Imrada. We'll be riding there together."

Neither Asturian had expected to have a woman commander, but both knew she had to be very smart and extremely competent to have earned such a position. Kellan took an instant liking to Caitlin, who had a pleasant demeanor and an alluring, if somewhat nasal, voice. And there was a self-confidence and an aristocratic bearing to Caitlin that he found both intriguing and unsettling—unsettling because in his present state he felt unkempt and unsophisticated.

Stoney caught Caitlin's glance. "What can you tell us about Imrada?"

"You'll want to settle in, maybe even get some sleep," she said. "After dinner, we can have a cup of coffee—or something stronger—and I can tell you what I know about the job on Imrada. As first-time miners, there are some things you'll need to adjust yourselves to." Caitlin looked back toward where the shuttle was docked as though looking for someone else. "I seem to be missing one miner. I'll catch up to you later," she smiled as she left them to walk to the shuttlecraft.

"She didn't answer me," said Stoney. "Do you think she is hiding something?"

Kellan did not hear Stoney's question. He was more interested in Caitlin, the first woman he had become excited about since Auburn. "Interesting lady. Attractive, too."

"Too thin," said Stoney dismissively.

Kellan took a last look at Caitlin's long legs as she disappeared down the corridor. "I don't know about that. I could learn to love tall and slinky."

5 | The Return of Julian Alfiri

The central government of the Holy Asturian Empire and the hierarchy of the Asturian Church were located in Capital City, housed side by side in two white towers connected by a 100-foot-high, glass-enclosed atrium. The atrium was equipped with the most sophisticated holographic display in the Empire, produced by a series of large projectors running up four sides of the atrium. It created images of the twin stars Poltare-Major and Poltare-Minor so sharp and three-dimensional that it appeared as though the two tall blue stars, as represented in the Imperial insignia, had been shrunken and transported here. Some Asturians upon seeing the display for the first time became convinced that any race capable of producing this wonder had to be God's chosen people. And even a frequent visitor to the Imperial Complex might stop to marvel at the image before stepping through the bright rays of the stars to reach the elevators leading to the tower offices.

Into the atrium, which was filled with government workers on meal break, tourists, and groups of children on class trips, walked the great Julian Alfiri and his two closest aides, heavy-set Harlan Knorr and a young redheaded woman named Jelinka Talbot. Trailing several steps behind them were three pairs of technicians, each pair wheeling a large storage box and some smaller containers marked: "Fragile: Computer Equipment."

The younger people in the atrium did not recognize Julian Alfiri, and a few may not have known who he was. But their parents and teachers and the government workers knew the great man—the man, who as a colonial governor, ran a model government, built thriving new industries, and funded the pharmaceutical research that eliminated the Asturian plague; and as Commander-in-Chief of the Space Service, revitalized the fleet and was the scourge of the Republicans, defeating them in three small but significant wars that preserved the Empire's borders; and as a policy advocate, championed public health, general education, and social equality.

Alfiri soon became the center of attention in the Atrium.

In his mid 60s, Julian Alfiri had a round face with a fleshy neck, a stocky build that made him appear shorter than he actually was, and eyes that seemed to notice everything. As was his prerogative as a retired Commander-in-Chief, Alfiri wore his uniform whenever he visited the Imperial Complex. But the uniform, light blue slacks and a dark blue jacket with a silver double-star insignia over the left breast and white braid on the shoulders, was too tight. And several of the silver buttons looked strained to the point of popping.

Surrounded by people wanting to meet him and shake his hand, Alfiri took the time to greet his admirers and to pose for photographs although he was on his way to a meeting that would, in all likelihood, put him back in the center of Imperial politics. He also went out of his way to say hello to the Imperial Guards he recognized from his days with the Space Service, calling each by name, a feat of memory that astonished Jelinka, the younger of his two aides, who had not been with him during the glory years.

Harlan Knorr, worried about how little time there was to prepare for the meeting with The Triumvirate, slipped through the crowd to stand next to Alfiri and whispered that they had to move on. "I must be going," Alfiri smiled as he shook a few more hands and waved goodbye to the crowd.

Alfiri and his entourage crossed through the atrium star hologram and took an express elevator to the top floor, where they were shown by Imperial Guards to a three-room suite. Harlan and Jelinka remained in the first room, where they immediately began setting up their computer equipment, while Julian continued to the second room to review the script of his presentation. A team of technicians went to the third and began to reassemble the android Bellycold. The team had put the robot back together once before, but taking no chances, Alfiri decided to disassemble him and smuggle him into this meeting.

Harlan barely had time to turn on his computer when his pocket communicator buzzed. Julian wanted to see him. He could not find the special contact lenses he needed to wear and was not fully satisfied with the script Harlan had prepared. He never was. Alfiri demanded perfection in both content and style, and when he insisted on changes, even the aide who drafted the document had to admit that his suggestions were always correct. Harlan expected to be making revisions until the last possible second. And indeed, he and Jelinka spent a busy and tense hour putting the finishing touches on Alfiri's presentation, which was ready just as he was about to leave for his audience.

The audience was with the three most powerful people in the Empire—although it was often said that there was an unofficial fourth member of The Triumvirate, Analeigh Dundane, wife of the aged Marc Dundane. Dundane, a gifted man in his youth but in declining mental condition now, was the political representative to the governing body of the Empire. Bishop Baggio was the ecclesiastic representative, and Clifford Riddenauer, the leader of Asturias' most important family of industrialists, the corporate representative. Alfiri was confident that a businessman like Riddenauer would vote for his proposal just as he knew that Bishop Baggio, a conservative cleric and old rival, would oppose him. The swing vote was Marc Dundane, or more accurately Analeigh Dundane, and when Julian entered the posh semicircular room referred to as the Throne Room, he gave her an especially warm hello.

Julian went to the podium at the front of the Throne Room, bowed, and said, "Your Excellencies." After decades as one of the most important people in the galaxy, Alfiri found his forced retirement—"his exile," as he called it—difficult to endure. He was a military leader, statesman, and policymaker; it was his hobby as well as his profession, and he had filled the empty hours of his exile working on plans and projects that might lead to his comeback. Now he was here, back at the apex of power.

Alfiri had a miniature microphone clipped to his collar and a mini-camera disguised as a label pin—both devices intended to help his aides assess how his presentation was going. Back in their suite of preparation rooms, Harlan and Jelinka, seated before their computers, became more attentive as Julian clicked a button on the podium that activated his holographic presentation space. Alfiri would use holograms to illustrate his remarks, but he could also use the technology to read both his speech and notes from his aides because that text would be visible only to him through the special violet-colored contact lenses that Harlan located in his briefcase and helped him insert.

"I come to you today on a matter of utmost importance," Alfiri began like a lawyer addressing a panel of High Court judges. "I think you will also find the matter that brings me here today both astonishing and exciting. But I must begin, with your indulgence," he said with a slight bow, "by reviewing a situation already well known to you."

This was the signal for Jelinka to activate a three-dimensional projection, which appeared in the air before The Triumvirate. The hologram was of their galaxy, and it followed the conventions of two-dimensional Asturian maps with bright stars concentrated primarily in the northwest region and a thick black band, The Void, running the length and width of the star map in the east. Near this Edge of the Universe, were, disproportionately large, the twin blue Poltare stars, marking the heart of the Empire.

Alfiri used the hologram as an illustration to restate what every member of the Empire already knew, that the Empire had its back against The Void and its outward expansion blocked by the increasingly powerful Federated Republics.

The Dundanes seemed interested in Julian's remarks or at least in the elaborately done hologram. But Riddenauer paid only polite attention, and Baggio, who already knew part of the reason behind Alfiri's requested audience, gave the appearance of being bored. Baggio considered Alfiri's liberal views on social issues and morality, and his enormous personal popularity a threat to the Church. And before Baggio himself had ascended to The Triumvirate, the two men had sparred on many issues, ranging from the funding level of the space fleet to whether the Church should continue to play its traditional role in Asturian politics. The Bishop was not happy to see Alfiri back with another plan to create more turmoil.

Noticing Baggio's expression through Alfiri's hidden camera, Jelinka entered a note into the hologram that only Julian could see, suggesting that he skip ahead to the proposal itself. Julian, however, knew that Baggio was a lost cause. This presentation was intended primarily for the Dundanes, and so he continued with several graphs showing how the balance of power would tilt even more heavily in favor of the Republicans over the next 25, 50, and 100 years.

"This data shows the state of affairs in the future," said Alfiri with great emphasis, "assuming there are no major changes in current trends. However, what I will propose here today is to alter those trends quite drastically." That remark caught the attention of both Riddenauer and Baggio. Marc Dundane did not hear it, causing Analeigh to repeat Alfiri's boast into her husband's ear. "Before I make my proposal, allow me to present to you an explorer of sorts, a robot with the unlikely name of Bellycold."

The door to the chamber opened, and in walked the reassembled android. Bellycold first bowed in the direction of the Dundanes, both of whom were as delighted as children to see such an unusual robot. He then turned to Clifford Riddenauer, who smiled and returned the robot's bow. Bishop Baggio, however, turned his face away before Bellycold could greet him.

While having only a general idea of what Alfiri might be proposing today, the Bishop clearly understood his strategy: The clown robot was here to impress Analeigh Dundane, who with her dyed hair and excessive makeup was, in Baggio's opinion, clown-like herself in appearance. The Bishop resented her because as her influence over her weakening husband increased, it diminished Baggio's ability to orchestrate, if necessary, a two-to-one vote against Riddenauer, who like many Asturian businessmen could think and act like a Republican if there was a profit to be made. Undercutting this android was just one of the ploys Baggio would use, but he was prepared today, if he must, to concede a victory—a temporary one, to be sure—to Alfiri.

"Bellycold has been on a most fantastic voyage," said Julian, undaunted by Baggio's reaction, "a voyage that promises a bright new future for the Holy Asturian Empire. This remarkable android was part of a secret mission that I authorized more than a dozen years ago when I first became Commander-in-Chief of the Space Service, a mission to explore The Void."

Baggio became indignant. "This mission, I assume, was approved by The Triumvirate before it was launched."

"Yes, indeed," answered Alfiri, unable to hide his pleasure at besting an old enemy, if only on a single point. "Your predecessors approved the exploration and ordered it kept secret pending its outcome."

Riddenauer was clearly intrigued by this claim. "Are you telling us that the ship actually entered The Void and the robot survived?"

Baggio interrupted before Alfiri could answer. "Why then is there no record of this—this venture?"

"My dear Bishop," smiled Riddenauer, "you cannot expect the Commander-in-Chief to be responsible for the failings of Triumvirate clerks. If we have no record of the voyage, it surely is not Julian's fault."

Alfiri, seizing on this opening to continue his presentation, resumed reading from the prepared text on the hologram. "As you know, travel within The Void was considered impossible. The first problem is that The Void has a very strong magnetic field that makes electronic devices, that is to say, navigation devices unreliable. The second problem is that travel at light speed is only possible in the vacuum of space, and the black cloud is hardly that." Julian paused while Analeigh repeated most of what he had just said to her husband. Then Alfiri triggered the next hologram, which showed a space vehicle with a white halo around it. "We in the Space Service set out some 15 or 16 years ago to solve this second problem and began constructing an experimental spaceship that generated a vacuum around itself."

Riddenauer first smiled at this news, then appeared to be puzzled. "But wouldn't a ship traveling at or near light speed fly beyond its own vacuum field?"

"Good question," answered Alfiri, pointing to the hologram of the ship. "However, you should think of the vacuum as being part of the ship, a second skin that moves along with it in the same manner that the hull does." Julian smiled in a self-satisfied way. "The system worked better than we could have hoped for, and because we were traveling at light speed and—as I will explain to you in a moment—over a very short distance, the cloud's magnetic field presented no problems."

Even Marc Dundane was alert enough to be impressed by this claim, but Bishop Baggio continued to be antagonistic. "So you did actually send a ship into The Void?" Alfiri nodded yes. "With this robotic machine?" Julian nodded again. "And was there a human crew sent into this most dangerous of situations?"

Alfiri hesitated. In fact, the crew of volunteers knew they were undertaking a very hazardous experiment and did so for God and the Empire. "There was, indeed, a human crew," he answered finally.

Baggio tried to exploit this vulnerability. "Then where is the human crew now?"

Riddenauer interrupted, saying that Alfiri should be allowed to tell his story in the sequence that he wished. Analeigh, in an unusual break in protocol, spoke for her husband and seconded Riddenauer's comment.

With a nod to his supporters, Alfiri continued his story. "I will answer the good Bishop's question in a moment or two, but first, allow me to tell all of you the best part of the story." He returned to the hologram of the galaxy. "We learned that The Void, that is, the galactic black cloud, is long and wide but flat—pancake shaped." To the amazement of his audience, even Baggio, Julian rotated the hologram to show that The Void was relatively two-dimensional in shape. "Our experimental ship not only entered The Void but exited the other side." Julian waited for this bombshell to sink in, then said matter-of-factly to the android, "Tell us please, Bellycold, exactly what you saw there, that is, on the other side."

"Millions of stars, new stars, the rest of the universe," the android answered without hesitation. "And new planets too. In fact, we got a good look at a couple of them."

"Yes," added Julian, "including a giant water planet, which I, with your permission, have named Dahai."

The term "water planet" struck Baggio with force although he managed to conceal it. Water meant there was almost certainly life on the planet. "But your crew is dead!" Baggio's comment had the desired effect, dampening the enthusiasm for Alfiri's accomplishment, if only for a moment.

Alfiri admitted that there had been a technological problem in the experimental ship although the trouble had been with its standard technology and not the vacuum generator. While cruising near Dahai, the vessel's sensors were too slow in picking up a meteor shower, and before the conventional shield deployed, one small meteor deflected off an exterior hatch, and a second, even smaller one, penetrated the hull. The vessel developed a tiny oxygen leak that went unnoticed until the ship began its return voyage across The Void. The ship lost power as well; its speed slowed; the vacuum generator shut down. The crew died from lack of oxygen, and the ship, bearing the marks of friction scorching, drifted for years until it re-emerged from The Void near the planet Gondar.

Baggio scoffed at this story and badgered Alfiri both about the death of the crew and the fact that no humans could attest to the truth of Alfiri's story. And when Alfiri explained that the exploration ship itself had been destroyed in a collision with Gondar, and therefore, even the spacecraft could not be presented as evidence, Baggio said as sarcastically as he could, "How convenient!" But Baggio knew he would not defeat Alfiri on this day. Dead crew or not, a second expedition through The Void would be warranted, and his best hope was to control that voyage or let it fail under its own weight.

Baggio abandoned his attack as Alfiri intrigued the rest of The Triumvirate with his proposal of a large-scale, manned exploration of the other side of The Void, one that would open a whole new world, countless new planets and moons that would provide mineral and biological resources for the Holy Asturian Empire, enough to once again overtake the Federated Republics in economic and military power. Alfiri then outlined his plan for an exploration fleet, which, to Baggio's consternation, he wanted to command himself. Julian showed holograms of projected costs and possible profits and returned to the charts that showed how far the Empire would fall behind the Federated Republics if something drastic were not attempted. Analeigh Dundane was firmly in his camp, and therefore, so was her husband, Marc. Riddenauer, as Julian expected, saw the potential payoff in the exploration, and the boldness of the plan suited his sense of business daring.

Baggio now voiced his reluctant support of the expedition but added, "The Church has always taught that The Void represented eternal damnation. It will take some time to prepare the faithful for a new revelation about what lies beyond The Edge of the Universe. If an expedition such as Commander-in-Chief Alfiri proposes were to be undertaken, I would suggest that it be kept secret until such time as the exploration fleet returns with good news and the Church has had the time to do what it must do."

Julian, sensing a victory, smiled, "I concur with the good Bishop's suggestion and believe secrecy is wise for other reasons as well."

"Perhaps," said Baggio smugly, "my colleague, Mr. Riddenauer, who chairs the military and space subcommittee, could tell us how prepared the space fleet is for a mission of the scope that Commander-in-Chief Alfiri suggests."

Riddenauer's expression grew more serious. "Three to five years to assemble such a fleet, I would say off the top of my head." At Julian's age, a three-to five-year wait could virtually eliminate him from any significant involvement in the voyage of exploration. Riddenauer quickly summoned an aide, who brought data on the size and composition of the Empire's commercial fleet, its deployment across the galaxy, and long-term contractual agreements. The conclusions were grim: the Empire's commercial fleet was small, aging, and overextended. Few, if any, long-range military vessels could be spared from their current assignments defending the frontier to make a journey of such length and risk. And finally, the time to gear up production capabilities to build an exploration fleet was at least five years and more likely seven or eight.

The opportunity appeared to be slipping away from Alfiri when the hologram began to flash again. It was another message for Julian from Harlan Knorr: Propose an expedition with privately owned vessels.

Julian, who was at his best when his back was against the wall, approached The Triumvirate members with new confidence. "Am I correct in saying that we all agree that exploration—and development—of this new world would greatly benefit the Empire and must be undertaken eventually?" Even Baggio could not disagree. "Further, we would agree that the only real obstacle is the shortage of appropriate ships. The question, then, is not IF but rather WHEN or perhaps HOW we can manage to send another expedition across The Void."

Julian looked at each Triumvirate member including Analeigh Dundane, the unofficial member, and still seeing no disagreement, he continued. "Yet, the R'Tanis have a massive fleet. And there may be some worthy vessels scattered among the Empire's many corporations. No matter whose ships we use, we, that is, The Triumvirate, would still control the mission because only we know how to build the vacuum-generating devices needed to cross The Void and return in less than an eternity.

"I, therefore, propose," said Alfiri, "that you authorize me to plan a moderately scaled and highly secretive mission, one that would be publicly denied if word leaked out. Further, I propose that you authorize me to seek—with the utmost discretion—the necessary financial and technological support from whatever sources I can muster. If acquiring a space fleet is the only obstacle to launching this smaller mission, leave the chore of cobbling together a ragtag but adequate fleet of spaceships to me."

Analeigh Dundane, again forgetting her place as her husband's advisor, spoke out in favor of Alfiri's proposal, but she was no more enthusiastic than Clifford Riddenauer, who had a vessel or two of his own to commit to such an enterprise. Baggio did not object; his time would come later.

The audience ended. Alfiri graciously took his leave, then marched down the hall to his suite of rooms like a man possessed.

Harlan and Jelinka were busy at their computers when Julian entered the room. "We've already started a database search for Asturian companies that might have the interest and the technology to support the mission," said Harlan.

"You will not find many," Alfiri said gruffly. "But there are Republican corporations that could supply the entire fleet, corporations that would scuttle the Federation itself if there were enough profit in it."

Jelinka waited for an indication that Julian was joking, but Harlan knew better. His eyes returned to his computer screen, and he began to call up Intelligence Service files on Republican space research and development companies.

6   A Hellish Night on Imrada

The alarm on Kellan Blake's wristwatch buzzed, startling him awake. He lifted his head and opened his eyes, then reached under his pillow and found his plastic "wake-up" vial. Lifting it to his mouth with his eyes still closed, he bit off the top and squeezed the contents into his mouth. In a minute or two he would be fully awake.

Adjusting to the 16-hour days on Imrada was impossible without the aid of a stimulant at the start of each wake period and a sedative at its end. The sleeping liquid was especially important for Kellan, who continued to suffer from the insomnia that had plagued him since his encounter on the death ship. And even during his drug-induced sleep, his nightmares continued. Only a few days before he had had a particularly vivid one. This time all three corpses from the derelict ship were attached to him by umbilical cords that could be stretched hair-thin but not completely severed.

His daily life now consisted of six hours of drug-induced sleep; nine hours of hard work, which had to be performed when Imrada's deadly sun was down; and one hour for everything else including a shower at the end of a shift and the one communal meal the base crew ate in the cramped mess hall.

There was only one bright spot in his week, when Caitlin Cormack, the base commander and its only woman, held her regular staff meeting with the mining team leaders. On that day Kellan was sure to shave and have on a clean uniform. He usually sat to Caitlin's immediate left and enjoyed studying her profile, particularly when she smiled and showed her pure white teeth. She had a great sense of humor and managed always to keep the meetings light as well as informative, and he marveled at how she never once showed the strain of being on this miserable planet. Caitlin seemed to like him as well, often glancing at him from the corner of her eye or giving him a discreet wink. But he saw little of Caitlin, who spent her work periods in the command center and took her meals in the Captain's suite.

On this base there was no time and, other than the mess hall, no place for recreation or informal social encounters. In addition to the tight work schedule, everything here was cramped because the base had been built under 500 feet of solid rock to shield the mining teams from the harsh conditions on the planet's surface, conditions that were, contrary to the prediction Kellan had made on the R'Tani freighter when he decided to sign up for this job, considerably worse than those on the Imperial moon base where he had served two years.

At least he had his own quarters, a tiny room consisting of a bureau, chair, and wall cot, which, when open, filled more than half the room's floor space.

In its effort to increase the speed of its mining survey operation here, the company, the Space Exploration and Development Corporation, more commonly known as SED-Corp, crammed a crew of 24 into a base designed to hold only 18. Individual rooms were only as long as they were high and half that in width; just big enough to stack a couple of coffins was how the crew described them. The 12 crewmembers who lost a lottery were forced to double up in rooms just large enough to hold bunk beds. And with six extra crewmembers, common facilities such as the mess hall, the bathroom, and the combination locker room/equipment storage area were strained well beyond their design capacity.

Kellan, checking his watch, finally got up, folded his bed against the wall, and as he did every day, he glanced at the sign pasted to the bottom of his bunk by Gordon Stoney, who was now part of his four-person mining team. It read:

> Welcome to the Imrada Resort Club.
> Estimated survival time if you decide to:
> Absorb radiation—a little more 14 hours
> Sun yourself—definitely less than 6 minutes
> Breathe the atmosphere—4 seconds if you're lucky
> Bathe in a lava pool—we don't recommend it
> Enjoy your day,
> The Management

Rather than just splash water on his face from the basin on his bureau, Kellan had gotten up a few minutes early to treat himself to a cool, early shower that would help lower his body temperature for the start of a hot night's work on the surface. Dressed only in undershorts, he draped a bath towel over his shoulder, grabbed his soap from the bureau, and left for the bathroom.

Sleep was a precious commodity on Imrada, and to avoid waking the other crewmembers, Kellan tread softly on the metal floor as he walked down the narrow, gray corridor. At this hour, he expected to be the only person awake other than Caitlin, who was probably already in the command center sipping her first cup of coffee of the night. As he approached the shower, he thought he heard someone softly humming but dismissed it as his imagination. He entered the bathroom and walked past the row of sinks to the shower area. A naked woman suddenly emerged from one of the shower stalls, casually drying her long blond hair with a large towel. The woman's white skin had turned pink, red in a few places, from the warm shower water. And the flesh of her ample breasts rippled as her hand worked the towel over the hair down the back of her neck. What a fabulous shape, he thought, as his eyes moved from head to toe and back up again. He had already checked out every visible part of her body when she noticed him. "Hi, I'm the new crewmember," she said, seemingly oblivious to her nakedness. "I arrived yesterday and slept in."

Kellan, unable to think of anything to say, clever or otherwise, merely smiled and nodded toward her. He had heard that in the Republics men and women often bathed and showered together, and were generally much more liberal about sex. Seeing this naked woman caused him to remember that before this instant he had not even seen a picture of a nude woman in the months since he left the moon base.

"I'm Vickie Webb," the woman said. Then realizing that he was studying her too closely, she wrapped the towel around her waist to cover the lower part of her body, leaving her top still exposed. "Sometimes I forget where I am. I attended a university where the guys and girls all lived in the same facility."

Kellan was embarrassed that she caught him gawking at her, then became even more uncomfortable when he remembered that he was in undershorts. "I'm Kellan Blake," he said, awkwardly lowering his towel to cover the fly in his shorts, "and I sometimes forget where I am. I'm from the Empire, where people hardly ever go naked, even in the shower when they are all by themselves."

"Really!" said Vickie.

Kellan explained that he was only joking. Then he told her that she must have been assigned to his crew, replacing Fahd Keifedes. The official report on Keifedes was that he had been sent home as a precaution after failing a routine heart examination, but Kellan believed that both the man's physical health and mental condition had quickly deteriorated under the harsh conditions of life on Imrada.

He wondered whether Vickie Webb, with her soft body and gullible nature, would fare any better.

Vickie was talkative, asking many questions about the work on the planet's surface and Kellan's life back in the Empire. He was enjoying their conversation—and the fact that she was standing half-naked before him—but they would have to leave for the surface soon, and when he tried to sneak a look at his watch, she caught him. "I should go and let you take your shower in private," she said. Vickie smiled as she opened her towel to rewrap it and cover herself from the neck to thigh. In doing so she gave him another good look at her. And he took full advantage of it. Vickie smiled again and left the bathroom.

It had been deliberate, he decided. She had given him another look either to torture him or as a come-on. Maybe he would get lucky today. Maybe Vickie would appear at his room after work clad in only a towel. Something like that could never happen back home, but Republican girls, it was said, could be very aggressive.

What a pathetic life, thought Kellan as he finally entered the shower. Encountering a naked woman was the best thing that had happened to him in a long time. He had not seen the sun in more than four months and had not breathed fresh air for a year and a half, not since his last leave from moon base. He once considered himself optimistic and lighthearted, but now he was often morose, obsessed with his own mortality, especially at the end of a work shift when he was lying in his dark, little room waiting for the liquid sedative to take effect. And he had become a slave to his work, driving his mining crew hard, believing that the sooner SED-Corp made some rich strikes, the sooner he could use his share of the anticipated profit to buy his way out of his contract. Only then, when he could return to a world of light, fresh air, and women, could he expect to resume his life. But that would not happen for approximately eight Asturian months or 320 Imrada days—days that, though shorter than those back home, usually dragged by without any high points, without laughter and affection, without the opportunity to lose his accursed consciousness in any engaging activity.

The locker room was the one part of the base approaching normal proportions. Circular in shape, its walls were lined by narrow benches and wall lockers, each with an environmental suit hanging inside it. Piled on the floor and against one wall were dozens of rectangular green-and-white metal boxes containing the various tools that the survey crews brought to the surface with them.

Kellan's team was already suited up when he arrived in the locker room: Stoney, who had become almost as depressed on this planet as Kellan had; an affable Republican named Warren Simmons, who always called Kellan "Chief;" and the newest member, Vickie Webb, whose marvelous body was now hidden under an environmental suit.

The environmental suits, which were thick with insulation and moisture absorbing pads that had to be replaced each day, were white with two-inch-wide green stripes down the arms and legs, and had the word SED-Corp written in green block letters across the front. High on the right side of the chest was the emblem of the Federated Republics, a rainbow arch with forked lightning crossing from upper left to lower right. On the back of the suits were one large tank containing compressed oxygen and a second, slightly smaller one, holding two gallons of water. A thin tube ran from the water tank to a small C-shaped piece that hooked just inside the mouth. Because the planet was so hot, even in the thermal suits, dehydration was a problem, and there was a small flow of water constantly running into the body. Two gallons were far more than anyone would possibly need in a nine-hour shift, but a margin of safety had been built in as there had been with the oxygen supply.

The large helmet, also white, had a cylinder the size and shape of a thermos bottle on either side just above ear level and a clear plastic visor over the eyes that doubled as a projection screen. The cylinders were stereo microwave sensors that penetrated darkness and fog like radar, and projected a three-dimensional black-and-white picture onto the helmet visor. The helmet was also equipped with a satellite-positioning device that projected computer images of satellite-generated surface scans. Using it was like following a road map that was overlaid onto the road before them.

While Kellan hurriedly began getting into his environmental suit, Stoney and Simmons checked out their equipment, and Caitlin Cormack called to the locker room over the intercom, "Who's first on deck? As if I didn't know."

Kellan pressed the intercom button near the monorail control panel. "First as usual, Caitlin."

"Kellan, do you have Ms. Webb with you?"

"Yes, we have a full crew," answered Kellan, looking over at Vickie, who seemed lost inside her bulky suit. "What about the weather?"

"Shouldn't be anything special. The monitoring station, however, says there is a chance of volcanic activity but far enough away that it needn't concern us, not today, anyway. But keep your eyes open—as open as you can."

Simmons leaned over Kellan's shoulder and shouted into the intercom, "You know our Chief. He's Mr. Cautious. He'll get us all back."

The other survey teams were now arriving, but they would have to wait their turn for a ride to the surface as Kellan's group, dragging boxes of equipment, gathered by the airlock that led to the monorail. Just as he was about to put on his helmet, Kellan decided to double-check Vickie Webb's equipment. The company had a thorough orientation program, but you could never be too careful, not on this planet. She stood at attention while he walked around her, making certain that her suit was sealed and that her life support systems were active. It was a good thing that he checked. Although the suit, including the helmet, had been properly sealed, and the oxygen flow started, she had forgotten to activate her water supply. Kellan shook a finger at her and turned the water flow on.

"It won't happen again," she said, her voice muffled by her helmet.

Kellan donned his own helmet and led Vickie to the monorail terminus, which was just big enough to hold the four of them and their two long boxes of equipment. The 1500-foot tunnel leading to the surface was not tall enough for a person to stand in, and the cylindrical monorail car that traversed it on a 30-degree incline was appropriately low and narrow. The crew loaded their equipment and strapped it down, then ducked their large helmets under the monorail door and entered one at time, climbing on all fours to their seats.

Sitting in the first seat, the controls just above his head, Kellan pulled one lever, and the back door closed. When he pulled a second, an electric motor kicked in, and the car started slowly to move. "We're on our way," he reported over his helmet radio, and Caitlin answered, "Good hunting."

The monorail car traveled smoothly for about 100 feet, shuttered once, and moved another 50, then the motor whined and shut off, leaving them stuck in the tunnel in total darkness.

"We're trapped!" shouted Vickie, panic in her voice.

"Happens at least twice a day," said Stoney in a sarcastic tone. He did not like getting stuck in the tunnel either, and it made him ornerier than normal. "Better get used to it, Honey, if you're gonna run with the big boys."

Stoney hit a raw nerve with her. "Big boys, my ass," Vickie shouted angrily. "And don't you dare call me 'Honey'."

"Anything you say, Sweetie."

Kellan interrupted. "We can always hand-crank our way up, Vickie. It just takes forever." He pulled the throttle back and pushed it forward again. Nothing.

"Is the monorail acting up again?" asked Caitlin over the radio.

"Has there been a day when it hasn't acted up?" Now Kellan's frustration was showing. "Sorry, Caitlin, I know it's not your fault."

Caitlin let out a rare sigh of exasperation. "I'll have the mechanic look at it again after everybody's up. And I have a new motor on order although until we have a real strike, we're not at the top of the company's priority list."

Kellan threw the throttle handle again, and this time the monorail resumed moving. Talking more to himself than to

Cormack, he mumbled, "We'll probably make it, but I bet somebody ends up hand-cranking it."

The upper terminus of the monorail was under a protective roof near the enclosed stalls where the land vehicles were kept. When the car reached the surface, Kellan opened the front door and got out. Even with the thermal suits, it felt like entering a blast furnace. The atmosphere, dark gray in the beams of their helmet lights, was thick, and because there was no wind, the heavy fog was eerily still, except for the small eddies created by their own movements. They unloaded the monorail car and sent it back for the next surface crew.

Knowing exactly which of the five land vehicles he wanted, Kellan walked toward stall number 2, waving his hands before him, trying to clear away enough fog to get a glimpse of what was a few feet ahead. He lifted up the stall door, and behind it sat a raft-like vehicle with a V-shaped front, open passenger compartment with room to seat eight, and a large storage area and motor in the rear. Called a "Float," the vehicle, when started, lifted three feet off the ground, suspended by a magnetic field that enabled it to cross any kind of rough terrain with ease. Each vehicle had a trailer attached for carrying additional equipment and the more promising samples of dirt and rock they would collect. The Float's thrust was provided by a solar-charged battery engine.

That was the only positive aspect of exploration on Imrada: the intense sun, after it burned through the night fog, would fully charge the solar batteries in half an hour.

They stored their equipment in the Float's trailer, got in, and Simmons, who enjoyed driving, started the motor. The vehicle gently lifted up to its cruising height; Simmons engaged the thruster and inched the Float out from under the base roof. Beyond the roof it was even hotter, and there was still no wind to stir the thick clouds; so they had only a few feet of visibility. They turned on their microwave imagers, which cut through the fog to produce 3-D images like charcoal drawings, all blacks, whites, and grays, portraying the boulders a short distance off as black lumps and the hills in the distance as dark gray shadows. Simmons pushed the Float to two-thirds throttle and headed into the hellish night of Imrada.

A half-hour's trip took them to the site they had been assigned for the night. Once there, Simmons shut down the Float's engine, and the vehicle gently came to rest on the ground. They climbed out and turned off their microwave imagers. It was still foggy although there was now some wind occasionally parting the mist to let them see a dozen yards in one direction or another and giving them glimpses of the large rocks that stood like monoliths all around them.

While Stoney and Simmons began to unload equipment, and Vickie tried but failed to make herself useful, Kellan turned on his satellite-positioning device. His helmet screen filled with red, blue, and yellow patches of color representing a satellite infrared imaging map. He could adjust the device to view the terrain in a scale that ranged from a few square yards to a square mile, and as his head turned, the map turned with him. He spent a few minutes deciding where they would go first, then led his crew to the first test site. They opened an equipment box and assembled a laser drill, a device that could bore a thin hole to a quarter of a mile below the planet's surface, gathering up tiny samples of dirt, rock, and hopefully some metal ore or fragments of precious stones. The long, tube-like drill was centered in a lightweight, ten-foot-high, aluminum tubular frame and would be retrieved by means of a pulley system at the top.

"Kellan?" Caitlin's static-muffled voice was barely audible over his helmet radio.

Standing surrounded by patches of dark fog, Kellan paused in an effort to hear her better. "Caitlin, you're not coming in well."

The static worsened, then suddenly disappeared altogether. "I'm getting reports of volcanic activity in your general vicinity," she said.

Kellan looked up toward the low clouds moving overhead and noticed that his helmet visor was dirty. He rubbed his glove across it, creating a dark smear. "Caitlin, we're getting ash."

"You shouldn't be," came the answer, "not unless you have a pretty good wind out there."

Kellan looked at the fog blowing by. "Yes, we're getting some wind now."

"Maybe you ought to call it a night." Caitlin sounded concerned.

But Kellan was not. "We got a light dusting of ash, that's all. It seems to have stopped. Let us stay out a while longer unless you see something bad coming our way."

"It's your call, Kellan," answered Caitlin. "I'll keep a good watch."

During the remainder of their shift, they managed to take a dozen core samples, each one requiring that the laser drill and its frame be disassembled, moved, and reassembled again. And each sample was carefully placed in the Float's trailer for return to base, where a technician working the day shift would run a computer analysis of what they had found and map out the next night's survey.

"It's that time, Kellan." They had been working in silence, and so Caitlin's voice was somewhat startling.

He checked the time read-out on his helmet display. They were actually approaching the short end of their safety margin. "We're just about finished." They were in the middle of taking their last core sample, the one that Kellan felt was most promising. "Let's finish up quickly, guys," said Kellan, then added, "Vickie, pack up the rest of the equipment." Just then he felt the laser drill jam. He tried to get it moving forward again, and when that failed, he tried to move it backward. "It's stuck," he said to Stoney, who was working alongside of him. "Try shaking it to get it free." That failed as well. Next Simmons joined them, and through the combined effort of all three, they managed to dislodge the drill and began to retrieve it along with its precious core sample.

"Look at that!" Simmons pointed to the ground where a large cinder burned dark red.

The wind was now blowing in volcanic cinders as well as ash, and a single cinder could burn through an environmental suit with fatal results. Kellan called to Vickie over the radio to return to the Float quickly, and he and the other two men began disassembling the drill frame and packing the laser and core sample with frantic speed.

"Are you on your way back?" called Caitlin over the radio.

"We're leaving now," answered Kellan, but he knew they were cutting it close. The laser was an expensive piece of equipment, worth almost half a year's pay for the entire survey team, and they had no intention of leaving it behind and allowing it to be destroyed by Imrada's intense sun. The cost of the laser and any other damaged equipment would be deducted from their salaries or would have to be worked off through a mandatory contract extension. No one wanted that.

As they hauled the equipment and core samples back to the Float, Kellan checked the time and saw that they were at the absolute limit of their safety margin.

Caitlin, who had been bringing back the other four surface crews, realized that she had not heard a report from Blake's group. "Kellan!" she called, clearly worried now. "You should be well on your way back by now."

"We're on our way," he answered. And it was then that he realized that there were only three of them. Vickie Webb was missing. "Vickie," he called frantically, "Vickie, respond immediately." There was no answer from her, but there was lots of chatter on the radio. Caitlin was asking what was wrong; Stoney was saying that she was lost, and they might have to leave her behind; and Simmons was confident that she had to be nearby because he had heard Kellan order her back to their vehicle.

Kellan looked at his time display again. Imrada's sun was rising, and although exposure to it would not mean instant death, especially not when it was just climbing into the sky, several minutes of it would give them a dangerously high dose of radiation, overheat their environmental suits, and would most likely be fatal.

Kellan climbed into the Float's driver's seat. "Get in," he shouted to the other two, ignoring Caitlin's insistent requests to be told what was happening. Kellan started the engine with one hand while activating the screen on the vehicle's control panel with the other. Each Float and crewmember had a special radar pulse beacon for just such emergencies. Kellan fiddled with the tracking device on the control console until a flashing green light representing Vickie's wrist beacon appeared on the display screen. "She never left her work site. Her damn helmet receiver must be out." He then turned the vehicle in Vickie's direction and went after her.

Caitlin was on the radio again. "I've got your position on the satellite. You're heading away from base. You're not going to make it."

"We'll make it," mumbled Kellan.

With Stoney complaining and Simmons trying to calm him, Kellan quickly closed the distance to the flashing green light. Vickie, oblivious to the danger and unable to hear the radio conversation, did not see the Float until it was a few feet in front of her coming out of the fog. She did not realize what it was at first and screamed into her helmet microphone as Kellan pulled alongside her. Because she was too stunned to move, Simmons and Stoney reached out and pulled her into the Float, while she shouted, "What the fuck is going on? What the fuck do you think you're doing?"

Webb went headfirst into a seat, and as soon as her legs were inside, Kellan turned the Float around and began the mad dash to the base. "I got us into this, and I'll get us out of it," he said, as he opened the throttle full, and the Float shot forward. There were only 23 minutes until sun-up. They would have to cut six or seven minutes off the time it would normally take reach to the base from here.

"Simmons?" shouted Kellan.

And Simmons leaned over the back of the front seat next to Kellan, "Yes, Chief?"

"Divide the trip back into thirds. We need to cover each third in no more than seven or eight minutes tops. Give me markers."

"Right, Chief."

Vickie tapped Stoney on the shoulder. "What's the matter?"

"We're about to be fried," he answered with his typical gallows humor. But Vickie, who could not hear anything over her helmet radio, pointed toward her ear, then held her hands palms up. Stoney moved his gloved thumb across his neck as though he were cutting his throat.

"You're full of shit," she said angrily, thinking he was teasing her. "Stoney's trying to tell me something bad is happening." When Kellan looked back at her without making a gesture of any kind, she understood how serious the situation was. "I knew I shouldn't have come to this planet."

"None of us should have come," said Stoney, who was certain they were going to die. "I'd have been better off having to face my old man on Asturias."

No one responded to Stoney's comment, and except for a few brief exchanges between Kellan and Caitlin, they now rode through the thinning fog of Imrada's dawn in complete silence. They covered the first third of the trip in 9 minutes, 16 seconds, a fact that was duly noted by Simmons.

"Not good enough," said Kellan, who still sounded calm. "Stoney, disconnect the trailer."

"Chief, the trailer and the equipment in it will cost us at least another half a year," said Simmons.

"Fuck it!" shouted Stoney, who began to undo the trailer hitch.

Simmons went to help him. "Maybe, if it isn't completely melted, we can come back and get it tomorrow night."

They did not feel like they were moving much faster without the trailer, but the speedometer indicated that they were, and they covered the second third of the trip in 7 minutes and 29 seconds—better but still not good enough.

Kellan kept an eye on the Float's control panel display, making sure they were on course and steering the shortest possible route. Every now and then, he would press his hand against the throttle in a futile effort to milk a little more speed out of the vehicle. He watched as the clock counted down to 6 minutes left, then 5, and 4.

The only other mining crew still on the surface had just reached base and was starting down the monorail. Kellan and his group could hear the leader of the other team complaining over the radio that the monorail motor had stalled out. What else could go wrong?

Three minutes left; they were too far away. For once, time on Imrada was moving too quickly.

Overhead the sky was showing the first signs of light, and the fog was turning a much lighter shade of gray. There was almost no time left, and the roof of the base was just coming into view.

Simmons looked up at the sky and again at the base roof. "It's about that time, Chief."

Kellan, his hands gripping the wheel tightly, was hot and soaked with perspiration. The overheat light on his helmet display was flashing red. The sky was getting bright.

Caitlin Cormack was urging them on; Vickie Webb was crying.

The Float's one major shortcoming was its breaking mechanism. Essentially it drifted to a stop with some help from two small reverse thrusters. Risking shooting past the base roof, Kellan kept the throttle open as long as he dared, then let up on it. The nose of the Float glistened with near-blinding sunlight. He engaged the reverse thrusters, and they glided under the protection of the roof.

"Okay Chief," shouted Simmons, clapping his hands. "We did it."

"That's the last time I'm taking a ride with you," said Stoney, who was calm enough now to crack a joke.

Vickie was sitting in the rear seat with her eyes closed. Simmons touched her arm. "Are we safe?" she asked, and he nodded yes.

They climbed out and ran to the monorail entrance, where they had to wait for the car to be hand-cranked up from below. Beyond the roof, brilliant white light was penetrating the fog, giving them their first look at daylight on Imrada. The monorail car finally arrived, and they hurried into it. Kellan took a last look at the outside world, which was becoming as bright as a star burst. He closed the door and began to hand-crank the monorail down to the base.

* * *

His body soaked with perspiration, his chest pounding as though he was about to have a heart attack, Kellan lay on his bunk in the dim light trying to recover from their near-fatal experience on the surface. He had come extremely close to killing himself and three other young people on this day. And he was beginning to suffer from claustrophobia. Now that he had seen the surface when it was being struck by sunrays as bright and deadly as laser beams, the base had become impossibly small. He was 500 feet underground, encased in solid rock, connected to the surface by a single long tunnel and a malfunctioning monorail. He needed more space and was having trouble breathing, and as his little room began to close in on him, his thoughts began to spin out of control.

"Get a hold of yourself," he said aloud, and he tried taking deep breaths.

What if this was what death was like? The body decayed, but the consciousness remained buried in a place like this without any physical stimuli of any kind. The mind would turn back on itself, knowing that it had an eternity of trying to futilely divert its consciousness from where it was. He would mercifully go insane. Perhaps that was what death was. Not utter annihilation, which he also feared, but rather an insane consciousness locked 500 feet under solid rock.

There was a tapping at his door, the first time that had happened during his entire stay on Imrada.

"I'll be right there," he called as he sprang out of bed. He was a wreck and would not even let Stoney see him in this condition. He stripped, toweled off the perspiration from his face and body, and put on fresh underwear and a clean pair of slacks. "I'm coming," he called again as he used his fingers to bring some order to his wild hair.

Kellan opened the door to his small cabin and was surprised to see Caitlin standing in the corridor. She appeared shaken. "Come in, come in," he said, motioning toward his bunk, the only place in the cabin to sit down. "Have a seat."

Caitlin walked over to the bunk and sat on the edge. He sat next to her, feeling awkward to be enclosed in such a small space with a good-looking woman who also happened to be his boss. "I want to apologize," she began with difficulty, "for letting you down today."

There was a vulnerability in her now that he had not previously seen. "It was all my fault," he said. "You had five crews to worry about. I had one."

She started to shake her head in disagreement. He could see tears welling up in her eyes, and he put a hand on her shoulder. "I let you down," she said as a single tear rolled down her cheek. Kellan gently brushed it away with the back of his hand.

"It was my fault," he insisted, "but regardless, we all got through it."

Caitlin looked like a child who needed cuddling, and despite feeling overmatched by her, he wrapped his arms around her. She leaned against him, but when he squeezed her tighter and kissed her first on the cheek, then square on the lips, she pulled away.

"This is a small base," she said, "and I'm the base commander. We have to control ourselves."

"Okay, we'll control ourselves but stay like this for a little while longer." He pulled her close again, and she rested her head on his shoulder.

7 | Unholy Allies

Harlan Knorr, his fleshy cheeks flushed red, sat anxiously outside the office of Kit Dreyer, the head of SED-Corp, the Republication exploration and mining company. A half-hour earlier, Harlan delivered a personal letter from Julian Alfiri to Kit Dreyer and had been sitting here anxiously ever since waiting for an answer. Next to him sat Bellycold. It had been Julian's idea to send the android along on this mission to recruit a possible Republican partner for the expedition "Beyond the Edge of the Universe," as Alfiri called it. He thought that Bellycold's sophistication would impress Dreyer, but Dreyer had not seen Bellycold. Instead it was Harlan who had been impressed by Dreyer's robot, the one with the model number 8-O stenciled on his chest and back. It was a sentry robot, and it stood across the room "keeping an eye on them," in the words of Dreyer's male assistant.

Otto, as the robot was called, was programmed to engage in combat—either by direct command or as an automatic response to prescribed situations—and he could destroy property and injure, even kill animal life including humans. There were no such robots anywhere in the Empire. Otto, who was about six feet tall, was fearsome looking, especially standing where he was in the shadow of the unlit portion of the waiting room. Harlan found the robot's color, a metallic dark purple with black undertones, and its lack of a complete face unsettling. Otto's face was T shaped. The eyes, the horizontal part of the T, were a continuous two-inch-high band of hexagonal light-sensing elements stretching from ear to ear. The vertical part of the T, the large nose-like compartment, Dreyer's assistant was careful to point out, contained several types of nerve gas, all but one lethal, as well as a tiny speaker, which Otto rarely used. His arms and legs were on the thin side, like pipes with elbow and knee joints, but his torso was broad and deep. He held a laser pistol in each hand, and from small doors in his shoulders, chest, and back additional blasters could quickly be put into action. Because he could use all these weapons simultaneously and with computer speed and precision, Otto was equal to a dozen or more human guards.

Otto heard the approaching footsteps before Harlan did and turned toward the door to Dreyer's inner office as the administrative assistant finally reappeared. The assistant crossed the room and handed Alfiri's letter back to Harlan, which Harlan took to mean that Dreyer had rejected Julian's invitation to a private meeting aboard a neutral R'Tani spacefreighter. But Harlan was wrong.

"Ms. Dreyer agrees to the meeting," the assistant said matter-of-factly. "She insists, however, on bringing Otto here as well as a human escort."

This was very good news, except for the part about Otto. Harlan was hoping he would never see the sentry robot again, but he was not empowered to refuse this condition. He looked at the dark purple robot and swallowed hard, "That is acceptable."

Bellycold, who had been mercifully quiet until now, put a large hand on Harlan's shoulder, "Hey, the more robots the merrier." Harlan frowned at the android.

Harlan and Bellycold retreated to the spaceport where their ship was waiting. A few minutes later they took off. Not long afterwards Kit Dreyer and her escort, including Otto, were following behind in a SED-Corp vessel.

In preparation for their meeting, Julian Alfiri sat in the conference room aboard the R'Tani vessel, rereading the file that Harlan and Jelinka had prepared on Kit Dreyer. In her late 60s,

Dreyer was tough, smart, and painfully direct. She knew her business, asked good questions, but was often cranky and abrupt. She could also be charming at times, although in her case, the mere absence of abrasiveness could masquerade as charm. Dreyer's aggressive and competitive nature had won her few friends as a youth but turned out to be a great resource for her when, as one of the first women in the Republics to start her own corporation, several conglomerates tried to snuff out her fledgling SED-Corp. Now, more than 25 years later, her company was one of the largest and most successful in the galaxy. Dreyer had the ships and equipment to complete the fleet that Julian was assembling. She also had the independence and daring to risk such a venture.

The only negative that Julian could see, other than Dreyer not being a loyal citizen of the Empire, was a conflict that happened 13 years earlier. The Republicans had taken over an Asturian colony on the frontier and had set up several mining operations, one of them belonging to Dreyer. Alfiri, as Commander-in-Chief of Space Service, had sent in a regiment of Imperial Rangers to recapture the colony and expropriate the mining facilities, which is exactly what the Republicans would have done had the situation been reversed. But that was a long time ago. And as Julian was fond of saying, "Profit, not revenge, is the favorite dish of a Republican corporate executive."

Julian was uncharacteristically nervous about this meeting because he felt that it was the last major obstacle to his becoming the discoverer of new worlds and being ultimately responsible for swinging the pendulum of galactic power back in the Empire's favor. During his entire adult life he believed that no achievement was beyond his grasp, and even in his forced retirement, he was always confident that he would return to prominence one day, perhaps even replacing the aging Marc Dundane as a member of The Triumvirate. Now that his expedition was close to becoming a reality, he worried that the opportunity might somehow slip away, and he glanced at his notes one last time only seconds before the Republican group arrived.

Kit Dreyer made her entrance accompanied by her entourage. The SED-Corp head had wrinkled skin, hollow cheeks, thin lips, and a sunken mouth, and because she had decided against wearing her glasses, she squinted often. However, despite her aged appearance and snow-white hair, she looked fit and almost military in her green-and-white SED-Corp uniform.

Julian stood to greet her. "It is a pleasure, Ms. Dreyer," he said, extending his hand. "I hope you did not find my note too informal and the request for this meeting too inconvenient."

Dreyer shook hands with Alfiri, glancing around the room suspiciously. "It was inconvenient, but I was interested enough to come,"

she said, finally looking at Alfiri. "I've heard a lot about the great Julian Alfiri, and I must I admit I never thought I'd meet you, not under these conditions, not as a possible partner," she said emphasizing the word "partner." "Wouldn't your brothers in the Church consider this something of an unholy alliance?"

"Some might," smiled Alfiri as he and Dreyer sat down opposite each other at a small white circular table that had only two chairs. "I'm hoping we can rise above that kind of attitude for mutual gain." Dreyer's escort, including the robot Otto, lined up behind her as Alfiri's aides, including the android Bellycold, took their positions behind him.

The R'Tani conference room, with star charts decorating the walls and a dome-shaped observation window overhead, was quite pleasant, but Dreyer paid it no attention. "Your letter said that you and I have some business to discuss," began Dreyer, not waiting for Julian to set the stage for their conversation. "I'm a busy woman, and you're a busy man. So why don't we get down to it?"

"As you wish," said Julian graciously, but he was slightly annoyed by her impatience and impertinence. During the next few minutes, Alfiri was in top form as he outlined to Dreyer the possibility of becoming the first Republican company to be permitted to search for and develop natural resources in the Holy Asturian Empire. At first, Dreyer raised her eyebrows in surprise at this suggestion, for she was being offered an opportunity that no Republican corporation had been granted in more than a half a century. Then she threw a dart at Alfiri's proposal by saying that she did not think the Empire had any natural resources worth developing.

"Circumstances prevent you from being aware of the great wealth there is to be found and developed in the Empire. If this were not so, we would have no need of your ships and equipment."

"So that's it," said Dreyer, nodding her head. "You need ships and equipment."

"Indeed," smiled Julian, "interstellar exploration ships, large cargo ships, and land exploration and mining equipment, the most sophisticated technology that you have at your disposal and everything that you can spare." Dreyer appeared somewhat shocked by this statement. So Julian, added, "Rest assured, you will profit very handsomely from the arrangement."

Dreyer paused for a moment, then said in a skeptical tone of voice, "All this sounds very interesting, but I must say, it leaves me with more questions than answers. And I don't do business when I have too many unanswered questions."

The discussion was about to reach its most critical point. "There is only so much I can explain without giving away my bargaining leverage," said Julian.

"I appreciate your position," replied Dreyer. "But I hope you understand mine when I say that I have to know exactly what I am getting into before I commit one ship or even a single mining laser."

Julian had been in far tougher negotiations. Dreyer, he decided, was goading him. If she were not interested in pursuing this partnership further, she would have left the room by now. Such was her reputation. "Of course, you have to know what you are getting into," said Julian coyly. "But must you also remember what you are about to learn?" Dreyer seemed confused by the remark. "I suggest that the two of us continue our discussion alone and with one stipulation. Are you familiar with this?" he asked, placing a small vial containing a yellow liquid on the table.

"Not unless it's a urine test," said Dreyer.

"It is a harmless drug," he said, looking her directly in the eye. "It prevents the brain from storing information in the long-term memory. A small dose will prevent you from retaining 20 to 30 minutes of information but in no way interferes with other cognitive abilities. You will be able to evaluate the information I give you and make decisions the way that you would under normal circumstances. I can tell you fully what you need to know to make an intelligent decision, but before you leave, you will find that everything you heard here has left your mind." She appeared genuinely startled by this proposal. "Perhaps, Ms. Dreyer, you have the same drug in the Republics."

"No, we do not," she said, shaking her head. "At least, I've never taken it."

"Madam," said Julian, his tone becoming more forceful. "If you were familiar with this drug, you would have no hesitation in taking it. Since you are unfamiliar with it, let me tell you in the strongest possible terms that I have nothing to gain by tricking you, and I would not waste your time—and mine—bringing you here if I did not think we were likely to reach an agreement. Nor would I make an agreement that I would not live up to."

Dreyer paused for moment, staring at the yellow liquid, then asked, "What's this stuff called?"

"Dynalixosolin."

"Dy-what? Never mind." Dreyer pulled a small transmitter from her pocket and placed it on the table. "If this damn drug is necessary, have your eggheads pull some journal reports and chemical diagrams of the stuff, and I'll have my eggheads, who are listening in on this conversation, take a look at it."

The negotiation was interrupted for five minutes while Harlan and Jelinka scanned their computer databases for the necessary information and transferred it to a minidisk. Jelinka brought the minidisk to Julian, who gave it over to Kit Dreyer. She, in turn, called Otto to her side and inserted the minidisk into a small slot at the base of his neck. The information was radioed by Otto back to the SED-Corp ship, and a short time later, Dreyer's advisors informed her that she could safely take the drug. She drank it, and as a sign of good faith, Julian withdrew his hidden microphone from under his lapel and placed it on the table along with Dreyer's. He then removed the batteries from both devices and asked all the people and robots present to leave the room.

Julian waited for Dreyer's eyes to dilate, an indication that the drug had taken effect, and he began his presentation, as usual, with a bit of personal history. "For some years, as you know, I was Commander-in-Chief of the Asturian Space Service. During my tenure in that position, I sent several unmanned probes into what we Asturians call The Void, but none was ever recovered—until very recently." The Republicans were not as obsessed with The Edge of the Universe as the Asturians were; it was not a physical barrier to their expansion, nor was it of any metaphysical significance. But Dreyer listened with interest nonetheless. "That last expedition, the one that returned, was manned. It also included the android Bellycold, whom you have seen in this very room a few minutes ago. The problem inside The Void was twofold: How to achieve and safely maintain light speed in a fairly dense cloud. And how to navigate within a magnetic field that renders computers almost useless at times." Alfiri paused for effect. "But my research team," he continued, "came up with a development that made crossing The Void possible—a vacuum generation device that makes travel at light speed possible within the cloud."

"And the magnetic field problem?"

"It had a negligible impact on our vessel although we cannot be certain exactly why. Perhaps it was a side effect of the vacuum generator. Perhaps its was travelling at light speed."

"So you went into the cloud?"

Julian smiled. "Our ship not only entered the cloud but exited the other side, in a sense going beyond the edge of the known universe." Dreyer's eyes lit up. "As you might expect, we found new stars and star systems and planets. A few of the most promising planets and moons were surveyed from space. There are some details that I will spare you such as the meteor storm that the ship encountered, something that could have befallen any vessel anywhere in space. But let me describe some of what we found in this new world." Julian paused to be certain he had Dreyer's attention; he did. "There is a moon, a large one, that appears to have the greatest deposit of uranium yet found anywhere." Dreyer was nearly jolted out of her seat by this claim. "We also detected an element on an asteroid that we were unable to identify, perhaps a new metal that does not exist in this part of the galaxy." Alfiri pointed up to the observation dome above them, and Dreyer's eyes followed. "On to how many worlds has the human race expanded?" he asked, looking at the stars.

Dreyer hated being quizzed on obvious questions and normally would have said so, but she wanted Alfiri to keep talking. "Counting military bases and small mining operations, I would say 125 or so—although only about 20 are really livable."

"Of that," continued Alfiri, "how many can naturally sustain life? How many have indigenous life?"

"Only nine have enough water to be of consequence. The rest have engineered water systems and massive recycling."

Julian dropped his eyes from the observation window to look directly at Dreyer. "Now there are 10 water planets, as you say, of consequence. We have found a planet that is bigger than any two of the other nine major water worlds combined. It has abundant water and plant life, and most likely has animal life as well. I have called it 'Dahai' after the mythical paradise in Asturian Holy Book."

The possibilities ran wild through Kit Dreyer's mind, and she thought: Name the planet anything you like; we can always change it later.

Their conversation lasted a while longer and was mostly concerned with the numbers and types of ships and equipment Dreyer agreed to provide, and the precautions intended to ensure that neither side would take advantage of the other. All the while, Julian kept repeating the key concepts to keep them fresh in her mind: The Void had been crossed; new worlds existed; one of them was a large water planet called Dahai; they would undertake a joint exploration and development project. Finally Kit Dreyer signed the contract that Harlan Knorr had prepared in advance, and Alfiri and Dreyer, the new partners, shook hands.

As Dreyer left Alfiri, she was barely able to conceal the smirk on her face. Earlier she had put on a show for him, hoping to lower his guard. There was, in fact, a memory blocking drug in the Republics and also a counteragent, which Dreyer had taken before she had left her ship to attend their meeting. She had been able to retain the important points of their conversation—or so she thought. When she reached into her memory for the details, they were beyond her grasp. She was suddenly at a complete loss to explain why she was on an emotional high or to remember even one significant detail of the conversation. In fact, she would not have known that she had signed a contract if she had not been carrying a copy of it in her hand.

But she had one more ploy: there was another microphone hidden in the upper plate of her dentures. As soon as she reached the SED-Corp vessel, Dreyer pulled out her upper plate and tapped it in her hand until a small transmitter fell out. "These infernal teeth are uncomfortable enough without this damn thing inside," she complained as two of her advisers hurried to her side. "The counteragent didn't work," she told them. "Were you able to pick up the conversation?"

Mather, the more senior of the two advisers, shook his head. "No, it was jammed. Alfiri and his people rarely miss a trick."

"Well," said Dreyer, waving the folder paper in her hand, "I just signed a contract, and I must have had a damn good reason. A lot of equipment is involved. Let's get every available mind working on figuring out what I've gotten us into and how we can best take advantage of it."

* * *

As Julian Alfiri and Kit Dreyer were concluding their business, another meeting was just beginning across the galaxy on Asturias, between Bishop Baggio and one of his senior aides, Prelate Carlo Asana, a lean man in his early 50s whose pockmarked skin, thick glasses, and thin, oiled-back, gray hair combined to give him a particularly stern appearance. Baggio, who at 63 years old looked almost as young as his aide, sat at his antique mahogany desk, a priceless carved ivory depiction of the Well of Life on the wall behind him. He considered Asana, who sat across from him, ambitious and ruthless, which made the Prelate a perfect choice for the assignment Baggio was about to give him.

Baggio tossed a folder across to Asana. "The most recent composite report."

Asana opened the folder and browsed through it without really reading anything. "I can imagine: Revenue down again; more churches closed; monasteries crying for novices to fill out their dwindling ranks." Asana closed the folder and slid it back toward Baggio. "It is an age of cynicism and irreverence. And now Alfiri is back."

Baggio was bothered by the hint of condescension in Asana's tone as well as the remark about cynicism and irreverence, as though Asana were offering an excuse—and a weak one—for Baggio's guardianship of the Church. Just how ambitious was the Prelate? the Bishop wondered. And he was beginning to think that, for his own sake, it would be good to get Asana out of Capital City for an extended period of time. "Yes, Alfiri is back," the Bishop said finally, "back and dealing with Republicans. We seem to have a theocracy in which nothing is sacred any longer. I never thought I would utter these words, but the greatest threat to the Church is within the Empire, not outside it."

Asana, as he often did when he was agitated, flushed dark red. "Perhaps the time has come for a crackdown, a return to the values and ways of the past."

"No, no, no," said Baggio, shaking his head. "My dear Prelate Asana, if there is one thing that history has shown us, it is that tightening the ropes when the flock is acting rebellious usually causes much of the flock to break free altogether." Asana clearly did not like being contradicted. Too bad, thought Baggio, I'm still the Bishop, and you, the Prelate. "It is better to let this kind of energy dissipate on its own or perhaps to channel and control it."

Asana was one of the few members of the Patriarchy who knew about the planned expedition across The Void. "The faithful," the Prelate said, "are not ready to learn that The Void is just an astrophysical anomaly with no metaphysical significance. It will take years, perhaps a generation or more, to prepare people for that news."

"I'm well aware of that fact," said Baggio sharply.

"If Alfiri's infernal robot is to be believed—and we dare not chance disbelieving it—there is a whole world on the far side of The Void."

"That is correct. The robot also claims to have observed a giant water world, which Alfiri had the gall to name Dahai."

Asana's eyes opened wide at this news. "That means life."

"Yes indeed, life."

"It could even mean intelligent life, human or otherwise," said Asana as he leaned across the Bishop's desk. "You and I can understand that an all-powerful Creator is capable of creating two very different worlds of intelligent beings, both meant to be flocks of the Church. But many would have their faith seriously challenged by such a discovery. Such a discovery would appear—on its surface—to invalidate core aspects of the Holy Book. And I can imagine even worse. What if the basic laws of physics are different on the other side of The Void? The absence of gravity or magnetic fields as we know them? There might be other physical forces that we cannot even begin to imagine. Would there be anything left of what we now believe that anyone could trust as being true?"

"Let's not get carried away, Prelate Asana," said Baggio calmly. "It seems very unlikely the rest of the universe is much different from what we know of our own galaxy. On every world explored in both the Empire and the Republics, the laws of physics have always been exactly the same, and never, never, never has any other intelligent life form been found. In that regard," said Baggio pointedly, "the Holy Book is quite literally correct in its description of creation."

With that comment, Asana realized that he had to be more careful or risk being accused of being heretical for challenging the truth of the Holy Book. "Then you intend to allow Alfiri to make this expedition?"

Baggio leaned back in his chair. "I will oppose him no further. That is," he added with a smile, "not openly." He paused a moment, then looked his somewhat puzzled aide in the eye. "You, my dear Prelate Asana, are about to be given the opportunity to serve your God, Church, and country in a most extraordinary way." Asana became very attentive in anticipation of what the Bishop was about to say next, and so Baggio let him dangle for a few seconds before saying, "You are going with Alfiri as my representative."

8 | A Hard Offer

Caitlin and Kellan got up from the small couch in her quarters and went to the door. He put his hands on her waist; she rested her arms on his shoulders; and he kissed her on the lips. She kissed back, then drew away. Emboldened by the flask of rum he had shared with her—a gift from Stoney, who managed to sneak a relatively large store of liquor onto their underground base—Kellan kissed her a second time on the lips, then a third time, then on the base of the neck, which caused Caitlin to react as though she had been jolted by electricity.

"Time to go," she said as she withdrew her arms and took a step backwards. "We both have an early day tomorrow or an early night, to be more accurate."

Another disappointment for him, another date when their romance, or near romance, as Kellan thought of it, was not to be consummated. "One last hug," he said as he embraced her again.

"A last hug," she agreed, pressing her cheek against his.

"Just stay like this for a minute."

"But only a minute."

Everyone on Imrada was sleep-deprived, and stealing an hour, even a half-hour, to socialize at the end of a work shift was difficult. Nonetheless he and Caitlin had managed to get together five times—he knew the number exactly—over the past few weeks. This was the first time she had invited him to her cabin, which was why he had been hopeful. But this relationship was beginning to remind him of his frustrations with Auburn. The encouragement came during their staff meetings and whenever he bumped into Caitlin in the mess hall. She would touch the back of his hand to emphasize a point or lean her shoulder against his, and on one occasion she sat with her knee touching his. The reluctance came when they were alone. She was usually responsive to his kisses but only cautiously so, apparently fearful of becoming too passionate. That must mean that she had some kind of romantic or at least sexual interest in him, but she was dealing with her feelings more like a schoolgirl back on Asturias than a woman from the liberated Republics.

Kellan give her a last squeeze, then a final kiss, and said good night.

As he walked softly through the corridor that ran down the center of their sleeping base, Kellan decided he was being too harsh on Caitlin. She was, after all, the base commander, his supervisor, a high-ranking woman in a field that was almost the exclusive domain of men. An affair with a subordinate could ruin her career with SED-Corp and follow her the rest of her working life. Of course, she had to be cautious.

On the other hand, he wondered if the distance he sometimes sensed between the two of them meant that he was simply her best alternative on a desolate planet. And at times he felt that might be all she was to him.

The one certainty was that he would spend another sleep period alone.

It seemed like only a short time later when Kellan had to arise, drink his wake-up liquid, and hurriedly eat a small breakfast bar. He rushed to the locker room to meet his crew—Stoney, Simmons, and Vickie Webb—and face another hot, bleak night on Imrada. Tonight, however, their shift might be more than routine because his team was closing in on a silver deposit, not a large one, but something that would help pay for the equipment that was destroyed during their race with Imrada's rising sun.

Caitlin called to the locker room over the intercom, sounding the same as always. "Who is up first? As if I didn't know."

"We are, Caitlin," Kellan responded. "We'll bring you back enough silver samples tonight to make you a bracelet."

"You know I love jewelry," she laughed.

Kellan and his crew finished putting on their environmental suits and climbed into the monorail for the long ride to the surface. The old monorail motor had been replaced by a reconditioned one that was only slightly better, and it nearly stalled out twice before they reached the top.

On the surface the fog was thicker than usual, and they had to turn on their microwave imagers to see even a few feet in front of themselves. Kellan, ever mindful of their brush with death, selected the Float that he considered the most reliable and checked the time on his helmet display every few minutes. With Simmons at the controls, they started out for their silver deposit, arriving at the site more than an hour later.

They had just unloaded the first equipment container and were about to lift its lid when Caitlin called over the radio. "Imrada Base 3 to all surface crews." Kellan had never before heard Caitlin make so formal a radio call, and he thought her voice lacked its characteristic sparkle. "We've got some company. I want all crews to return one at a time in 15-minute intervals. Kellan, you were first out, and you're first back in. Head to base now. Please acknowledge."

"Roger, Captain Cormack," said Kellan, adopting the formal radio etiquette that Caitlin was using. "We hear you and are heading back now."

They returned the unloaded equipment box to the Float, climbed onboard, and began the trip back in complete silence, understanding that an important member of SED-Corp's management must be sitting next to Caitlin and able to hear any radio transmission they might make. Kellan was sure that they would not have been abruptly pulled from the field without good reason, and when they reached base an hour later, they found a somber-looking engineer waiting for them. There was, indeed, a visitor from SED-Corp headquarters, and they were instructed to meet with Captain Cormack individually, starting with Kellan, who took off his environmental suit and hurried to the command center.

Sitting next to Caitlin at the communications console was an older woman with gray hair and a wrinkled mouth but with a rugged looking body and a hard look in her eye. After taking in the visitor, Kellan's gaze moved to Caitlin, whose expression was more serious than he had ever seen before.

"Kellan," said Caitlin, "this is Ms. Dreyer." Kit Dreyer nodded at him but made no move to shake his hand. "Kellan is our top mining team leader," said Caitlin as he dropped into one of the chairs by the computer bank and sat facing them. Caitlin gave him a stern look. "Kellan, Ms. Dreyer, who is the chief executive officer of SED-Corp, has an interesting proposition for you, and I think you should hear her out."

This was bad, he thought. Caitlin was warning him not to lose his temper.

"I have a deal for you," Dreyer began. "It's a good offer but also a hard offer because you have no choice but to take it. I know the conditions on this planet are terrible, worse than I could endure, and I know the pay is good but not the greatest. And the prospecting hasn't been the best."

Kellan tried to contradict her. "We were about to sink an exploratory shaft into what might be a decent silver deposit." Before he completed the sentence, he was sorry he had spoken. A minor silver deposit was not going to change what Dreyer was about to tell him.

Indeed, she dismissed his comment with a wave of her hand. "I saw the numbers." Dreyer pointed to Caitlin. "Captain Cormack here, in whom I have the utmost confidence, showed me the projections. They don't look that good. Listen," she said, holding up her index finger. "I've got a lot of people to talk to; so I'll come to the point. I'm closing down the mining operation on this planet." Kellan was not sure how to take this news and hoped that it might mean that he was going home. He could not have been more wrong. "There are two issues involving you, Mr. Blake," continued Dreyer. "One, you owe me for some expensive equipment that you destroyed, and two, if you read your contract carefully, you'll know it is for a full year whether on this planet or elsewhere."

Kellan looked to Caitlin, and her expression seemed to say "patience."

"That's the bad news," Dreyer continued. "Here's the good news. I've got a new project, a major exploration and development project, and I can use good men like you. Good women, too," she added, looking back at Caitlin. "So here's my offer. I've got you under contract for more than six months one way or the other, and it could take you another six months of working for nothing to reimburse me for the equipment you destroyed. But I'll forget the cost of the very expensive laser drill that you let melt, triple your base pay, and double your percentage of your team's gross take if you extend your contract for another year."

Another year! He was getting farther and farther away from ever returning to Asturias.

"It's the best option, Kellan," said Caitlin, who evidently wanted him to accept the offer. "You might even end up someplace where there is fresh air and plenty of sun. And you certainly couldn't find a worse world then right here on Imrada."

"That's what I said when I left the moon base where I was stationed to come here." Kellan turned from Caitlin to Dreyer. "Where would we be going?"

"I can't tell you where, not exactly. What I can tell you is that it is a joint expedition with Julian Alfiri."

The name Julian Alfiri set off a stream of associations in Kellan's mind: the robot Bellycold, the derelict spaceship, The Void, and home. Dreyer's project had something to do with that ship, he decided. "Alfiri is involved?"

"Yes, and my offer is a good one," said Dreyer. "I made a similar proposition to your commander, and she accepted. But as I said at the beginning, it's a hard offer because you don't have much of a choice."

"I'd like to think about it," he said, but what he really wanted was to talk it over with Caitlin.

"I don't see what there is to decide. You either owe me a year and come out broke, or you agree to put in a year and half and come out rich." Dreyer shook her head. "Besides, I need an answer now. I have 20 some people to see on this base, not to mention the other bases on Imrada, and my other mining operations on other worlds. So what's your answer?"

"There is no middle ground on this offer, no compromise?" Dreyer shook her head no. "I would have kicked myself later had I not asked." Kellan sighed. "I guess I'm in."

The hint of a smile formed in the corners of Dreyer's thin lips, and Caitlin looked relieved.

Kellan headed toward his room to pack his few belongings. Then he thought of his friend Stoney and worried about how he would react to Dreyer and her offer. Stoney was having problems, and although he did not speak about them much, Kellan guessed that even out here he was worried about his demanding family. Kellan also wondered if Stoney might be also dealing with a mortality crisis of his own, perhaps sparked by his experiences on the derelict ship. Whatever the cause, the result was that Stoney was getting drunk during most rest periods instead of going directly to bed, and the alcohol and loss of sleep were taking their toll.

Kellan hurried to Stoney's room, where he found him sitting on the edge of his bed, toweling the perspiration from the back of his neck. "The head of SED-Corp is here," said Kellan. "She's probably going to make you an offer that will take you off Imrada."

"I can't think of anything I want more than getting off this hellhole," he said nonchalantly.

"She is a tough lady, Stoney, a no-nonsense lady. You'd better hear her out, and you'd better be on your best behavior."

"Best behavior! Then I'll need a sip of hooch."

"Why don't you skip that?" said Kellan as Stoney reached under his bed and pulled out a bottle of whisky.

"Trust me, Kellan. I'm at my best after three or four drinks." He took a swallow, then offered the bottle to Kellan, who declined. "Or am I at my best after five or six? Problem is I get bad after 10 or 12."

"Then promise me you'll stop at four."

Stoney held up the bottle in a toast. "I promise. Four and only four."

And he did stop at four, primarily because he was paged over the base communication system a few minutes later. He was slow in getting to the control room to meet Kit Dreyer but agreed to her offer in even less time than it had taken Kellan.

One by one the rest of the crewmembers were called to meet Dreyer, and when the last was finished, Kellan went to Caitlin's cabin. She saw him coming through the partially open door and called to him, "I was just about to go looking for you." He entered the room and closed the door so they would not be interrupted. "I hope you understand," she said, "that I had no idea this was coming, or I would have warned you."

"I know," he said softly.

"And I think you made the right decision. It's the best option for you."

"And for you?"

Caitlin took a deep breath. "For me it's a great opportunity, a chance to discharge a long-standing obligation." She did not intend to explain her comment because it was a subject she rarely discussed.

Caitlin Cormack was actually born in the Holy Asturian Empire, and her father had uprooted the family when Caitlin, the eldest of four sisters, was 18. Mack, as her father was known to everyone including his own children, took them to a Republican colony near the Empire's edge and invested his considerable savings and far more in borrowed funds in a digital publishing venture. It was his ambition to publish the works of all the great thinkers and writers, even the most obscure, regardless of whether they were from the Empire or the Republics. Even renegade Asturian theologians would again be given their voice. And Caitlin, whom he treated as a son and primary heir, was to be his right hand in this enterprise.

The first years, while Caitlin was completing her education, were lean, and just as it looked as if the business might start approaching a breakeven point, Mack suffered a stroke. Without him, the business began to slide, but saddled with a long-term property lease, labor contracts, equipment, and copyrights that had cost Mack a small fortune, the family had no choice but to try to make the business succeed.

The four sisters did everything they could to fulfill their father's dream while Mack was still alive. But the business never did make money, and after a few more years, they realized it was holding the family hostage. The sisters along with an uncle and several cousins worked long hours for low wages just to keep the business from going bankrupt. Eventually it was decided that Caitlin, the smartest and best educated of the family members, would work outside the business to bring in more investment capital. And Caitlin, in turn, decided that their best hope was to build up the company just enough to be able to find a buyer for it.

The bonus Caitlin was able to negotiate from Kit Dreyer to join her new expedition would allow her to get the business in saleable condition—it would allow her to set her family free.

She turned away from Kellan, her eyes tearing as she remembered how happy Mack was on the day years ago when he showed her the property he had just leased for Cormack Publishing. "Yes," said Caitlin, "it's a great opportunity for me."

"Well, I won't be sad about leaving this place, and we'll be able to spend time together on the transport ship."

Caitlin turned back toward him. "Actually we won't. I'm supposed to travel on Dreyer's command ship."

Kellan, noticing that her eyes were moist, put his arms around her and pulled her close. "Even so, we'll stay in touch."

"At least I'll be in position to look out for your best interests," she said as she put her head on his shoulder.

They did not have much time; the shuttle was leaving in 10 minutes. He gave her one last hug; then she pulled him back and gave him one more. A short time later Kellan found himself aboard the shuttle lifting off Imrada for Dreyer's interstellar transport ship.

* * *

"These figures don't look right," said Julian. "Harlan," he shouted, "Jelinka." Both aides hurried into Alfiri's office. Without looking up at her, he handed Jelinka a sheet of electronic paper. "Better check these. They don't look accurate to me." Jelinka, noticing that Julian's eyes were lowered, made a face at him to express her frustration at his wanting her to double check yet another fact or number. "Is Prelate Asana here yet?" he asked about Bishop Baggio's emissary, the man who would be Julian's second in command during the expedition across The Void.

"He is on his way up now," answered Harlan.

"Then why don't the two of you sit down. You'll need to meet him."

Julian felt that he had, in large measure, been restored. His new office on the 27th floor of the Imperial Complex and his new title, Special Advisor to The Triumvirate, were more than acceptable to someone who had just returned from a forced retirement. His status would further improve after the successful completion of his voyage of exploration, but this day had already presented one major threat to his voyage, and Asana would probably present some obstacles of his own.

That morning Julian learned that Marc Dundane, the aging and frail Triumvirate member, had been hospitalized with a virus. Dundane was in stable condition, but if the worst happened, and his position on The Triumvirate were filled with someone as conservative as Bishop Baggio, Julian's voyage would be ended before the first ship could blast off. Julian had cornered the Bishop into backing this exploration and had gotten the other members of The Triumvirate to agree to Kit Dreyer's participation before broaching the idea with Baggio. After outmaneuvering the Bishop, Julian immediately attempted to appease Baggio by eagerly accepting Asana as his deputy. However, Baggio was probably still angry with him, and now, with Marc Dundane's health in some jeopardy, Julian had to face Asana and needed to win him over.

The communicator on Alfiri's desk chimed. The Prelate was finally here. The office door opened and in walked Carlo Asana, a severe-looking man who nonetheless broke into a smile the instant he saw Alfiri.

Julian stood up to greet him. "A pleasure to meet you, Prelate Asana," he said, extending his hand.

Asana, who knew that he was not pleasing to look at, had long ago learned to exude charm. He wrapped both his hands around Julian's. "Carlo. Please call me Carlo." Asana then introduced himself to Harlan and Jelinka as "Carlo Asana," grasping their hands as he had Julian's.

The two aides, who were surprised and pleased by Asana's informality and friendliness, took their leave so that Julian and the Prelate could speak in private.

Alfiri gestured toward a chair, and Asana sat down opposite him. It was then that Julian observed the star-shaped medallion hanging from the Prelate's neck. He was certain that it contained a hidden microphone that transmitted to a recording device or perhaps directly to a receiver in Baggio's ear. Julian began the conversation by paying a number of compliments to Bishop Baggio and expressing his thanks for the Church's support of his expedition.

Asana returned the praise on Baggio's behalf. The Prelate then got down to business, reaffirming his role as the clergy's representative on the voyage. "I don't need to tell you, Commander…"

"Please call me Julian."

"I don't need to tell you, Julian, that every voyage of discovery in the history of the Empire has had a clergyman along to tend to the spiritual life of the crew." Alfiri nodded his agreement. "And this is a most unusual expedition both because of where it is going and the nature of the partnership that you have arranged. Bishop Baggio, in all candor, does not trust the Republicans and worries that we might lose control of the expedition to our ancient rival."

Julian smiled confidently. "Let me put your mind and that of the good Bishop at ease," he said softly. "Only we can manufacture the vacuum generators that make crossing The Void possible. Our engineers will install them on the Republican ships, and our computer technicians will program them once for the voyage across and a second time for the journey home."

That comment caused Asana to frown. "Why can't the Republicans take the devices apart and reverse engineer them?"

"The devices are booby-trapped. Any attempt to tamper with them will cause a miniature LEDD, that is, a Localized Electronic Disruption Device if you are unfamiliar with the term. . ."

"I am familiar with the term," said Asana.

"The LEDD would detonate, destroying the vacuum generator and making it impossible for the ship to return to this side of the universe within the life span of the crew on board. In addition, we can trigger the LEDD's remotely by radio signal should the need arise."

Asana nodded his satisfaction with this information. "And I understand that you plan to include some soldiers among the land crews."

"Not just 'some,' my good Prelate Asana, a full company of Rangers." Julian folded his hands together on the table and leaned toward his new deputy. "The Republicans will be completely overmatched if hostilities break out on any of the planets."

Asana's expression hardened. "Very good, but I would suggest that you include some of Bishop Baggio's own Special Rangers among those troops." Asana folded his arms across his chest, a pose Julian thought was meant to convey an air of power or perhaps defiance. "I can arrange that for you."

Julian thanked Asana for his offer and politely tried to decline it. But Asana was insistent, and Julian felt that he had no choice other than to agree. And there was more. Asana explained that he had been trained by the Black Robes, an ultra-orthodox order of monks, and that he, as the spiritual officer on the voyage and the representative of the Church, intended to enforce all the traditional codes of conduct, including eliminating the unnecessary mingling of the sexes. "We'll start with your aide," said Asana. "Surely you don't plan to allow an attractive young redhead to be with a group of lonely men on a long space voyage?"

Julian tried to put Asana at ease. "Jelinka will be quite safe."

"That's not the point," Asana said forcefully. "Lust is a sin. Why provide the temptation? Fornication is a worse sin. Why provide the opportunity?"

Had Marc Dundane not been taken suddenly ill, Julian would have thrown the arrogant Asana out of his office. For the present he would have to accede to his demands. Jelinka would be sorely disappointed, but he would have to leave her behind. Once the expedition entered The Void, however, the black cloud's magnetic field would make contact with Asturias impossible, and Alfiri's mission would continue regardless of what happened to Dundane and despite any additional obstacles Baggio and Asana might try to present. And it would continue on Julian's terms.

* * *

Kit Dreyer was in her cabin in a bathrobe when she was called to the bridge of her transport ship on a matter of utmost importance. The heels of her loose-fitting slippers slapped against the metal floor as she made her way to the command center. "What's the problem?" she asked.

"No problem," said the duty officer. "We received a message. . ."

"A message! Is that all?" she shouted. "You have me come out here looking like an old fool dressed like this, thinking there is something terribly wrong with the ship, and all for a message!"

Despite her tirade, the duty officer did not back down. "It has the seal of The Triumvirate."

Dreyer silently surveyed all the faces on the bridge including Caitlin Cormack, the newest member of her think tank. "First, Julian Alfiri wants to see me. Then, The Triumvirate sends me a message. I'm getting to be very popular. What does the message say?"

The duty officer explained that they had received an encrypted holographic message, and when they decoded it and began to play it, the image of a seal bearing the twin blue stars Poltare-Major and Poltare-Minor appeared. At that instant they stopped the hologram and sent for Dreyer.

"Somebody must have gone to a lot of trouble to send it to us," said Dreyer as she sat down in the captain's chair. "I guess we ought to hear what they have to say." The duty office activated the hologram, and the ghostly image of a portly, heavily made-up woman appeared in midair before them. "Who is this old lady who is trying to look 20 years younger than she is?"

Before anyone could answer, the hologram started to speak. "Please listen carefully. This message will play once, then self-destruct." The room was completely silent except for the low hum of the computers. "Some important people in the Empire are opposed to the joint voyage you are undertaking. Our problem, I hasten to add, is not with you but with Julian Alfiri and his intentions. We do not plan to stop your voyage—although we could—but rather wish to offer you a better partnership arrangement than the one you have with Alfiri." The holographic figure paused, and Dreyer listened with great interest when it resumed speaking. "Your current arrangement is a 50-50 split. We offer you 75-25—in your favor, of course. In return we ask for total control of one planet out of the scores you will visit. It is a good arrangement for both sides because our interests are very different from yours."

The message ended abruptly with instructions on how Dreyer could transmit an answer if she wished to engage in a discussion of this proposal.

"What do we make of that?" Dreyer asked.

"In case you didn't recognize her," said Caitlin, "that was Analeigh Dundane, wife of Triumvirate member Marc Dundane."

Dreyer frowned. "What sense does it make that she would contact us?"

"Asturian politics are bizarre." Caitlin shrugged her shoulders. "But from everything I have ever read or heard of Analeigh Dundane, this doesn't make any sense. She and her husband are not Alfiri's adversaries."

"It might not have been her," offered the duty officer. "It might have been an electronic simulation made to look and sound like her."

"That seems reasonable. Why should someone as important as Dundane's wife risk coming out in the open? Can't we find out for sure whether that was her or not?" asked Dreyer, looking back at the duty officer.

"Not if the hologram has self-destructed."

Dreyer remained motionless for a few moments, apparently lost in thought. "How seriously do we take this offer of a new agreement?" she asked finally, directing her question to Caitlin.

"There is no reason not to take the next step, not to speak to Analeigh Dundane or whoever is really behind this," Caitlin answered. "At least it might give us better insight to Asturian politics. Alfiri's enemies could be our allies, or they could be our enemies as well. It would be good to find out, if we can, which is the case."

9 | Into The Void

Radar screens throughout the Holy Asturian Empire lit up with the blips of more than a dozen Republican space vessels crossing the frontier and heading toward the mother planet, Asturias. Leading the procession was Kit Dreyer's command ship, a Starhawk spacefighter bearing the emblem of the Federated Republics. Following behind were six survey vessels, each paired with a gigantic cargo ship. Shaped like seagoing aircraft carriers and almost two-thirds of a mile long, the survey ships carried a variety of planetary exploration and shuttle vehicles, ranging from small land-and-sea Floats to large Omnihauls that could hoist an entire land base to and from orbit. The cargo ships, each a mile-and-a-half long, consisted of a bullet-shaped crew area up front, eight cylindrical cargo sections, and a tail with six enormous rocket boosters.

Near Asturias, Dreyer's ships rendezvoused with the rest of the exploration fleet that Julian Alfiri had assembled, including four other Republican ships of the same scale and technological generation as Dreyer's SED-Corp vessels, and two smaller commercial vessels supplied by Triumvirate member Clifford Riddenauer. Three more ships, long cylindrical vessels, were tankers belonging to the Asturian government; they were used to siphon water from rivers and lakes into space, where the liquid froze and was towed in enormous icebergs to irrigate dry planets. The final vessel was Alfiri's own command ship, a large-scale version of the Defender long-range spacefighters used by the Asturian military.

Never in the history of the galaxy had so many jumbo space vessels been assembled in one place, and as they continued toward the "back door" of the Asturian Empire, dozens of small shuttle vehicles, carrying technicians and land crew members, started to crisscross among them.

Aboard one of cargo ships, The Nemesis, Kellen Blake watched the panorama of space vehicles through the 360-degree wall of windows that lined the observation deck. It buoyed his spirits to see that so many other ships and people were making this voyage—he and the rest of The Nemesis crew only recently learned that they were making a journey of exploration beyond The Edge of the Universe. It helped that he heard the news among a group of Republicans who, unlike Asturians, attached no religious significance or superstitious beliefs to The Void.

But Kellan had seen the only ship that had ever entered The Void and returned, and he doubted that anyone really knew what was in store for them on this voyage. He could imagine all sorts of terrible things, especially after his experiences on Imrada, and knew that he had to block out such thoughts. There were dangers ahead, to be sure, but his poor condition, both physical and psychological, was causing him to magnify his problems. He had not seen Caitlin since they left Imrada, and during the long days he spent aboard The Nemesis, he had grown lazy, doing little but eating, sleeping, and reading—a reaction to the inhumane schedule and conditions on Imrada. As a result of his compulsive snacking and lack of exercise, he gained 10 extra pounds and felt uncomfortable in his tight-fitting clothes. He intended to begin a diet and start using the ship's gym regularly, but he was not ready yet. He wanted to feel more settled in his new situation first.

At least his Imrada survey team—Gordon Stoney, Warren Simmons, and Vickie Webb—had been kept together, and they were good company for him. They would soon be joined by some

Asturian crew members because each surface team was supposed to have an equal or near equal number of Asturians and Republicans as a means of allowing the uneasy allies to keep an eye on each other. Kellan, an Asturian by birth, was amused to learn that he was classified as a Republican, a mistake attributable to the fact that he worked for SED-Corp on Imrada. As long as he was on a Republican ship and under contract to Kit Dreyer, there was no reason to correct the mistake.

Nemesis flight control announced that a shuttle was approaching. The rest of Kellan's land team was supposed to be aboard it, and so he went to the docking area to greet them. When he reached the docking bay, he could already hear the clank of the shuttle being locked into position and then the whir of the ship's hatch opening. The Asturian contingent began to file into the bay, and Kellan was surprised and delighted to see that Bellycold was among them.

The large, silver-faced robot hurried over to him. "Hi, I'm Bellycold," he said, shaking Kellan's hand, and Kellan understood that he should not let on that he knew the android. Bellycold motioned over his shoulder to two men who were following him. "This is the rest of our surface team, Alexander Reed and Darin Wallace." As Kellan shook hands with each man, he decided there was something out of place about them. Reed, who had a beard, was supposed to be a zoologist and Wallace, who wore his hair long and shaggy, was supposed to be an environmental specialist. But despite the beard and shaggy hair, they had the solid, well-conditioned bodies of professional soldiers, and Kellan thought they would look more natural clean-shaven and in military crew cuts. It made sense that the Asturians would want to hide a few Rangers among the land crews, but Kellan was not certain that these two would pass for scientists.

The robot put his arm around Kellan's shoulder and led him down the corridor away from the other men disembarking from the shuttle. "Julian is appreciative of the help you gave me," Bellycold whispered. "He'll get you back home when this expedition is over." That was great news to Kellan, but they still had to survive the expedition. The android looked over his shoulder to be certain he could not be overheard. "Julian doesn't completely trust the Republicans. Who does? We saw you listed as a Republican and thought it wouldn't hurt to keep it that way."

Kellan nodded his agreement, then asked, "Can you tell me what this voyage is all about?"

"I'll tell you what I can later when there are fewer people around."

"At least tell me if you think it's possible to actually cross The Void safely."

"Sure it is," said Bellycold, gently slapping him on the shoulder. "The problem is that we almost didn't get the chance. We thought for a while that Marc Dundane might die and ruin everything. But he's okay now. Not only that, we also had to deal with a guy named Carlo Asana. But that's another story," he said as Kellan led him to the crew's quarters.

* * *

As part of their contractual arrangement, Julian Alfiri and Kit Dreyer agreed that no arms would be brought on this journey except the laser cannons on each partner's command ship, the weapons needed by their joint security force, and the laser rifles and pistols carried by the land crews exploring planets that might have indigenous life forms. And so each ship was to be inspected for, as Dreyer called them, "rockets, bombs, and other tricks." On The Nemesis the Asturian inspection would be carried out Alexander Reed and Darin Wallace, who were not just professional soldiers, as Kellan had guessed, but rather Special Rangers loyal to Bishop Baggio. As soon as they stored their duffel bags in their new quarters on The Nemesis, Reed and Wallace began their inspection with the help of a Republican guide who identified himself only as Mallory. Mallory, who was affable and accommodating, and who looked too young to be taken seriously, was actually one of Kit Dreyer's top aides. He led the Asturians on a tour of the bridge, taking great care to describe the functions of all the ship's power controls, navigation systems, and communications centers. Then he took them to the crew quarters, where they briefly encountered Kellan, Bellycold, and others of their own team. Occasionally, either Reed or Wallace would open a bureau drawer, look under a bunk, or shine a pocket light into a ventilation duct. Nothing was the least bit out of order.

Mallory was about to take them to the first of the ship's eight 300-yard long cargo sections when Wallace noticed a room they had missed. "What's in there?" he asked, pointing to the door.

"The briefing room," smiled Mallory. "Almost forgot it." He opened the door and ushered them inside.

There was little to see in this room, just chairs and a few drawerless desks, apparently no place to conceal anything of importance. There were, however, two large doors, moveable partitions of some kind, on the rear wall. Reed walked toward the doors. "What's this?" he asked as he scratched his beard.

"Oh that?" said Mallory in a dismissive manner that made Reed suspicious. "Just a projection screen for viewing star charts and engineering diagrams, that's all. You don't need to see that, do you?" Reed gave Mallory a stern look. "I guess you do need to see that," said Mallory, answering his own question. He inspected one of the doors and tried to slide it back by hand. "Won't budge."

"It looks like it needs a key," said Reed sarcastically.

"Right you are," smiled Mallory. "I'll go get the key and be back in a minute."

As soon as Mallory left the room, Wallace joined Reed at the partition to check it himself. He tried the door; it was locked. Then he gave his partner a quizzical look. "Do you smell coffee?"

Reed sniffed the air. "Yeah, but it's awfully sweet smelling coffee."

The coffee smell was accompanied by a barely audible hiss.

Suddenly things began to move in slow motion. The room lights dimmed, and Mallory and three other men, all wearing gas masks, entered the room and came up behind Wallace and Reed, who were now standing frozen in place.

"We can continue into the cargo area." The voice was Mallory's, but it was coming from a miniature speaker in the ceiling, not from him. "But you'll need to wear some safety equipment." Helmets containing virtual reality equipment were placed over their heads. "You'll also need magnetic boots because there's no artificial gravity in the cargo holds." They were handed boots and gloves, also containing miniature electronic devices, which they put on as instructed. "Let's see the cargo areas, shall we?" said Mallory's recorded voice. The two Asturians, without looking around to see who had them by the arms, let themselves be moved gently onto two small treadmills that had raised out of the floor.

What Wallace and Reed saw inside their helmets was a flawlessly realistic recreation of the room they were in and of Mallory standing by the door, a smile on his face, motioning them forward, "This way. Follow me." The virtual reality displays in their helmets were keyed to the motion of their treadmills so that as they walked, the doorway before them came closer. And when they finally reached the exit, they saw the corridor leading to cargo area.

The illusion for someone in a drug-induced stupor was perfect.

Mallory opened the door to the first storage area, which was a cylinder 75 yards in diameter and 300 yards long, and mostly empty except for an Omnihaul and some equipment boxes. As they walked through the storage area, their footsteps and Mallory's voice echoed, and when they touched the equipment with their electronic gloves, it felt solid. Reed even lifted the lid of a toolbox and looked inside to see an assortment of hand-held mining equipment. All the while Mallory continued his narration as they walked through eight cargo compartments, all identical in that they were largely empty except for the kind of cargo-moving equipment and storage pens one would expect to find in the hold of a large spacefreighter.

Reed and Wallace walked a mile and half without leaving the treadmills they were on. At the end of the last cargo compartment, they climbed aboard an electric cart—or thought they had—and Mallory drove them back to the crew area. They then returned to the briefing room, where Mallory took their helmets, gloves, and boots.

"How about some coffee?" asked Mallory, but they did not respond. "Fine, let me get you some. Why don't you sit down and rest after all that walking?" And the two Asturians sat down.

Mallory left the room with the other three Republicans, and when he finally returned, Reed and Wallace were almost back to normal, Reed, commenting on how large the ship was and Wallace, complaining about how his feet were tired from all the walking.

"What did you think of the ship?" asked Mallory as he carried in a tray of coffee, milk, and sugar.

"It's a very big ship," said Reed, reaching for a coffee mug, "a big ship with a lot of empty space."

* * *

There was a loud crackling sound followed by a high-pitched mechanical hum, and the entire ship seemed to shutter. Carlo Asana, who was in his cabin praying, looked at the ceiling as though expecting to see cracks suddenly appear. He never remembered just how much he hated space travel until something like this happened, a strange noise or some turbulence that caused him to fear that the ship would crash or break apart or that the life-support systems would fail. Asana remained quiet for a few moments; there were no more odd sounds or vibrations, but he decided to go to the bridge anyway.

The command center, with Julian Alfiri sitting in the pilot's chair, was full of activity, crewmen closely monitoring their computer screens and calling out terms and numbers that had no meaning for Asana. "What's going on?" asked the Prelate.

"Ah, Carlo," said Julian, who was still trying to befriend the man. "Just in time."

"For what?"

"We just activated the gravity generator and will be entering The Void shortly." The color drained from Asana's face. "Sit down," said Alfiri, pointing to the co-pilot's chair, "I've reserved a front-row seat for you."

With everything else he had to think about, Asana had not devoted much attention to The Void, the great hell of the Holy Book, and in fact, he had thought they were at least a few days from actually entering it. As he walked to the co-pilot's seat, Asana felt unsteady, and his legs wobbled slightly. He was not a man of great courage when faced with physical danger, and he despised Alfiri for being so calm. Men like Alfiri were born with every advantage. They possessed the confidence that comes with being the children of aristocrats. They never experienced deprivations or hopelessness, and therefore, their lack of hard experiences left them less courageous than naïve about the possible harm that could befall them.

Alfiri smiled condescendingly at him. "I assure you, my dear Prelate, everything will go smoothly."

Asana realized that he was in a cold sweat and in danger of embarrassing himself before the arrogant Alfiri and the entire bridge crew. "I'm fine," he protested. But, in fact, his hands started to quiver.

When Alfiri said they would be entering The Void shortly, Asana thought he meant within minutes, but as Alfiri now explained, they had to activate and thoroughly test the vacuum generator while they were still a distance from The Void. And so it was not until an hour and 15 minutes later, time during which Asana had nothing to do but squirm in his seat, that Julian Alfiri announced that they were actually about to enter the black cloud.

* * *

"Kellan Blake! Yo Blake! Where the fuck are you?"

Kellen hopped out his bunk and threw open the door to his cabin. There was Stoney in the corridor, pounding his hand on the wall, screaming Kellan's name, and drunker than Kellan had ever seen him. "Hey, Stoney, did you forget which cabin was ours?"

"You missed the party, man." Stoney's eyes were watery, and he slurred his words. "Actually, the party is still going on. So you're still missing it."

A special dinner was being held in The Nemesis' mess hall to celebrate the ship's crossing of The Edge of the Universe, which was about to happen soon. Kellan, however, had spent most of the last few hours in the ship's library, where he had gone almost every day on this voyage, to read works of theology, philosophy, psychology, and anthropology, anything that might improve his outlook on life and death. He had begun working out in the gym as well, all part of his effort to get himself back together. The problem was that he was not eating. He had put himself on a crash diet and in a dozen days lost five of the 10 pounds he wanted to lose. Then, when his weight stabilized and he could lose no more, he decided to fast. Fasting was common among the ancient Asturian prophets, who used fasting and other physical privations to attain insight. Trying to lose weight and gain insight at the same time seemed like a good idea. But now Kellan was weak and listless and sinking into depression.

"They missed you at the party," Stoney continued, "but forget that now. Some of the ships are already in The Void—the spooky, spooky Void," he said, pretending to afraid. "Since you and I go way back, I thought we could go up to the observation deck and watch."

"You want to watch it?"

"Sure," Stoney answered, stifling a belch. "Don't you?" Kellan reluctantly nodded yes. "Then you'll need some hooch." He pulled a flask from his rear trouser pocket.

"Not on an empty stomach," said Kellan as Stoney shrugged his shoulders, then took a sip himself. "Tell me, Stoney, how the hell do you manage—no matter where you are—to keep yourself so well supplied with alcohol?"

As they started down the corridor toward the observation deck, Stoney threw an arm across Kellan's shoulders. "If you can't keep yourself supplied, you don't have the talent for being an alcoholic. It's that simple."

The observation deck was, to Kellan's surprise, completely vacant. That was a pity, he thought, because the view was striking. There was a sky full of stars behind them and nothing in front of them.

As they took seats at the forward windows, Stoney took another swallow of liquor. "So Kellan Blake, former Imperial Ranger Kellan Blake, did you ever think that two kids like us from Asturias would ever find themselves going into the spooky, spooky Void?"

"No," answered Kellan, his eyes on the empty sky before them.

"Me neither," said Stoney, who continued to drink.

It was not long before Stoney fell asleep, and Kellan, still feeling weak and depressed, was left to his own thoughts until he heard footsteps coming up the metal stairs. It was Vickie Webb approaching him with a tray of food and drink.

"When I didn't see you in the mess hall, I thought I'd find you here or in the library," she said. She paused when she saw Stoney slumped in a chair. "What's wrong with him? He looks dead."

"Dead drunk."

"He looks in really bad shape, and you haven't looked so good lately yourself."

"I'm not eating enough," he answered with no strength to his voice. "I think my diet has gone too far."

"Then eat," she said, glancing down at the tray she held. "It's real food in honor of crossing into The Void, and I don't think we'll get food like this again anytime soon."

"You're right, Vickie," he whispered. "I need to eat. If I can't feel any better than this, there is no point in being alive." He took the tray from her and rested it on his lap. "It was really thoughtful of you to bring me this food," he said as his attention was suddenly drawn to an orange on the tray. He could not remember the last time he had fresh fruit, and he decided to eat the orange first. Taking a knife, he sliced it in half. Like a man under the influence of drugs, he became fascinated by its color. There was no other color like orange, he thought; it was so different from the gray metal bases and spaceships where he had spent so much of his time. He was even more fascinated by its geometry, spherical when whole, circular surfaces when cut in half, but an interior consisting of triangular wedges. And somehow the different shapes all fit together. He also started thinking about genetics. There once was an advertisement for a Republican fruit company showing a baby lizard hatching out of an orange. The caption read, "If it doesn't have our name on it, you don't know what you are getting." But he could slice open a million oranges and never find a lizard, only these little wedges. Amazing how that worked.

"Are you gonna eat that orange, or sit there staring at it?" asked Vickie with mock annoyance.

Kellan's reverie was broken. She was right. Just eat the damn orange, he told himself, don't analyze it.

The orange was tasty and sweet. It only took a few bites of orange, some of the vegetable casserole, and a sip of wine to bring his mood up from the depths.

"You're beginning to look human again," said Vickie. "I thought you were in a trance."

"I was. I've been obsessed with perception," he said, taking another sip of wine.

"Perception!" Vickie laughed. "Is that why you were staring at the orange?"

"Sort of." He felt a little embarrassed that she was not taking him as seriously as he meant to be taken, but there was no stopping the philosophical mood he suddenly found himself in. "Asturians used to think The Void was actually hell. Now we know it's just a black cloud, a very unusual cloud, but there is nothing metaphysical about it."

Vickie, whose eyelids were droopy from having drunk several glasses of wine at dinner, held up both hands. "Glad I'm not an Asturian." she said without thinking, and then she became apologetic, "I didn't mean to be offensive."

He took another bite of the orange. "Don't worry. I'm not offended," he said, chewing and speaking at the same time. "Think back to Imrada," he continued, determined to make his point, "to how we used microwave imagers to get around—all form and everything in blacks, whites, and grays. Yet the satellite infrared scans were all color almost without form. Both views were accurate but also incomplete at the same time."

"Are you sure you didn't start drinking before I got here?" she smiled. "Eat more of the food I brought. Maybe you'll make more sense."

But he was too involved in his own thoughts to change the subject. "Did you ever play ball with a dog, then grab the ball, and hide it under your shirt?" For emphasis he pulled out the front of his knit shirt and stuck his fist underneath. "There's the ball bulging out plain as day, but the dog's head is turning from side to side because he can't figure out where the hell it went." She nodded that she knew what he was talking about but still was not taking him very seriously. "So have you ever thought about what we humans might be missing?"

Vickie laughed. "No, what is it that we humans are missing?"

"I couldn't possibly know, and that's the point. Why worry about what you do see if you know that you can't see everything there is? There are lots of limitations—to our senses, our brains, our consciousness. So I'll tell you what all this means." Kellan smiled as he waved an orange slice in her face. "Eat the damn orange; don't analyze it."

"You're almost as drunk as Stoney is."

"Probably," he said, looking around the observation deck. Outside the ship there was only blackness in all directions, not a star to been seen anywhere. "Good lord, we're in The Void."

"I thought we'd feel something."

"I was hoping we wouldn't." Kellan reached over and shook Stoney's shoulder. "Wake up. You're missing it." It was no use; he was unconscious.

The lights suddenly went out, leaving them in complete blackness. The lights flickered, went out again, then came on, and stayed on. Vickie looked frightened. "The Void has a magnetic field," said Kellan. "We must have just entered it. No cause for alarm." But he neglected to tell her that Bellycold claimed The Void's magnetic field should have no effect whatsoever on their ship. "We should relax and enjoy the ride. The ship didn't burn up when it entered the cloud, and it isn't shaking apart." He looked all about the deck again. "Of course, there isn't much to see up here now."

Kellan continued to eat while sharing his wine with Vickie, and after a while, traveling through The Void seemed no different from any other space journey. When he was finished his meal, he looked up at Vickie and thought she had a look of expectation on her face.

"Remember the first time that we met on Imrada?" she asked, putting her hand over the back of his. He nodded yes and noticed for the first time that she was wearing a tight-fitting tee shirt. "You were staring a me then too," she laughed. "Don't start blushing on me. I didn't mind."

He was wrong more often than not in matters of this sort, but he was reasonably certain that this was a "come-on." Acting impulsively, which was out of character for Kellan Blake, he reached out both hands and touched her breasts. When she did not draw back or complain, he pulled out the front of her shirt, reached up and under her bra, and began to caress her bare flesh as she closed her eyes and titled her head back. "Not here," she whispered. "Let's go to your cabin."

He straightened out her shirt, grabbed her hand, and gently pulled her to her feet.

"What about him?" she asked, motioning toward Stoney.

"Let him sleep it off. I'll come back for him later," Kellan said as he led her off the observation deck to his cabin.

10 | The Other Side

Perhaps nothing in their lives would match the sight of seeing The Other Side for the first time, of exiting The Void to find a sky full of stars, different constellations, of course, but a sky not unlike their own except The Void was now behind them in the western sky.

But the view they had now of the great water planet Dahai was also spectacular, an enormous lavender-and-blue planet overlaid with swirls of white clouds and circled by a broad, thin network of rings. From the angle of The Nemesis' approach, Dahai's three sets of rings—two of them wide with a narrow one sandwiched between—crossed the planet from the upper left to lower right and tilted forward 30 degrees like the lip of a great saucer. As the ship moved into orbit, one of Dahai's three moons, a craggy white disk, became visible from behind the planet, the moon's small size and plainness underscoring the splendor of its mother planet. Dahai was a planet with a lavender atmosphere, dark blue oceans, and pure white ice caps, and it had more water, the most valuable commodity in the universe, than any of them had ever seen before.

All the surface crews on The Nemesis, including Kellan Blake and his team, crowded the observation deck for a look at the place where they expected to spend the next 100 days. On this first trip to The Other Side, they would explore and mine the most promising portions of the land masses, collect samples of any new vegetation and animal life they encountered, and siphon off water to be carried back to Asturias to, in Julian Alfiri's words, turn his dry home planet into a paradise.

The surface teams, eager to get down to the planet, were forced to wait while The Nemesis completed a half dozen orbits of Dahai so that the planet could be mapped and infrared images could be taken. There was an additional delay while the aerial survey data was analyzed, and the surface team leaders convened to decide where to establish their first bases on the planet's surface. These were considered low-risk decisions because the land bases could be moved in a matter of hours. Indeed, as the data from the land crews and orbiting sensing devices continued to be analyzed, it was expected that most land bases would be moved several times before large-scale mining operations began.

Kellan's team was assigned to Dahai's southern continent, to a region near the planet's equator where several distinct types of ecological systems existed within a short distance of one another. His crew would have the distinction of being the first to descend to the planet's surface and therefore, would operate from "Base 1." They would be dressed, at least initially, in bulky environmental suits (although Dahai appeared to have a breathable atmosphere) and were shot up with or forced to swallow every type of immunization and anti-bacterial agent known.

Their transportation down to the surface was an Omnihaul, a long, sleek vehicle that had short retractable wings behind its nose for better stability, large swept-back primary wings, and a three-part tail fin. The bridge was just above and behind the nose of the craft, and a long narrow passenger compartment ran along the top. The Omnihaul had a front, a back, and a spine but no belly, and it was here in the hollow underneath the passenger compartment that a large payload could be attached, either a small mining installation, a large cargo container, or, in this case, an aluminum land base.

Kellan, dressed in an environmental suit and holding his heavy helmet with both hands, stood at the Omnihaul's entrance, checking in his surface team. In recent days he had felt much better both physically and psychologically. In addition to abandoning his severe diet and continuing his reading and physical exercise, he had added an occasional sexual encounter with Vickie Webb to his list of recreational activities. Every time he thought of Caitlin, he felt guilty about Vickie, but the truth was that he and Caitlin were, so far, only good friends, and he felt justified in taking advantage of any diversion, anything pleasurable that would help him get through The Void and pull him out of his funk.

Vickie's attitude toward sex was as cavalier as his. When they slept together for the first time, she admitted that, although she had several other "conquests" aboard the ship, she always "had an eye" on him. And she probably had conquests after Kellan as well because she was no more serious about him than he was about her. And they both agreed that once they were on the surface of Dahai, their jobs would come first, and the sexual encounters would have to stop.

Simmons was the first of his team members to check in and board the Omnihaul. He was followed by Vickie, who gave Kellan a warm smile as she walked by; then the Rangers Wallace and Reed, who still looked no more like scientists than when Kellan first saw them; and finally Bellycold, who was telling everyone who would listen that he could not wait to a get a breath of fresh air. Members of the other two surface teams scheduled for this flight continued to arrive. But no Stoney.

Kellan was worried about his friend and went to find him. Stoney often wore his drinking binges as a badge of honor, but his overuse of alcohol was getting serious. Unless a space traveler imposed a strict regimen on him- or herself, which Stoney had not, a journey such as this could cause a person to lose all sense of time and biological rhythm, to suffer psychological as well as physical atrophy. Stoney, like Kellan, was watching his life slip away on this odyssey, which began when Captain Zeitz asked them to escort Bellycold back to Asturias. Stoney must have felt that he should be back home now finishing his first term of law school. Instead he was on this voyage. But now the first part of the journey had ended, and he should have been eager to join in the exploration of Dahai.

Kellan hurried to their cabin, where he found Stoney sitting on the edge of his cot staring blankly.

"Hey, man," said Kellan with as much cheer as he could muster. "For the first time in how long? A year and a half? Longer? We can breathe real air and feel the warmth of real sunshine. And you're just sitting here!"

Stoney looked up and smiled bitterly. "That's the problem. I once had a pet bird, and the one time I accidentally left its cage door open, it wouldn't come out. You know why? Because it had become accustomed to being in a protected environment."

Kellan gave him a playful slap on the shoulder. "Come on, you'll have a laser in your hand. You can blast anything down there that tries to eat you."

"Can you blast a virus or bacteria? I'd rather be eaten by some giant fish than be infected by some microbe that will slowly turn my body into green jelly before it kills me." Stoney took a deep breath. "But don't worry, Chief," he said, imitating Simmons. "I'm goin'."

Kellan and Stoney were the last two to enter the Omnihaul, and they strapped themselves into their seats just in time to hear the final radio conversation between Nemesis Flight Control and the Omnihaul's crew. The dome covering the launch pad lifted up and back, and their pilot engaged four vertical-thrust engines that lifted the Omnihaul gently off the flight pad and into position for blast off. The large rear engines then fired, and the Omnihaul lifted away from The Nemesis.

The first part of the flight was smooth, but when the ship entered the planet's atmosphere, they experienced turbulence. Kellen never enjoyed these flights, and he was happy a few minutes later when the turbulence ceased, and they were cruising over a dark blue ocean and approaching a large landmass.

Kellen was in a window seat, and Vickie, who was sitting just behind him, tapped him on the shoulder and motioned for him to take a look at the ground directly below as the Omnihaul began to slowly circle. "A yellow lake! Isn't that unusual," she said, and her comment caused Kellan to take a closer look at what was below them. It certainly looked like a yellow lake, a large patch of yellow, unbroken by hills, rocks, or trees, and waves appeared to be rolling across its surface. But as they dropped lower, he could see it for what it was. "That's not water," he said to Vickie. "It's tall yellow grass rippling in the wind."

"I'll be damned," she mumbled as she leaned against the window for another look.

The Omnihaul slowed, then stopped all forward movement as it began a vertical descent to the surface. As the ship landed, its legs deployed, flattening the tall grass and digging into the moist soil. The rocket engines shut down.

Standard procedure called for the flight crew to announce that the ship had been secured before any of the passengers left their seats, but Kellan, without waiting for clearance, put on his helmet, hurried to the passenger compartment door, and threw it open. Led by him, the members of the three land crews began climbing down the rungs built into the exterior of the Omnihaul.

Kellan was enthralled by Dahai. The planet's gravity was uncomfortably greater than he was accustomed to, but otherwise, Dahai struck him as an artist's rendering of a beautiful alien world. The grass, which was almost as tall as they were, was lemon yellow; the sky ranged from dark purple in the cloudy portions to light violet where it was clear; and the sun was reddish orange. And in the southwest there was a giant stone arch in the sky—a section of Dahai's rings.

All two dozen members of the three land crews, including Stoney, climbed down to the surface and were walking slowly around the Omnihaul, pushing their way through the tall grass, their heads tilted up at the sky like tourists getting their first look at a tall mountain range.

Vickie ran a gloved hand up a five-foot tall blade of grass. "I wonder if everything on this planet is giant-sized?" she said to herself, but her comment was broadcast over her helmet microphone to the others.

"There could be a million giant snakes out there, and we wouldn't be able to see them in this grass," said Stoney teasingly, and more than a few of the others stopped in their tracks to look around their feet.

"Damn it, Stoney," said Vickie. "Did you have to mention snakes?" If the height of the grass was any indication, she thought the snakes on this planet might be 100 feet long.

Ignoring the chatter that Stoney had provoked, Kellan checked the outside temperature reading on his helmet display and saw that it was 85 degrees, about the same as the hot days he enjoyed back home. Next he took out an atmosphere testing kit. Working awkwardly with his bulky gloves, he fumbled as he opened a box containing a stack of rectangular cards. He took out a card and pulled its seal tab, unveiling two dozen dots the size of pencil points arranged in neat rows, each with the name of a chemical element written above it. The test showed that the air was not only breathable, but that it was almost pure oxygen.

Vickie stood next to him and glanced down at the test results. "Are you sure you've given it enough time?"

"Yes, but let's try another card." When the second card showed the same excellent results, Kellan pulled off his helmet. He took a deep breath of the fresh, sweet air and sighed. Then he tilted his face up toward the orange sun and closed his eyes as he felt the warmth of its rays.

The crew of the Omnihaul, who had a schedule to maintain and no time to sample Dahai's atmosphere, unloaded the land base by unbolting it from the underbelly of their ship and hydraulically lowering to the ground. The long, white aluminum structure was large enough to house more than two dozen people. It had several doors big enough to accommodate a person in an environmental suit and dozens of small windows in the front section; the rear section consisted of a utility shed containing scientific equipment, six Floats, and two power generators. Once the base was anchored to the ground, a radio antenna was raised from one corner of the building. In less than two hours, the base was fully operational, and the Omnihaul lifted off to ferry the next ground team to the surface.

That first afternoon on Dahai was intended to be slow and relaxing, a chance for crew members to get used to their new surroundings, to regain their land legs, and most important, to slowly adapt to the planet's gravity. In the late afternoon, the entire human crew—except for Stoney, who was happy to let the others do the exploring—left the base without their environmental suits and walked around in the tall, yellow grass. Reed and Wallace went along too, and Kellan had the distinct feeling that the two Rangers were keeping an eye on the others although he was uncertain what they were on the watch for.

Kellan thought Dahai was the best place he had ever been, better even than his own sunny Asturias. The air itself was invigorating, but the combination of sun, wind, and gravity tired them all quickly. And soon they had to return to base. The exercise had given most of them a big appetite, and dinner that evening, plain though it was, was met with great enthusiasm. As they were finishing their meal, Kellan, eager to go outside again, suggested they watch the sunset.

"Sounds like fun, Chief," said Simmons, "but it got pretty cool out there the last time I checked."

"We can build a real wood fire," offered Vickie enthusiastically.

But they could not build a wood fire because in all their wanderings outside the base no one had come across any trees, and there was no wood on the base, not even in the tables and chairs, which were plastic. They settled on using a large battery-operated heater/lantern instead. Four of them—Kellan, Vickie, Simmons, and a member of one of the other land crews—grabbed coats and blankets, and took their after-dinner coffee outside while the android Bellycold, always wanting to be seen as just another member of the group, followed them carrying the heater. Wallace also left the base a minute or two later, but he remained near the door, leaning against the base wall, sipping coffee from a large mug.

They walked a short distance from the base, sat down on the grass around the heater, and watched the sun, which seemed redder now, descend in the sky and leave a trail of bright purple beams in the clouds overhead. Soon the temperature dropped but only a little, and the wind picked up, rustling the grass all around them. They sat listening, not even the talkative robot saying a word until Vickie said, "Hey, look—in the sky."

"What is that?" asked Bellycold.

"It looks like a night rainbow."

The sky was now completely dark. One of the planet's three moons appeared, and like moonlight falling on a lake, it lit up the section of Dahai's rings in the western sky. From the way the rings sparkled, Kellan guessed they must have contained chunks of ice as well as rock.

The scene could not have been more pleasant or more peaceful. They talked for a time and listened to the wind, which was now howling through the tall grass.

Simmons was the first to stand up to leave. "Think I'll get some shut-eye." The end of his comment was almost drowned out by a loud and very strange sound in the distance.

Vickie sat upright and grabbed Kellan's arm. "My god, what was that? A lion?"

Kellan turned in the direction of the sound. "That wasn't a roar. At least, I don't think it was." The strange noise was heard again. It was definitely an animal call but more of a snort than the growl of a large cat or the howl of a wolf.

"Whatever it is, Chief, it sounds really big. Like I said, I think I'll get some shut-eye. I don't want to end up some creature's late-night snack. Good night all."

"That's one of the many advantages of being an android," said Bellycold. "You don't have to worry about becoming somebody's snack."

"How do you know," smiled Kellan, "that the creatures on this planet don't eat metal and silicon?"

The robot processed this idea for a minute, then stood up, grabbed the lantern, and followed the others back into the base.

* * *

Kit Dreyer's Starhawk command ship was in orbit around Dahai. The SED-Corp head was on the bridge, sitting with Caitlin Cormack at a bank of computers, observing the positions and progress of the landing crews on this planet and the other planets and moons they planned to explore. Reports from the various exploration vessels, after a slow start, were coming in at a brisk pace now, and although Dreyer was checking the situation on Dahai, Caitlin managed to glance at Dreyer's computer to see the confirmation that Kellan's team had landed successfully on Dahai's southern continent.

On the other side of the bridge, the communications officer was monitoring the many radio transmissions that were arriving from the surface of Dahai and from other ships. He suddenly sprang to his feet and hurried to Kit Dreyer's side. "It's her," he said, meaning the voice that was supposed to be Analeigh Dundane.

Dreyer gave a puzzled look. "On this side of The Void?"

"I can't imagine that she would have made this journey," said Caitlin. "It proves that someone is using an electronic device to conceal their own identity, and perhaps picked this particular voice to confuse us or maybe just to tweak our noses a little bit."

"Better put her through," said Dreyer, "and see if you can trace the origin of her transmission."

The communications officer returned to his post, and a few seconds later a woman's voice came over the speaker on Dreyer's computer. "Can you read me?"

Caitlin shook her head and whispered, "I'll bet Analeigh Dundane never said 'Can you read me?' in her life."

"I can read you," answered Dreyer. Caitlin reached over and activated the microphone on Dreyer's computer. "I can read you," Dreyer repeated. "But is this transmission secure?"

"Of course, it is secure."

"I didn't expect that you would make the journey across The Void."

The voice ignored the comment. "Your command ship is circling Dahai."

The communications officer was approaching again. Caitlin reached over and turned off Dreyer's microphone while the communications officer reported, "Julian Alfiri is on the radio, and he sounds upset."

"What is it with these damn Asturians?" Dreyer grumbled, knowing the reason for Alfiri's call. "They all panic because my ship is orbiting Dahai. I'm beginning to be sorry I ever got involved with them. Well, damn it, tell the great Julian Alfiri to wait."

Dreyer turned back to her computer, this time remembering to activate her microphone. "Yes, we are circling Dahai. We're making certain that our surface crews get down to the planet without any problems."

"And does this also mean," asked the voice, "that this is where you intend to carry out your part of our bargain?"

"We haven't decided about that. You said it had to flow organically. I think those were your exact words." Dreyer looked to Caitlin, who nodded yes. "For something to be organic, it has to grow from something else, and there hasn't been time for that something else."

"I'll be watching with great interest," said the voice, and the radio connection was severed.

"That's it! What the hell was that supposed to be about?" asked Dreyer, and Caitlin shrugged her shoulders. Then turning to the communications officer, Dreyer shouted, "Were you able to trace that transmission?"

"There wasn't enough time. What about Alfiri? Should I put him through?"

Taking a moment to gather her thoughts, Dreyer decided she would handle this situation by doing her best imitation of Alfiri's gracious manner of speech, which she considered superficial and annoying. "Okay, put him through." Dreyer cleared her throat. "My dear Julian," she began. "How are you? Had a good flight, I trust?"

"I must tell you that I am concerned," came his response, uncharacteristically direct. "I am concerned that you have taken orbit around Dahai."

Dreyer, losing her composure momentarily, made an obscene gesture at the computer speaker but then said as pleasantly as she could, "I'm as good here as anywhere. It's where you and your command ship happen to be. Besides I like looking at the planet. The colors are quite beautiful. You may not realize it, Alfiri, but I have quite an appreciation of color." Dreyer turned toward Caitlin and smiled at her own wit.

If Alfiri caught the sarcasm in her voice, he did not react to it. "But we never agreed that you would be part of the Dahai contingent."

"We never agreed otherwise." Then she added in a sharp tone of voice, "Read your copy of our contract addendum. We agreed to the positioning of every survey and cargo ship, even to the positioning of those infernal water-sucking Asturian monstrosities. But nothing in the contract covers the location of my command ship. I'm free to go wherever I wish, and here is as good a place as any." With that remark she flipped a switch that severed their radio contact without the courtesy of a sign-off. "That Asturian," she said turning to Caitlin, "vastly underestimated me when he thought I couldn't figure out where his precious expedition was going." Caitlin had heard this before but listened attentively to Dreyer again. "Every child who has studied geography knows there isn't even an asteroid in the Empire worth developing. Maybe I didn't see it immediately, but I did figure out that the Asturians had crossed The Void—took 'em long enough—and that they found something there. And what does the Empire need more than anything else?" Caitlin knew that she was not expected to answer the question. "Water, that's what. It didn't take a genius to figure out that the Asturians had found a water planet. And how could I not also be interested in a water planet, especially that one?" she said, pointing to the lavender-and-blue sphere visible from the window at the front of the bridge. Dreyer hesitated as a more serious thought crossed her mind. "Do you think we should deploy our 'eggs' now?"

"We could," said Caitlin. "But we could also wait a few more hours or a few more days or even longer for that matter."

"I'd rather do it sooner than later," said Dreyer. "In fact, let's drop the eggs now. I'm sure to sleep better once they are in place."

Although Caitlin was not pleased by this command, she activated the microphone on her own computer and turned on an audio scrambling device. She called Mallory on The Nemesis and gave him the prearranged message, that "they needed some powdered eggs." A few minutes later a door on the tail section of The Nemesis opened, and a black object the size and shape of a rain barrel spun out into space and unfolded four fan-like panels.

* * *

Because Stoney overslept, Kellan's team was the last of the three land crews to leave base on the first morning they explored Dahai. One crew went north to the foothills of a mountain range, a second east toward the ocean, and Kellan's group southwest to a rainforest. There were seven in his group, including Bellycold, in two large Floats, each with a trailer containing camping gear, food, water, and surveying and sample-collection equipment. They all carried laser pistols for protection, and Stoney took a laser rifle as well, joking that he planned to shoot some fresh meat for supper.

Their Floats, similar to the ones Kellan used on Imrada, were open-topped with a V-shaped nose. And once their engines were started, they rode three feet above the ground on a magnetic field. But because the grass surrounding their base was five feet high and taller, the explorers felt as though they were on rafts riding on a carpet of vegetation. Kellan, accompanied by Stoney and Bellycold, drove the lead Float. Simmons, Vickie Webb, and the Imperial Rangers Reed and Wallace followed in the second. They navigated by using a microwave imager on the Float's instrument panel, which gave them a 240-degree view of what was ahead and would show in outline form any trees, rocks, or other obstacles that might be in their path. There seemed to be nothing ahead of them, only an ocean of grass as far as they or the imaging device could see.

For more than an hour the scenery never changed except the lemon-colored grass rose occasionally to eight and nine feet high, some of it turning brown at the tip, which caused Kellan to remark that the grass was beginning to look like "overripe bananas."

They were miles away from their base and finally approaching the edge of the rainforest when Bellycold said, "Well, what do you know?" The android pointed toward the microwave-imaging screen. "There is the first feature on this plain. A hill, I guess. Anyway, it's something besides grass."

Kellan took a closer look at the dark image on the screen. It was either a mound of dirt or perhaps a large boulder lying by itself a half mile off. As they approached it, Kellan kept an eye on the screen, but when they were less than a hundred yards off, it was Bellycold who announced the change, "The hill just got bigger."

Kellan also observed the change. "It did get bigger," he said thoughtfully, "as if it stood up."

The words "stood up" hung in the air. In the rear seat Bellycold, who was taller than his two human companions, grabbed the seat support in front of him and stood to his full height. He looked over the windshield of the Float, above the top of the tall, lemon-colored grass. There looking back at the android was a pair of red eyes framed by two long, sharp horns. "Good lord!" shouted Bellycold. "It's got horns."

Kellan looked up at the robot. "Horns?"

"Horns," Bellycold repeated. "And red eyes that bulge right out of its head."

A worried-looking Stoney released the safety catch on his laser rifle as Kellan asked, "Is it a mammal or a reptile?"

The android shrugged his shoulders. "Either one, or maybe an insect."

Kellan had to admit that he was both excited and frightened at the prospect of encountering a new and apparently strange life form. "That's why we're here," he said. "We should take a look at it."

"Couldn't we start with something smaller?" asked Stoney.

"I thought you wanted fresh meat?" said Kellan.

"But I'm not hungry enough for something that size."

Kellan kept them on a direct path toward the dark form on the microwave screen, which was growing larger by the second, and radioed to the second Float that they were approaching some kind of large life form. The Float's engine ran almost silently, and Kellan cut their speed in the hope of being able to sneak up on the creature. They were less than 30 yards away when the creature let out one of the loud snorts they heard the night before and followed it with a long, low, rumbling grunt.

"This is close enough," shouted Stoney, and Kellan turned the Float away from the creature. While the beast gave another loud grunt, Kellan radioed the second Float to follow him in taking a wide detour around the red-eyed creature in the grass.

For the remainder of their journey in the Float, they kept an eye on the imager and checked all around for more of the creatures but saw none. Eventually the tall grass began to thin out, and it gradually gave way to swampland. A few oddly shaped trees with brown bark and blue leaves began to appear here and there. Then came short, wide bushes with gnarled limbs and feather-like leaves. And when the trees and bushes began to increase in density as well as variety, the Floats had to be slowed to a crawl, and eventually they could no longer navigate what had become a jungle dense with all kinds of vegetation. Kellan informed his crew that they would have to get out and walk, which was not a very pleasing prospect because the water was at least thigh deep and was as murky as dark blue ink.

Bellycold was the first out of the Float to test the water, and he pronounced it safe. "At least, it's safe for a robot," he added. Kellan and the Rangers Reed and Wallace were next out, and soon the entire crew was busy unpacking and securing their vehicles to trees, activating the Floats' homing signals, and preparing for a long hike into the rainforest.

With the human crew loaded with heavy backpacks and the android Bellycold dragging a large sample-storage box that floated on a magnetic field, the expedition waded through the dark blue water, feeling their way carefully because they could not see more than an inch or two below the surface of the water. Reed and Wallace knew almost nothing about plants, and so it was left to Kellan, who had done well in his two biology courses at the Academy, to decide which species of plants looked sufficiently unusual to warrant collection. In fact, much of what Kellan saw looked new, and he found himself stopping every few minutes to add a leaf or an entire plant to the sample box.

Others of the crew merely walked along enjoying the scenery and the lavender sky, while Vickie and Stoney kept on alert for slimy creatures that might be crawling around in the water near their legs.

Vickie was attracted by an odd-looking section of tree trunk growing out of the water and up the side of another tree. The part that was sticking out of the swamp was two feet long and six inches in diameter, and its bark looked like thin parchment stretched over a wire mesh frame, the ribs of which were protruding. Vickie moved to within a few feet for a closer look, sloshing water as she walked. The last thing she expected was for that part of the trunk to move, but that is exactly what it did, bending around and turning in her direction as though it knew she was there. She let out a loud gasp. The creature opened its mouth by separating six wedge-shaped flaps and made a whooshing sound.

Vickie's head and shoulders were instantly covered with a clear, smelly, gooey substance. Too shocked to move, she stood breathing heavily and moaning between breaths while the goo ran down the front of her shirt. Kellan, who saw what happened and watched as the creature disappeared underwater, rushed to her. Vickie began wiping her face with her hands. When Kellan reached her, he grabbed her arm and dragged her down to her knees and into the water. "Keep it out of your eyes and mouth," he said while splashing water on her chest and arms, and helping wipe the goo from her face and head.

"What is this stuff?" she asked nervously. "Am I okay?"

"You're okay," said Kellan reassuringly although he noticed that her skin was red in several places. "It's apparently more smelly than caustic."

At first, she had not noticed the sour smell of the gooey substance, but now its odor assaulted her. "Make sure it's all out of my hair. Oh god, I'll never get the smell out of my hair."

"What happened, Chief?" asked Simmons, who with the others had gathered around Vickie.

"Something spat on her," said Kellan.

"A big worm," said Vickie, her face and chest soaked with water, her hair and the collar of her shirt still dripping with goo. "I come half across the universe and cross The Void only to get spat on by a big worm."

11 | Strange Encounters

High above him in the rainforest canopy, dozens of birds were giving their exotic morning calls, and occasionally Kellan would hear a moaning sound that he guessed came from some kind of large tree mammal. The evening before they had cleared just enough space on the jungle floor to erect seven one-person tents—Bellycold needed his own tent to protect him from the rainforest's excessive moisture—and Kellan now sat on a folding stool, having his second cup of coffee of the day. The others were still in their tents except for the android, who stood by a tree removing a yellow-orange mold that must have worked its way into his ankle and knee joints when they were walking through the swamp the day before.

Kellan had never heard or seen anything like the sounds and sights he encountered on this planet, and he was beginning to love Dahai and its life forms. They were everywhere on this planet. Some living thing seemed to have invaded every square inch of Dahai. During yesterday's long trek, which had been both fascinating and exhausting, Kellan filled his sample storage box with a variety of plants he collected along the way including several fruits and vegetables that looked like distant cousins of varieties they had on Asturias. These, however, were much larger because of the abundance of water on Dahai.

The task for today and for the next week or more was to find some real wealth, to penetrate the rain forest another 30 miles south to a spot where an aerial survey indicated there might be a petroleum deposit. Once there, they would erect a laser device, exactly as they had on Imrada, and drill down far enough to see what was there. But that could wait. For now Kellan would continue to enjoy the sights and sounds of Dahai, the smells that reminded him of cinnamon and sweet peppers, and the warmth of a patch of sunlight that had broken through the trees overhead.

Stoney, his clothes disheveled, his hair matted, and his eyes still droopy from sleep, made his first appearance of the day. Without saying good morning, he waved halfheartedly at Kellan as he headed into the bushes to relieve himself.

Bellycold, who was so humanlike that Kellan could almost forget he was an android, began complaining about the difficulty he was having removing the mold from his metal body. But Kellan ignored him to concentrate on the sound of yet another bird, this one calling out a series of "oohs" and "aahs" that echoed throughout the forest. But he left his reverie when he heard Stoney shout. Kellan rose to his feet as Stoney hurried back from the bushes.

"Man, that was weird," said Stoney, who appeared more confused than frightened. "You should have seen what just happened." Kellan and Bellycold gathered around Stoney, who held out his right hand to illustrate his story. "I was just about to take a crap when I noticed a spider the size of my hand, maybe bigger. And man, it had these thick green-and-orange striped legs."

"Did it bite you?" asked Kellan.

"I didn't give it a chance. I stepped on it." Stoney gave Kellan a puzzled look. "Here's the weird part. When I lifted my foot, about a dozen little spiders ran out."

"It must have been a pregnant female," Kellan offered.

Stoney shook his head. "But there was no big carcass. I could understand the small spiders—maybe, but the carcass of the mother would still be there."

"I've checked my databank," said Bellycold, "and didn't

come across anything about a spider that could divide itself into smaller pieces."

"Try searching for composite life forms," said Kellan.

Bellycold was silent for a few seconds, then said, "Ah ha! This is interesting." Both Kellan and Stoney listened attentively. "There is a species of sea slug on the Republican planet Drakan. About a dozen individual slugs combine to form a composite creature that looks like a fish, or at least the stick figure of a fish, and each slug performs a specific biological function for the whole. When threatened," the android continued as though reading from a text, "the composite creature often disassembles, and the individual slugs disappear into the sand on the seafloor." The robot paused briefly then added, "Of course, the individual sea slugs don't look anything at all like the composite fish. So it's not an identical situation."

"It's close enough," said Kellan, hoping Bellycold's report would put an end to the discussion.

Stoney reached down for the pot of coffee that Kellan had made on a solar battery-operated burner and poured a cup. "I hate this place," he mumbled.

"I like it here," said Kellan, looking up at the small portion of sky visible through the trees. "I think it's a great planet. But like it or not, we've got to fulfill our contracts with SED-Corp to get a ride home. So I suggest we push through to this alleged oil field and find ourselves a large petroleum deposit."

Stoney took a sip of coffee. "Let's do it then," he said, wiping his mouth with the back of his hand.

During the next half-hour, the rest of their team awoke. Simmons was his usual cheery self, but Reed seemed cranky and spoke to no one. Vickie was the last to come to breakfast, and she arrived scratching the back of her neck. Kellan thought that her face appeared unusually red, probably from sunburn, but because of her experience with the worm the day before, he asked to examine the skin on both her face and neck. She had a dozen red, pimply splotches, more like a rash than sunburn.

And it itched, she said. He gave Vickie an ointment for skin irritations from the first aid kit, and a few minutes after she applied it, the itching stopped. By the time breakfast was finished, Kellan was convinced that Vickie's rash was not a serious problem, and so they broke down their camp and resumed their trek.

The first part of the morning's walk was relatively easy and uneventful except for a swarm of gnats they briefly encountered and the noise of an unseen but apparently large animal scurrying through the bushes just ahead of them. Then the vegetation became so dense that they had to start hacking their way through the saplings and twisted vines, making passages big enough to accommodate the large android and the sample storage box that he pulled behind him.

They had covered less than three miles when they came to a pleasant clearing surrounding a pond. Tired and hot, they dropped their backpacks and decided to break for lunch. It was then that a worried-looking Reed pulled Kellan aside, and they walked a dozen yards away from the others. "Something has been bothering me," the Ranger began in a whisper. "Wallace and me, we inspected The Nemesis for contraband and anything that might indicate that Dreyer might be up to some funny business."

"And did you find anything?"

"No, nothing." Reed's tone indicated that he was more than a little upset. "But ever since then, I can't help but think that something wasn't right."

"What does Wallace say?" asked Kellan with one eye on the pond, where Simmons was creating some kind of commotion.

"That I'm crazy, that I'm imagining things," he answered, the level of his voice rising. "But I know that something wasn't right about the inspection tour we took, even though I can't put my finger on what it was. I thought maybe since you were on the ship before us and worked for Dreyer, you might know or have seen something."

"No, I certainly don't know anything. And I didn't see anything either, but I was only in the front portion of The Nemesis."

Kellan wanted to be helpful. After his experience with the crew on Imrada, Kellan no longer considered Republicans the enemy, but he was still an Asturian, was loyal to Alfiri, and planned to return to Capital City when the expedition ended. Neither side, he believed, should be plotting against the other, and on a completely personal level, the last thing he wanted was the alliance to break apart and jeopardize the return trip across The Void. "The only thing I know is that there was a lot of shuttle traffic to and from The Nemesis, and there were some very large vessels—supply ships I would guess."

"How many?"

"Of the big vessels? At least five."

Reed's eyes opened wide at this news. "At least five!"

Kellan nodded his head. "Maybe more."

"But the holds were basically empty. So what was on the large supply ships that you saw, and where did the cargo go?" Reed looked really worried now. "I was thinking of going back to our land base and trying to get a message through to Alfiri to check out The Nemesis again."

"Yo, Chief, you got to see this." Simmons, a camera hanging around his neck, was calling to him and pointing overhead.

Just below the treetops, 75 to 100 feet above the crew, something white and shaped like a large tulip bulb facing downwards, floated gently like a parachute. Kellan walked closer for a better look, uncertain whether this was a plant or an animal. "It looks like a giant flower blossom, Chief, but I don't see where it came from." Simmons lifted the camera to his eye, craned his neck back, and snapped off several pictures.

Kellan saw that the white blossom or the white creature, whichever it was, was spinning and changing direction as it descended either from the breeze or by design. Then he noticed that it was larger than he originally thought, perhaps four or five feet in diameter, and it was dangling what appeared to be slender tentacles. An airborne jellyfish of some kind, thought Kellan.

Simmons continued taking pictures while the creature floated gently toward him.

When it was 20 feet above Simmons and directly over his head, the sides of the white creature folded like an umbrella, and it fell like a stone, opening again just soon enough and just wide enough to drop over Simmons. Covered from head to hips, Simmons staggered and fell into the pond as Kellan and Reed rushed to help him.

"Oh my god!" shouted Vickie. "Pull it off him, pull it off."

While Simmons thrashed about in the water, which was only a few feet deep, Kellan grabbed the creature's delicate-looking but leathery-feeling skin. He tried to peel the skin from Simmons, but it had a surprisingly strong hold on him. Stoney and Wallace joined them, and each grabbed a section of the creature's skirt. "When I tell you," shouted Kellan, "all pull at once and pull the skin up as though you were peeling a banana. Ready," he said, looking first at Reed, then at Wallace and Stoney. "Now."

They pulled, and the whole white skirt came back. But the creature was attached to Simmons with eight thin, spiny tentacles. Simmons' head was still covered, and he was struggling for air.

The android now joined them. "Bellycold," shouted Kellan, "can you take hold of the skin by yourself?"

"I can sure try," he answered as he wrapped his massive hands around the creature's white skirt, which had been bunched together above its head, underside out.

"When I tell you to," continued Kellan, "throw the damn thing as far as you can. The rest of you each grab two tentacles and peel them back. And be careful not to get pierced by them."

The four men crowded around Simmons and gingerly peeled back the eight tentacles. Simmons, gasping for air, slid out free.

"Okay," shouted Kellan, "on the count of three we let go, and Bellycold, you throw it as far as you can. Ready. One, two, three."

They let go of the tentacles, and Bellycold threw the creature about 15 yards. It smashed against a tree trunk and slid down to the ground. Then it used its tentacles to climb up into the tree with surprising speed.

Stoney ran for his laser rifle, but by the time he returned, the creature was hidden in the treetops. Stoney fired several shots nonetheless but only succeeded in blasting off a few tree climbs, which fell to the ground a dozen yards from where they were standing.

Simmons was badly shaken, short of breath, and covered with scores of tiny puncture marks. He looked drowsy and said that his arms felt stiff. Vickie brought the medical kit, and they tried smelling salts on Simmons, but that did not help. Then Wallace, who had some training as a battlefield medic, injected him with synthetic adrenaline, and Simmons began to feel more awake although still groggy.

Kellan had momentarily forgotten about Reed and his concern, but Reed, despite the attack of the "aerial jellyfish," was still focused on what had happened to him on The Nemesis, especially now that Kellan had told him about the large ships docking with it. When they could do no more for Simmons, Reed huddled with Kellan again, and after a long conversation, they decided to divide their team in two. Simmons, who appeared as though he could fall asleep at anytime, would need more medical attention than he could receive here and would have to be shuttled to one of the orbiting space vessels. Vickie Webb's rash had gotten bad again, and the ointment was no longer helping. She too should probably see a doctor. And Reed was certain that he wanted to try to contact Alfiri and suggest that he have The Nemesis re-inspected. These three would return to base, and Wallace would make the trip with them just in case he and Reed had to carry Simmons part of the way back to the Float.

The rest of the team, Kellan, Stoney, and Bellycold, would continue at least as far as the site of the possible oil field and laser drill a test hole.

* * *

The Omnihaul dropped through Dahai's upper atmosphere until it was cruising over a bank of clouds, which yielded here and there to give a glimpse of an ocean below. As they approached the large island in the northern hemisphere, where he had helped install Base 5 only a few days before, the Omnihaul's pilot slowed the craft and began to circle.

The island, like much of Dahai, was covered with vegetation, all but the narrow beaches that surrounded it and the tips of the jagged mountain peaks at its center. The ship continued to circle and drop its altitude as it approached the coordinates of where the base was supposed to be, nestled in a stand of palm trees a short distance from the ocean. Instead they saw only a large, black spot, which, from the air, appeared to be almost a perfect circle. The Omnihaul's right wing raised up, and the ship turned left to trace a slow loop over the black spot. It was the base, or what was left of it, but there was no sign of life nor any indication of what started the fire that had charred the area.

As a precaution, the Omnihaul landed 100 yards from the base. A joint security force consisting of three Asturian Rangers and three SED-Corp guards disembarked, all of them in environmental suits with lasers drawn. A light rain was falling although the sky was mostly sunny. As they walked down into the charred depression, raindrops thumped on their helmets and ran down their visors; the rain splashed on the black ash on the ground and glistened on the pale green lichen that was already rising out of the devastation. They approached what had been a highly sophisticated base and saw that the front end—the crew quarters and mess hall—had been obliterated, and the back portion containing the storage area and generator, melted and disfigured.

Benjamin Alomar, the Asturian co-leader of the team, a large man with combat experience during several so-called "skirmishes" with the Republicans, slowly advanced on the burned-out base.

The portion that was still standing was slanted to one side like a warped candle, and he bent down for a better look through the opening where the back of the base should have been connected to the front. "Whatever it was, it generated a hell of a lot of heat," said Alomar.

Just behind him stood Karina Hudson, the Republican co-leader of the tactical team. A slight-built woman, Hudson was a martial arts champion whose only exposure to battle was during holographic training videos. "I guess it could have been a laser blast," she said.

"Could be," answered Alomar in a matter-of-fact tone. "But it would have to be a laser with a 20-or 30-foot-wide beam, and I don't think any such device exists."

"Then a rocket hit," offered Hudson.

Alomar shrugged his shoulders. "That would be the most logical guess, but it would have to be some kind of incendiary warhead that I'm unfamiliar with." He looked at her through his rain-streaked helmet visor. "Do you have such a device in the Republics?"

Angered by the remark, Hudson took a step closer to the Asturian. "It was our base, Alomar," she said forcefully. "Why would we destroy it?"

He immediately became defensive. "I wasn't making an accusation."

"The hell you weren't. And the crew was half ours as well." Thinking of the crew took the edge off Hudson's anger at Alomar. "What about them? Do you think they are dead?"

"Nah," said Alomar optimistically. "They reported that they had gone into the field, but we'll know for certain when we are able to check for their safety pulse beacons."

* * *

Carlo Asana was momentarily startled by a knock on his cabin door; he never had visitors. "Coming," he said as he got up from his small desk and opened the door. It was Harlan Knorr, looking nervous. But then, Asana thought, Knorr always looked nervous.

"May I come in?" The Prelate ushered him in with an elaborate sweep of his arm. Harlan glanced around the cabin in a cursory fashion, "I hope you are finding your quarters comfortable."

"Don't give me that," said Asana, a smile on his face but an edge to his voice. "You didn't come here to make small talk. You're carrying a message, and it must be an unpleasant one."

Harlan took a deep breath and reminded himself that he was here representing Julian Alfiri. "No, not unpleasant news, not really. It's just that Julian feels—well, that you've spending a lot of time on the bridge and sometimes—well, that sometimes you question his judgment or appear to be giving him orders."

Asana's pockmarked face flushed red, but he held his temper and kept his voice down. "Alfiri thinks he is kicking me off the bridge?"

"No, not at all. He's just asking that you spend less time on the bridge, and that when you are there, you be more mindful of your position. . ." The Prelate's eyes opened wide at that remark, causing Harlan to quickly add, "Perhaps that was a poor way to put it."

"You fat prick!" shouted Asana as he exploded in anger. "My position! Just who the hell do you think you are to speak to me of my position." Harlan visibly quaked under Asana's verbal assault. "You're Alfiri's messenger boy, that's all, the one who handles his unpleasantries for him. Go tell your boss that if he has anything to say to me, to tell me face-to-face instead of sending a toady." Knorr, thinking Asana was finished with him, started to leave. "Where are you going?" Harlan paused in mid stride, and before he could say anything, Asana's expression and tone softened. "Stay a minute. Maybe I'm being too harsh. After all, you are just the messenger. Sit down," he said, pointing to the chair at his desk. "Go ahead, sit down." Harlan looked at the chair, then back at Asana, and sat down, his palms sweaty, the back of his neck damp with perspiration. The Prelate stood over him. "I've noticed something special about you, Harlan," he said, and Harlan did not know whether to expect a compliment or another insult. "What's special about you is that Alfiri, the Great Julian Alfiri, listens to you."

"He listens to me but not always," Harlan answered weakly.

"But more to you than anybody else."

"Probably so."

"Definitely so, and you're smart too, a little short on backbone maybe, but smart." Asana smiled. "Smart enough to know that you can't change the tide of events, smart enough not to stand in the way and be crushed by them." The Prelate took a step backwards and spread out his arms, palms up. "Look at me, Harlan, and tell me what you see." Not knowing where Asana was going, he merely shrugged his shoulders. "You see the Asturian Church. You see The Triumvirate of the Holy Asturian Empire."

Just then Harlan was paged over the ship's communications system. Alfiri wanted him on the bridge immediately.

Harlan stood and pointed to the door. "I've got to go."

The Prelate again smiled, and he put his hand on Harlan's shoulder. "He is lost without you, Harlan. You'd better go to his side. When you have a chance, come back, and we can finish our conversation."

Harlan hurried out of Asana's cabin, then paused in the corridor to pull a pill from his shirt pocket and pop it into his mouth. He felt trapped. He wanted to avoid Asana for the rest of the voyage but well understood that Asana could not be ignored. Perhaps the Prelate overstated his own importance when he said he represented The Triumvirate, but as far as the people on this expedition were concerned, he was the Church.

Harlan was paged again, and he rushed to the circular bridge of the Defender command ship, where he found Alfiri seated at the elaborate communications console, arguing with Kit Dreyer over the radio about the use of the Asturians' water vessels.

Dreyer began the conversation harshly, despite her promise to Caitlin, by saying, "You damn Asturians just suck the water, suck the life out of a place, without even doing a damn environmental impact study to determine how much water an ecosystem can lose before it is destroyed completely."

But Julian, ever the diplomat, answered in a controlled voice, "There is plenty of water. What we are taking is quite literally a drop in the bucket."

"Bullshit!" said Dreyer. "You'll suck the place dry."

"Read your copy of the contract," he responded. "We never specified how much water we would take or from where, and so we have a perfect right to do what we are doing."

Harlan, who was standing behind Julian, was approached by the commander of the Defender, Captain Goldschmidt. Goldschmidt whispered into Harlan's ear, and Harlan, in turn, immediately tapped Julian on the shoulder. "Excuse me, Julian," he said, nervously taking a swallow of air. "Everyone needs to hear this."

"Hear what?" asked Dreyer.

"Switch to Channel C," said Knorr. "Everyone needs to hear this."

Julian turned to Channel C as did Dreyer, and the Defender's communications officer asked Ranger Alomar to repeat his report. They all listened in silence as Alomar told them that Base 5 had been totally destroyed—charred and melted by some unknown high-temperature device or substance. Alomar also reported that the land crew had been away from the base at the time of its destruction and had been located traveling safely along an ocean beach in their Floats.

When the report was finished, Dreyer was the first to speak, "I suggest, Alfiri, that we both need time to analyze this new information and that our discussion about Dahai's water is best continued at another time."

"Agreed," said Alfiri, "but let's have our aides schedule another conversation soon. This situation is not good, and we are going to need to keep talking." Alfiri handed the microphone to Harlan, who found one of Dreyer's aides, Caitlin Cormack, on the other end of the radio proposing times for another conversation.

Julian left the bridge to gather his thoughts in private. He wanted to believe the best about Dreyer and the Republicans; after all, he was the one who proposed and arranged the alliance. It made no sense that Dreyer would destroy her own base—unless she wanted to provoke him. But why here, on the other side of the universe, was provocation necessary? Why not simply attack? There had to be another explanation; perhaps a generator or laser drill on Base 5 had accidentally exploded. He decided to arrange for Ranger Alomar to give him an in-person report on exactly what he had seen at the destroyed land base.

* * *

Caitlin's recommendation to Kit Dreyer was the only one that made sense: "We have to sit tight and do nothing until we know more. We can't use this situation to create a confrontation, not until we know the cause. We might be facing a common enemy or a strange natural phenomenon on Dahai." Caitlin went on to argue that they had no proof or even a possible motive for believing the Asturians had destroyed the land base. And even if they were to assume that Asturians were to blame, they could not say for certain whether Alfiri was responsible or the shadow group that Dreyer was dealing with. "We can't act," Caitlin said, "because we don't know against whom to act." It was against Dreyer's nature to sit tight, but she agreed that Caitlin's advice was correct. She would remain patient. But not for much longer.

As soon as she finished that conversation, Caitlin went to her computer to check on Kellan's whereabouts. Each land explorer carried a wrist safety beacon that could be monitored from orbit. But these beacons had to be relayed through the radio antenna of a land base. That was why Caitlin had suggested that the security unit be sent to Base 5 in the northern hemisphere—she lost the base's signal and had been unable to locate any of the crew's safety pulses. Now she checked on Kellan and his crew from Base 1, and found no sign of them either. She was on the verge of panicking and sending a security unit to go after Kellan when she thought to check the position of her ship relative to his base. What a relief! Base 1 was out of their transmission range. The Starhawk would have to progress at least another two full hours in its orbit before Kellan's transmitter could beam a signal up to them. She would check again then.

12 Back to Where He Had Never Been

Kellan fell asleep to the sounds of a gentle rain against the roof of his small tent. For someone who had spent most of his life on dry Asturias, it was an especially pleasant sensation. That afternoon they had traveled another difficult four miles through the wilderness, across an area that was more open than the jungle they traversed during the prior two days. Exhausted from the long trek, Kellan helped make camp, ate a large meal from their packaged rations, and went straight to sleep.

During the night, the rain increased in intensity, and occasionally he was startled awake by loud cracking thunder. So he was unusually cognizant of his dreams, dreams that were populated by new and interesting creatures including goo-worms, flying jellyfish, and large silver-and-red squirrel-like creatures. His dream squirrels, which were as large as medium-size dogs on Asturias, behaved exactly like the real ones they encountered near the end of the day's journey. The squirrels were very territorial and gathered in the trees above their heads, making angry clicking sounds at the three intruders. And when Kellan and the others continued slowly moving straight ahead, the animals began to throw large nutshells of some kind, shells that were especially hard, as Kellan found out when one struck him on the shoulder. The assault continued until Bellycold turned toward their attackers and gave his impersonation of a lion's roar. Despite his aching shoulder, Kellan laughed at how the android's antics scattered the squirrels back into the treetops.

Suddenly Kellan was tossed head over heels, then spun horizontally in a semicircle. At first he thought he was still dreaming, but then he was rolled over a second time and hit in the midsection by something hard. He tried to get up but could not find the ground beneath him and for an instant thought he was flying. It was the sound of thunder that helped him figure out what had happened. He was caught in a flood. His tent was being carried away by the water, tossed, and pummeled like a twig in a fast-moving stream, while his gear and food supplies were being thrown around the inside. And his tent's waterproofing was failing, allowing water to seep in. He was in a life-threatening situation and tried desperately to find the zipper to the tent flap so that he could escape. But the way he was being thrown around, he could not have worked the zipper even if he had been able to find it.

The tent stopped moving with a thud. It had caught against something. Kellan reached out in the darkness hoping to find his knife. He found his laser pistol instead. He took it in both hands and fired it while moving the pistol's muzzle in a horizontal line. The dim light of the Dahaian night shown through the opening he had cut in the tent wall. Feeling the tent dislodging from whatever was holding it in place, he quickly locked the safety catch on the laser pistol, stuck it down the top of his trousers, and started to climb out.

The rain was coming down in quantities he had never before experienced. He managed to get his upper body out of the tent and quickly studied the tree that was preventing his tent from washing away. He reached up and grabbed one of the tree's thick vines, and just as he was pulling his legs out, the tent was torn away by a wave that also submerged his head. He managed to hold onto the vine, and when the water receded several feet, he coughed out the water he had swallowed and took several deep breaths. Expecting another wave to hit at any moment, he pulled himself higher up the vine, and when he found a foothold on a low tree branch, he was able to climb several feet above the water level.

Pausing only long enough to take another few breaths and to assess his situation, Kellan climbed higher into the tree, thankful that there was so much vegetation on Dahai, and that it grew in such a tangled mass, that it provided him with a ladder to take him several dozen feet above the flood.

There was little light in the sky, except when the lightning flashed. Nonetheless Kellan shielded his eyes from the rain with his hands and tried to look for his two companions, whom he feared had been swept away. He could see nothing but jungle and rain, and he shouted their names. To his surprise he heard a response, and he shouted again. It was Stoney, who was a good distance away and apparently also esconced in a tree.

Kellan's relief at learning that Stoney was alive was tempered by the realization that the android Bellycold might be lost, and that all their equipment, including food, surveying and mining gear, their navigational and communications devices, even his wrist beacon, had been washed away by the flood. Unless they recovered some key equipment, or one of the orbiting space vessels was somehow able to monitor their situation, they were on their own in the wilderness of Dahai. They would have to live off the land and find their way back to their Float by the position of the sun.

Several times Kellan and Stoney tried to communicate, but they were too far away, and the rain was too loud for them to distinguish any more than a few intermittent words.

Kellan kept an eye on the water level, concerned that another wave would roll through. But none did. The heavy rain, however, continued to fall, and the water level rose noticeably. Occasionally thunder would crack overhead, and lightning would turn the sky brilliant white. After a period of time, which Kellan estimated at an hour or more, the rain began to slow, and he began to feel more confident that he and Stoney would survive until morning.

It was then that Kellan saw a brilliant light through the forest canopy. The thunder that trailed it was lower in pitch than what he had been hearing, and the light, itself, did not move at the instantaneous speed of a lightning bolt. As the light streaked across the sky, he saw that it was a large ball, not a ball of fire but rather one of intense white light. The thunder now echoed directly overhead as the great ball descended like a falling meteor. It hit some miles away with the impact of a bomb, strong enough to shake the tree he was perched in. White light exploded into the sky above the area of impact. And a short time later he saw the orange glow of a distant forest fire.

Kellan had heard of a phenomenon called ball lightning. He knew little about it except that it was supposed to be fist-sized, but he could think of no other explanation for what he had just witnessed.

Nothing on Dahai was exactly like it was at home.

The remainder of the night passed without incident. The rain slowed, then stopped altogether, and by morning the water level receded, although the downpour had created a muddy lake beneath him filled with floating tree branches and leaves. Kellan, who was soaked from head to toe, carefully lowered himself down the tree and tested the water level. It was about two feet deep and moving slowly; so he decided it was safe to make his way over to where Stoney was.

Although his joints were stiff, and his back ached from spending the night in a tree, Kellan felt strangely exhilarated. He had narrowly escaped being swept away in the flood by cutting his way out of his tent and pulling himself to safety. And he had survived an explosion of ball lightning—or whatever the phenomenon was. Rather than feel overwhelmed by the dangers on this planet, he felt masterful, unafraid of the next challenge Dahai might offer.

What a place, he thought as he looked at the clear lavender sky and bright reddish orange sun. The colors were so different from those of Asturias, and while whole areas of his home planet were dry and barren, some life form, and often a bizarre one, seemed to be growing out of every pore on this planet's surface.

Stoney, who appeared as upset as Kellan was invigorated, was just ahead, and he climbed down when he saw Kellan approach. "Man, I'm really sorry," he said as he lowered himself into the thigh-deep water.

Kellan was puzzled. "About what?"

Brushing his long, wet hair out of his eyes, Stoney said, "That I couldn't warn you guys. I was outside when the flood hit."

"In the rain!" said Kellan incredulously.

"Yeah. I was thinking about moving my tent to higher ground, but there wasn't any nearby," said Stoney, who explained that when he saw the wall of water suddenly approaching, he barely had time to grab onto the nearest tree limb. He had shouted a warning to Kellan and Bellycold, and watched helplessly while their tents were washed away. Now he felt somewhat guilty that he had not been more helpful. "I lost everything, even my laser pistol and my last two bottles of hooch," he complained, "and hooch and a laser are the things I need most on this crazy planet."

"Don't worry. I've got my laser," said Kellan, putting his hand on the pistol handle protruding over his belt. Then he looked at Stoney's wrists, which were bare. "You lost your pulse beacon as well?"

"Yeah. It makes my wrist sweat. So I keep it in my backpack."

"Me too." Kellan looked around. "Why don't we see if we can find Bellycold and anything that remains of our camp?"

They began to wade downstream, and at first there seemed to be no hope of finding anything. But after they searched for more than an hour, they came across a tattered tent wrapped around a thorn bush. Another few dozen yards away, they saw Bellycold face down in a tangled mass of tree vines and not moving. The android, a crease in his metal back and smeared with mud, was not moving and did not respond to their calls. Kellan was certain that, despite Bellycold's insulation, the robot's circuits and chips must be damp, if not soaked. He could only hope that when the android dried out, he would return to normal.

Bellycold was too heavy to move. So they left him as he was and searched his metal body for a service panel. Kellan found a small lever under the android's left shoulder, pulled it, and watched as the upper left portion of the robot's back opened, revealing a keyboard.

Stoney looked at the keyboard, then at Kellan. "I didn't think you knew anything about robots. Did you study them at the Academy?"

"Nope, didn't study them and don't know anything about them," said Kellan, deciding to do the only thing he knew how to do. "It's a computer, right? I'll reboot it." He began to fiddle with various keys, then started pressing two at a time. To his surprise, one of the combinations caused something inside the android to whir with a sound not unlike that of a computer hard disk starting up. The whir was followed by a series of beeps, then a minute or two of clicking. Kellan noticed the robot's yellow eyes light up. "Are you okay?"

"Of course, I am," came the android's answer. "I always rest in trees like this."

Kellan smiled. "Good old Bellycold."

"Course I am," repeated the android. "In trees—trees like this."

It could have been another of the robot's jokes, but he doubted that it was. Bellycold was stuttering, and Kellan could not begin to imagine what else might be wrong with him. The timing could not have been worse because they needed the robot and every other possible advantage they could muster to find their way back through the rainforest to their Float.

* * *

It was only a footpath, but Kellan had an intuition it might turn out to be the most important find they had yet made on Dahai.

Stoney disagreed. "It's probably an animal path of some kind, and if we follow it," he cautioned, "we might run smack into a pride of giant lions or worse."

"But what if it was made by humans or humanoid creatures or some other intelligent species?" asked Kellan excitedly. "It would be the first time that we discovered a life form capable of creating culture, laws, and religion that evolved completely independent of the Asturian Church. We have to find out. Another race of people might have a very different perspective on the world," he said and thought to himself, "and on the metaphysical world as well."

"They can't be any smarter than us. After all, we crossed The Void to find them, not the other way around. And with our luck, if we found people-like creatures on this planet, they would be primitive types that would take one look at us and see dinner."

Kellan was never certain how seriously to take Stoney. "Okay, I'll grant you that we must be technological superior. And I'll grant you that they could be hostile. But we have to take a chance. Next to crossing The Void, it could be the most incredible discovery ever made. Besides, we're lost in the jungle without navigation equipment and with almost no hope of finding our way out. Our best chance may be to have someone—or something—with intelligence lead us out. And remember we still have this," he said, holding up his laser pistol. "And him." He now pointed to the robot. "I plan to follow the path one way or the other to its end. You two have to make your own decisions."

"Don't go anywhere without me," said Bellycold. "If I stay here, I'll get covered with more of that mold."

Kellan looked up and down the path, then started in the direction he thought was closer to the place where they left the Float. Bellycold fell in behind him. Stoney hesitated for a few moments, then also took the path. "Okay, I'm coming too. But if we find anybody, they better be willing to share their hooch."

"I'm sure they will." Kellan looked over his shoulder at the robot. "And Bellycold will certainly scare the living hell out of any primitives we encounter," he said, hoping to lessen the tension.

"Hey! I resent-resent that." The android's speech, though still not perfect, was improving as his interior dried out.

The two human members of the party were not in the best condition themselves. They were sleepy from having been awake most of the night; their clothes were still damp from the flood; Kellan's boots had washed away with his tent; and the only edible-looking vegetation they found that morning, a green skinless banana, turned out to be too bitter to eat.

They followed the path for half a mile, then came upon several footprints in the mud. Kellan bent down to examine them. The toes and heel were clearly visible on several of the prints. "They certainly look human to me," he pronounced. Kellan was about to say that the prints belonged to either a child or a very small adult when he sensed a presence ahead of them on the path. He looked up to see four men, tall men with dark pink skin, dressed in white silk robes, carrying spears in their hands and long curved knives in their belts. Three of the Dahaians were young and had long black hair. The fourth was very old and had thinning white hair. All four had long thin noses and deeply cleft chins, and all four stood motionless, no doubt shocked to encounter two strange-looking men in odd clothing accompanied by a giant silver android.

As Kellan slowly stood up, Stoney also noticed the four men. "Kellan, get your laser out," he said as his body tensed in anticipation of a fight.

"Stay cool, Stoney," whispered Kellan. "They may be friendly."

"Let me handle this," said Bellycold. "I was in the diplomatic corps with Julian Alfiri."

"You'd better not." Stoney glanced at the android while keeping an eye on the four armed men before them. "You're a clown robot, remember?"

"That too—too," said Bellycold, taking a step forward.

The three younger Dahaians reacted to the android's approach by pointing their spears and shouting, and Bellycold had the good sense to freeze where he was, while Kellan slipped his hand toward the handle of his laser pistol.

The Dahaians were not only shouting at the intruders but seemed to be arguing among themselves in a language that was nothing like any Kellan had ever heard. Judging from how the old man was standing in front of his younger companions with his arms extended, Kellan guessed that he was urging the others to show restraint. One of the younger men seemed particularly angry, and he pointed at Bellycold with his spear and beat his chest with his free hand. Then he motioned toward the ground and began shouting even louder.

The footprints, thought Kellan; there was something about them that was upsetting this man.

A soft voice called from the bushes, causing the Dahaians to stop their argument. Then a small boy emerged from his hiding place. The boy was obviously one of them. He had the same pink skin, long nose, cleft chin, and black hair, which he had pulled back in a ponytail. All the Dahaians appeared relieved to see the child, who could not have been more than six or seven. The Dahaian who had been pointing toward Bellycold now moved toward the boy, but the boy extended his arms as if trying to keep the man away from him, and he spoke in a tone of voice that sounded as though he was complaining or giving a warning.

"The kid doesn't want to go with them," Kellan said to Stoney. "I think I understand what happened. The kid ran away, and they were looking for him. When they found us instead of him, they must have thought that we had harmed the boy."

While the humans in both parties were not certain what to do next, Bellycold took center stage, and the next few minutes belonged to him. To break the awkwardness between the two groups as well as the apparent conflict between the boy and the adults in his party, the android began a series of birdcalls that attracted the notice of all the Dahaians, who immediately became an attentive audience. Then the android blew a half dozen perfect smoke rings, which drew a giggle from the boy and nods of appreciation from the other Dahaians, who felt enough at ease to approach the robot. Next Bellycold cupped his large fist, pretended to blow on it, and seemingly from his empty hand, drew out a long string of brightly colored scarves.

As Bellycold's performance continued, the old man approached Kellan, and although Kellan could not understand a word he said or even distinguish the end of one word from the beginning of the next, he guessed that the man was apologizing for the threatening behavior of his group. Kellan smiled and bowed from the waist, hoping that he was able to convey an air of friendliness.

In addition to being able to perform magic tricks, the android Bellycold had another important skill: he could translate more than 100 languages and decode new ones. When his show had ended, the robot began talking to the Dahaians, especially the old man, pointing to such things as the grass, trees, sky, and their clothing, and then asking the Dahaians to give their word for it. But it was through sign language that the Dahaians invited Kellan, Stoney, and Bellycold to follow them for something to eat.

The man who seemed to be the boy's father took the child by the hand and led the way. The boy went with some reluctance. The other two young Dahaians followed, then came Kellan and Stoney, and finally Bellycold and the old man, who continued to exchange words, each in his own language.

After 10 or 15 minutes of walking, Bellycold caught up to Kellan and Stoney, and with the old man listening but not understanding a word of what he said, the android gave his report. "This will take time," he began. "It's a weird language. It seems to have only two vowels—the equivalents of our a and u—but it has a whole load of consonants, maybe three dozen of them or more. I'm still having a lot of trouble understanding it, but this is what I can make out from the old man. The little boy," he said, pointing ahead to the child, "calls himself Nuzalu. The others call him Udta, but he calls himself Nuzalu. Udta or Nuzalu, whichever you prefer, ran away. He wanted to return to his village, which is that way," said Bellycold, pointing in the direction from which they had come. "But the men say the boy's village is this way." Now the android pointed in the opposite direction. "And they say the boy has never been out of that village in his whole life. That's the crux of the dispute. I'll report more later," he said as he dropped back and resumed speaking to the old man.

Stoney shook his head as he watched the android leave. "I think the robot's brain is still waterlogged."

"Bellycold's translation may have been somewhat off," he said, more to himself than to Stoney. "But maybe there is something about the culture of these people that we don't understand that is making the translation sound odd."

The Dahaian village was much larger and more elaborate than Kellan anticipated. There were about 50 two-story wood houses with high peaked roofs arranged in neat quadrants. And the village was full of people, most of them tall, all of them with the same dark pink skin, and most with black hair. The women wore the same kind of silk robes as the men, only theirs tended to be more colorful, most decorated in floral or abstract patterns. The older children dressed like the adults while the youngest ran naked and barefoot. The village erupted into conversation when the strangers appeared. Children pointed to Bellycold, and several women raised their hands to their cheeks or mouths in gestures of surprise. At the urging of the Dahaians escorting the strangers, especially the old man, the villagers surrounded the visitors and talked among themselves excitedly.

Bellycold needed no encouragement. He immediately began his repertoire of magic tricks and birdcalls, and he soon, to use the android's own words, "had 'em eatin' out of my metal hand."

The Dahaians were so friendly that even Stoney started to relax. While the android continued his antics, the old man led Kellan and Stoney to his house, gave them silk robes and sandals to wear, and showed them where there were towels and a wash basin where they could clean themselves. When they left the house a while later dressed like Dahaians, they saw that Bellycold was still holding court in the village square. The android would point to a child, and the child would speak or make an animal sound. Bellycold would record the sound, and when he played it back, the crowd of children would react with delight. They never seemed to tire of it and were arguing over whose turn was next.

That afternoon, a large communal meal was prepared. The villagers carried wooden tables and chairs from their houses and arranged them outside in the village square in several long rows. Every family contributed something to the meal, and the visitors were, of course, the honored guests and sat at the center table with the old man.

As the meal was about to start, the Dahaians took their places, bowed their heads, and grew silent. The three Asturians, including Bellycold, did likewise. The old man then spoke, and Kellan guessed that he was saying a prayer of thanksgiving for the meal. Then the old man raised his head and talked in a more animated tone, gesturing several times in the direction of the visitors. When he finished, the villagers nodded their heads toward their guests while Kellan and Bellycold nodded back. Stoney, who felt uncomfortable dressed as a Dahaian and who had reservations about the food set before them, most of which he could not identify, merely looked down at his hands.

They began the meal, and Kellan found it delicious, especially the large, pink-fleshed crab that was the main course. Stoney nudged him and whispered, "Have you noticed that the people and the crabmeat are the same color? Do you suppose that's why the people are so pink?"

Kellan looked down at the crabmeat and up at the villagers across the table from him. The colors were remarkably similar. "I think you'd look better with a little color in your face," he laughed as Stoney pushed his portion of crab to the far end of his plate.

The old man was now looking at Kellan and speaking rapidly as Bellycold translated for him as best he could, "The old man says that the boy—Udta or Nuzalu—wants to see his mother and the rest of his family in the other village."

"Is this the village that he has never been to?" asked Kellan.

"Exactly," answered Bellycold, who then listened to the old man again before continuing his translation. "Of course, his father and family are also here in this village." The android hesitated, studying the old man's face carefully. "Sometimes things like this happen." Bellycold was now translating verbatim. "I told them, told the boy's family, that the little one will continue to run away unless they allow him to visit the other village and his other family. So soon we will take him to his other home."

Curious to figure out the puzzle of the two villages and two families, Kellan wanted to make that journey as well and was only a question away from getting that opportunity. Kellan waited for a pause in the conversation between the old man and the android, then said, "Bellycold, ask the old one if he can tell us how to get back to our Float, to the place where the tall grass is."

The android rattled off some Dahaian words, then listened to the old man's response. "Of course," said Bellycold, speaking for the old man. "The place of the tall grass is not far from Nuzalu's village. You can go with us when we visit there."

They spent the next two days in the village, Kellan learning everything he could about their culture and even making an attempt to learn their language. Bellycold performed for the children—and many of the adults—after every meal, but Stoney, a little shaky and irritable without alcohol, still felt uneasy among the Dahaians and kept to himself.

On the third day of their stay, the boy the villagers called Udta ran away again. The villagers knew where he was going and caught up with him, but they now knew they could no longer delay taking the boy on his journey.

13 | Assault on The Nemesis

The transmitter on the Dahaian land base that served as headquarters for Kellan Blake and his team had been within range of Kit Dreyer's command vessel for more than five hours, and still Caitlin Cormack, sitting at a computer on the ship's bridge, could find no trace of the crew's safety pulse beacons. Nor had she been able to reach them by radio. Caitlin was worried that Kellan's base had fallen prey to the same unknown force that nearly vaporized Base 5 in the planet's northern hemisphere. And she feared another destroyed base would cause Kit Dreyer to act impulsively, or Julian Alfiri or their shadow partner, who had yet to identify her-or himself, to take aggressive action of one sort or another.

Being one of Dreyer's senior advisers was a much more stressful job than Caitlin had anticipated. Keeping track of the space vessels and land crews on all the planets and moons being explored in this new world meant long hours at their mission control center. But dealing with the volatile situation between Dreyer and Alfiri was even more wearing, especially since Caitlin sometimes felt that she was the only person capable of getting Kit Dreyer to react rationally to a bad situation. And now there was a problem with Base 1. For everyone's sake but especially Kellan's, Caitlin hoped the security team that she was about to dispatch would find some problem with the base transmitter, but that the facility would otherwise be intact.

Caitlin checked the location of The Nemesis on her radar screen. It was almost in position. She turned in her swivel chair toward the ship's communications officer and called, "Mr. White." A young man in a green-and-white SED-Corp uniform turned to face her. "Please contact the Captain of The Nemesis and tell him to dispatch the security team now."

On the shuttle pad of The Nemesis, an Omnihaul carrying the security unit commanded by Karina Hudson and Benjamin Alomar blasted off. Neither said a word as their vessel cleared the deck of the mother ship, then descended from orbit and entered Dahai's atmosphere. Both dreaded finding another burned-out base; both feared what would happen to the uneasy alliance between the Asturians and the Republicans if another land installation had been destroyed.

The Omnihaul continued its descent, then leveled out over Dahai's dark blue southern ocean. Alomar pressed his forehead against the window and watched as the water below gave way to a green-and-brown landmass. The Omnihaul slowed and again began to descend. Soon they were circling above a large field of yellow grass, many square miles of it. Alomar noticed a flash of light, which he thought might have been a reflection from the metal land base. He strained for a better look, saw a second flash, but was too far away to make out its source.

A few minutes later the Omnihaul set down on the ground less than 100 yards from the land base's location. The six-person security unit scrambled out of the ship with lasers drawn, but from where they stood, the base looked normal.

None of the unit members had been here when the Base 1 was installed a few days before, or they would have noticed that something had changed. The yellow grass, which had stood five foot high and taller all around, had been cut down to ground level in a half-mile radius around the base.

Unaware of this peculiar change, the security team slowly approached the long, metal structure. They studied the base from the outside, and when they were close enough, they looked inside the base windows. Nothing seemed the least bit out of order until they went around to the back. There they found the radio antenna, a freestanding 40-foot structure that had been bolted to the base's rear wall, lying flat on the ground and bent in several places. In addition, there were peculiar dents and scrape marks on the base's rear wall. The main thing, as Hudson was quick to point out, was that the base had not been burned to ashes.

During the next hour and a half, the security unit, with the help of a winch on the Omnihaul, raised the radio tower to its upright position, reconnected the wires that had been detached, and reestablished the base's contact with both Alfiri's and Dreyer's command centers.

On the bridge of Dreyer's Starhawk, Caitlin studied her computer as the safety beacons of the base's land crews came to life on the screen. Something was wrong. Two teams were approximately where they were supposed to be, but there were no pulses in the rainforest where Kellan and his crew were last spotted. Then she noticed that four beacons were approaching the land base.

"Mr. White," called Caitlin, and the communications officer became attentive. "Please radio Commander Hudson that one of the Base 1 expedition teams, or at least most of it, appears to be approaching their location from the southwest."

As soon as she received the message, Hudson took out her field glasses, and with Alomar standing behind her shoulder, she scanned the horizon until she found them. "Yep, there is a Float heading back to base," she said. "Maybe they can shed some light on what happened here."

But when the Float reached the base, there were other things to talk about. Vickie Webb's rash had worsened, and she kept scratching it and making it more inflamed. Simmons was in the rear seat, sound asleep and snoring loudly. He appeared to be okay, but they were unable to wake him.

"As long as he is breathing normally," said Hudson, "we should probably let him sleep. As for you," she said, turning toward Vickie. "I'll check the Omnihaul's medical kit for something to relieve the itch."

As Hudson walked away, Alomar took the opportunity to speak privately with Reed. Alomar led him well out of earshot of the rest of the security unit but whispered anyway. "We were concerned about you," he began. "Another base was wiped out completely, burned to a cinder."

Reed was upset by this news and wanted to know if there was any evidence that Republicans were responsible. No, answered Alomar, but he said that Republicans were completely untrustworthy and could not be discounted as the cause of the destruction.

Now it was Reed's turn to talk about his suspicions, about how he was supposed to have inspected the cargo holds on The Nemesis but felt that he had been drugged or otherwise tricked. Now he could not swear that he had actually seen the inside of even one of the ship's eight cargo areas. And the most damning information of all was Kellan Blake's description of large space vessels docking with The Nemesis before the inspection took place.

It did not take much for the two Rangers to conclude that whatever destroyed the land base in the northern hemisphere was a secret weapon of some sort, probably a new and extremely powerful laser concealed in the cargo area of The Nemesis, and delivered there by the ships seen by Kellan Blake. And there might be other, even more menacing, devices hidden aboard The Nemesis.

"Is there any way to radio Alfiri?" asked Reed.

"Not without the Republicans overhearing; none of our radios have a scrambling device. Besides, if we're right, and there is something funny on The Nemesis, Alfiri will never be able get an inspection crew on board. We stand a better chance of finding out what's in those holds if we examine them ourselves when we bring Simmons and Webb back for treatment."

Reed took a deep breath. "I've done some intelligence work, and there's always a risk of getting into trouble. But in this case it could be riskier to do nothing."

"We'd better try then," said Alomar as he started back toward the others. Then he suddenly turned back to Reed and asked, "Do you think we can pull this off without being caught?"

"Yeah, maybe. But if we get caught, we have to play it as dumb as we can, claim we were just taking a stroll and wandered into the cargo area. After all, if there is nothing on The Nemesis that shouldn't be there, then they have nothing to be upset about. If there is something there, then we did the right thing."

A short time later, the Omnihaul lifted off the surface of Dahai and returned to The Nemesis' shuttle bay. As soon as the Republican team members took Simmons and Webb to the sickbay, Reed gave the Asturians their assignments. Two security team members were to remain near the shuttle bay to keep an eye on the Republicans in the sickbay. Alomar would wait near the bridge to watch for anyone coming from there. And Wallace would cover Reed as he entered the cargo area. Reed gave them all the same instructions: first distract or dissuade anyone from coming near the entrance to the cargo section; if that did not work, they were to give Reed a warning by singing loudly; and only as a last resort, should they use physical force.

Reed and Wallace headed for the ship's holds. Most of The Nemesis' crew was on the bridge or in the mess hall or was asleep, and the two Asturians were able to reach the entrance to the cargo section unnoticed. More important, there were no Republican guards near the ship's holds, which encouraged Reed to think that they might actually be able to pull this off secretly. The hatch to the first hold was a large circular door with a wheel lock at the center. Reed spun the wheel and unlocked the hatch. Then he and Wallace hurried inside the tubular connection tunnel that lay behind the door. While Wallace kept watch, Reed continued ahead to the next hatch, but this one had a magnetic lock on it. "It's locked," Reed said. "I'm gonna blast it off. If we're lucky, they won't learn about the lock for a while."

Reed aimed his laser pistol and fired a blast that cut the circular magnetic lock in half, but the remaining section managed to keep the hatch wheel from unlocking. He fired a second shot, blowing away more of the lock, then kicked the rest of it free with the heel of his boot.

At that moment, Mallory, Kit Dreyer's aide, was leaving the bridge, intending to go to the mess hall. He noticed Alomar standing at the end of the corridor and called to him, "I understand you found the Base 1 crew, and that they were okay except for some minor problems."

"That's right," said Alomar as he moved forward to engage him in conversation and keep him away from the cargo hold. Alomar was only a few steps away from Mallory when a pulsing buzzer sounded.

Mallory realized at once that the door leading to the cargo hold had been opened, and without saying a word to Alomar, he started to run in that direction. Alomar, a head taller and much heavier than Mallory, reached out, grabbed him by the shoulder of his shirt, and swung him against the wall. The slight-built Mallory reacted swiftly by bringing his heel down on Alomar's toes, then quickly slamming a knee up into his belly. As Alomar doubled over in pain, Mallory grabbed him by the arm, twisted it, and flipped Alomar to the floor.

At the entrance of the cargo hold, Reed, despite the buzzer, continued to pull the second hatch door open. He moved closer for a look inside and froze when he saw what was in there—the last thing he would have expected to find in the cargo hold of The Nemesis. "This is unbelievable," he said.

Wallace turned toward Reed. "What is it?"

"The place is full of people," he said in disbelief.

"What do you mean, 'full of people'?" asked Wallace as he hurried toward the cargo area.

Reed pointed through the hatchway. "See for yourself."

A voice behind them shouted, "Hey!"

Reed spun around, saw a figure running through the first hatch and instinctively fired his pistol. It was Mallory, and he went down.

"Shit!" shouted Wallace as he quickly closed the hatch to the cargo hold. "Ah shit," he repeated as he hurried to examine Mallory, who was dead and who was unarmed.

"I thought he had a laser," said Reed nervously.

Wallace began thinking how they might able to conceal Mallory's death or at least keep the Republicans from knowing for certain that they were responsible. But more alarms began sounding.

Reed, his eyes open wide with a mixture of fear and determination, tapped Wallace on the shoulder. "Come on. They'll come after us now, and our best chance now is to pick up Alomar and the others, and take the bridge."

* * *

Harlan Knorr rushed to the command center of Julian Alfiri's ship. Prelate Carlo Asana, appearing almost happy, was already there with Captain Goldschmidt, the Defender's first officer, and the ship's communications specialist. Julian was the last to arrive. "What is the trouble?" he asked calmly.

Asana pointed to the radio console. "It's Dreyer, and there seems to be a major problem," he said.

Julian sat at the console, straightened the jacket of his commander-in-chief's uniform, which had bunched up around his waist, and put on a communications headset. "This is Julian Alfiri," he said into the thin microphone that extended across his mouth from the earpiece.

"You son-of-a-bitch," was how Kit Dreyer began. "You wanted a confrontation, and now you've got one."

"Madam," said Julian forcefully, "I have no idea of what your are talking about."

"I'm not going to play games, Alfiri." Dreyer's voice was so loud in his earpiece that Julian winced in pain. "Tell your men to lay down their lasers and surrender."

"What is she talking about?" asked Julian, looking up Harlan and Asana. They were as puzzled as he was. "Look, Ms. Dreyer," he said into the microphone, "would you please explain what the problem is." Julian could hear someone whispering on Dreyer's end of the communications channel but could not make out what was being said.

"Okay, Alfiri, I'll explain," said Dreyer in a calmer voice. "I have a young man, one of my very best, dead from a laser blast fired by one of your Imperial Rangers. And your Rangers tried to take the bridge of The Nemesis but were held off. At this very moment, your trained killers are trapped but still armed in the crew section of my ship. I want them to surrender and face the consequences of what they—and you—have done."

Alfiri looked about the bridge. "Does anyone know what this is about?" No one did. "Ms. Dreyer, I and my senior staff are unaware of this situation. If an individual Ranger or even a handful of them has behaved in an aggressive manner—and I don't know that they have—they may have done so in self-defense. In any case, they have not acted on my orders."

But Dreyer would not relent. "If I pipe this radio connection into the area where your Rangers have barricaded themselves, will you tell them to surrender?" Julian did not answer. Agreeing to this demand might put his men in great jeopardy. "Alfiri?" called Dreyer impatiently.

Julian looked to Harlan, who had nothing to offer. Then he glanced up at Asana, who said in a most irreverent way, "Better not botch this, Alfiri."

While Julian was still considering his response, there was a commotion at the radar console. Captain Goldschmidt hurried to Alfiri's side, and as Julian removed his headset and covered the microphone with his hand, the Captain reported, "We picked up three laser blasts from unknown origins."

"Laser blasts!" Julian was in disbelief. "And what do you mean 'unknown origins'?"

The Captain extended his hands palms up. "I mean the blasts came from orbit but not from any ship that we can see on radar."

If they did not come from a vessel or from the planet itself, there was only one other possibility. "A satellite then?"

"Possibly," answered Goldschmidt, "but one that has to have a radar cloaking system."

Dreyer was back on the radio. "Alfiri, by now you may have figured out that we have severed the water suction lines on all three of your water tankers. I'm not playing games."

"She's a mad woman," Alfiri said to Asana, but the Prelate was unsympathetic.

The balance of power had changed. With her satellite or satellites Dreyer could blow his command ship out of orbit any time she chose. But Julian told himself not to panic, to think of something to negate the advantage Dreyer now had. Turning back to the ship's Captain and keeping his hand over the microphone, Julian asked, "Where are we in relation to Dreyer's Starhawk?"

"Our orbit is approximately four hours behind hers." Goldschmidt paused for a moment, then added, "Not close enough for a laser cannon shot if that is what you are thinking."

Asana interjected himself. "How long would it take to get into range?"

"We could sneak up on her and be in range in an hour or so—if she holds her speed."

"Then let's do it," commanded Alfiri, glancing at Asana from the corner of his eye. He turned back to the radio. "Ms. Dreyer, it is most unfortunate that you act so impulsively," he said. "One or more Imperial Rangers may have acted improperly—I don't know for a certainty that they have. But if any have, they have done so without my knowledge and authority and will face the severest discipline. However, that in no way, Ms. Dreyer, justifies your willfully attacking our water tankers. And I must add that putting laser satellites in orbit around Dahai was not part of our bargain and is most certainly considered by us a sign of aggression."

"I figure," answered Dreyer nonchalantly, "that the laser satellites begin to lessen the advantage you gained when you placed Imperial Rangers in the survey teams posing as scientists."

How did she know that? wondered Julian. And what else did she know? He began to worry that his glorious and beautifully planned expedition to the other side of the universe was on the verge of chaos. Alfiri uncharacteristically panicked and decided to play, or rather threaten to play, his biggest trump card. Julian cleared his throat and stretched his neck, then he again addressed himself to Kit Dreyer. "May I remind you that your technicians cannot program your ships for the return voyage, and if you ever wish to see home again, you will. . ."

"Listen, Alfiri," interrupted Dreyer angrily. "I'm an old lady. Maybe I don't have to see home again. In any case, crossing The Void again is far more important to you than it is to me. Refuse to program our vacuum generators, or blow them up with the LEDDs you put inside them. I don't care. Call my bluff."

She knew about the LEDDs too. Maybe she had even managed to remove them. But if the LEDDs were still functional, and he acted now, gave the order to disable the vacuum generators on Dreyer's ships, the mission would be destroyed because there would be no way to haul the precious cargoes back through The Void. Destroying the vacuum generators was out of the question, and the bluff, once called, was useless. Alfiri felt checkmated. An incident on The Nemesis, some laser satellites, a few words with Dreyer, and suddenly he was out of moves.

Julian turned away from the communications console and looked up at the faces that surrounded him. Harlan was in a cold sweat. But Carlo Asana appeared strangely confident.

"Mr. Nen," said Asana to the communications specialist, "ask Ms. Dreyer to stand by." Then he turned toward Alfiri. "I think it's safe to say that the Republicans have gained the upper hand, and this entire voyage is on the verge of disaster." The Prelate reached into the right front pocket of his trousers and produced a letter, which he now waved before Alfiri's face. "I have here," he announced in a voice loud enough for everyone on the bridge to hear, "written authorization from The Triumvirate of the Holy Asturian Empire granting me authority to take command of this expedition if the alliance between the Empire and Ms. Dreyer and her Republican corporation is broken, or is on the verge of breaking down, or if some other disaster is about to befall this expedition because of the negligence of its leader." Asana looked at the others who stood around the bridge, then at Alfiri. "I think we can safely say that at least one of those conditions has materialized."

Julian at first did not fully realize what was happening. "Is this a joke?" he asked as Asana held out the letter so that Alfiri could see The Triumvirate seal and the signatures of all three members. The seal and the signatures looked authentic, and therefore, Julian knew that Bishop Baggio must be the author of the document. "This makes no sense," said Alfiri as he took the letter and began to scan it. "Why would the Triumvirate give you this kind of authority?"

"Why?" Asana moved closer to Alfiri and stood over him. "Because you were in retirement before this expedition began," he said, causing Julian's eyes to burn with anger. "Because you made a deal with the devil and let the enemy inside the walls when you brought Republicans in on this voyage. It was only natural that The Triumvirate would want some insurance against a disaster. And this," shouted Asana, "is a disaster. Imperial property has been destroyed in an act that essentially means your alliance with SED-Corp has been broken." Julian tried to dispute that point, but Asana would not let him speak. "The Republicans have unauthorized laser satellites in orbit, and those satellites now have us at their mercy."

Julian finally got up from his chair and stood almost chin to chin with Asana. "And I say the picture is not nearly so bleak as you paint it."

Asana would not back down. "It doesn't matter what you think. The Triumvirate has empowered me to make that assessment. Read the letter," he said, pointing to the document Alfiri had in his hand. "It's all spelled out for you. But ask Captain Goldschmidt and the rest of the bridge crew if there is one man here who disagrees with my assessment of how the situation has changed."

Julian looked first at Goldschmidt, then at the others. No one came to his support. Even Harlan Knorr, who stood behind Julian, remained silent. "This can be straightened out," said Alfiri, shaking his head as though he could make these problems disappear. Mr. Nen, get Kit Dreyer back on the radio."

"Mr. Nen," said Asana, walking to the communications console, "leave the radio alone. And Mr. Alfiri, I'm going to ask you to leave the bridge."

"I will not leave my bridge," shouted Alfiri, who was now breathing heavily and in danger of losing his composure.

"You will leave, or I'll call security and have you confined to your cabin."

Alfiri was about to object, but Harlan Knorr, who had secretly sold out to Asana, now went into action. He hurried to Julian's side and whispered, "Concede this battle to win the war. Once you're confined to your quarters, you'll be unable to fight him. Everything will be lost if you are not free." Julian calmed slightly as he weighed Harlan's words. "You are Julian Alfiri. You fight smarter than this. We need a little time to think, to find away to get back your command—or at the very least, to negotiate a role for you in this expedition that will allow you to return to Asturias to the recognition you deserve."

Asana carefully observed their exchange, and when it appeared that Knorr was making headway with Alfiri, he said, "Mr. Knorr, please escort Mr. Alfiri from the bridge."

Julian Alfiri stared at Asana a long moment, then allowed Harlan to lead him away.

Asana sat down at the communications console and asked Nen to get Kit Dreyer back on the radio. Once contact was made, Asana gave the prearranged code words, "You are now hearing the voice..." He hesitated a moment, then said, "...of Prelate Carlo Asana, the new leader of the Asturians on this expedition."

"You are coming over loud and clear," said Dreyer, answering with the coded response that "the voice" had given her.

Asana emphasized the importance of maintaining their alliance and apologized for any problems that the Imperial Rangers might have caused under the previous commander. He was certain that their strained relationship could be repaired, and he would take the first step by asking the Rangers on The Nemesis to lay down their weapons and give themselves up. In return, Dreyer must agree to turn over the Asturians to Asana, and he assured her that proper punishment would be meted out.

Dreyer, after a short delay, agreed to that much.

"I'm also willing," said Asana, "to consider compensating you for the loss of life on The Nemesis and any damage done to the ship, but I have a much larger proposition for you to consider, one that will certainly convince you not to break the alliance that you have with the Holy Asturian Empire."

"Go ahead. I'm listening," answered Dreyer, who showed Asana no more respect than she had shown Alfiri.

Ignoring her insolent tone, the Prelate continued, "If you would agree to give over to us complete control of Dahai and its water, which is badly needed by the Empire, I could offer you a share of the proceeds from this expedition much larger than your current contract calls for, a 75-25 split—in your favor."

Dreyer, of course, sounded very receptive to this proposal. Indeed Asana's conversation with her was for the benefit of the bridge crew and the ship's log. The arrangement the Prelate was proposing was one that Dreyer had been offered and had accepted before the armada crossed The Void, only now the ill-tempered but clever woman realized that she had been dealing with the Church, and that Asana was actually the person behind the Analeigh Dundane hologram and radio messages.

Dreyer, according to their arrangement, had agreed to provoke an incident that would cause her alliance with Alfiri to fall apart, allowing this second deal to take force. The incident was supposed to evolve naturally and not be contrived, nor, if possible, was it supposed to cause death or serious destruction. But some overaggressive Rangers had created the provocation for her, unfortunately at the cost of Mallory's life. Dreyer was glad to get this confrontation behind her and to finally know, after all this time, just exactly who she was dealing with.

"I am, however, concerned about one thing," Asana said to Dreyer. "You put laser satellites into orbit around Dahai. We never agreed to that, and we must work out an arrangement on the laser satellites before I can agree to the rest of our bargain, that is the 75-25 split."

"I'll tell you why I used the laser satellites." Dreyer's voice was soft, her tone conciliatory. "You don't completely trust us, and we don't completely trust you. And with reason. You—or at least some of your men—attacked one of my ships and killed—murdered—one of my top aides. And how do I know that when I return across The Void, that the whole Asturian Space Fleet will not be waiting for me to take every last cargo ship away from me?"

She had a point. Bishop Baggio had considered that possibility. In fact, Asana could not be completely certain that the entire Asturian Space Fleet would not be waiting for her when she returned. "The last few minutes have been very emotional for both us," said Asana, realizing that it would be difficult to deal with the laser satellite issue solely through negotiation, at least as things now stood. "The matter of the satellites can be solved but not necessarily at this exact moment. I suggest that we continue to back off the precipice we found ourselves on a short while ago and complete this negotiation after the dust has settled a little more."

Dreyer agreed. A time was set for another conversation, and she signed off.

Prelate Asana leaned back in his chair, quite pleased with himself. He had helped Bishop Baggio bring down an old enemy.

He, in the name of the Church, would control Dahai, its water, and all the information coming from the planet; and they would suppress Alfiri's vacuum generation technology to prevent additional voyages across The Void until the Church was ready for them.

The only remaining problem, but a large one, was the orbiting lasers. Of all places, he did not want them around Dahai, and he worried that even if Dreyer agreed to withdraw them, it would be impossible to verify that she removed them all. Asana decided to proceed in two directions simultaneously—negotiating with Dreyer to remove the laser satellites and finding a way to destroy them. Kit Dreyer did not yet understand that Carlo Asana was not Julian Alfiri. Had he threatened to use the LEDDs, he would have been willing to push the button that would destroy the vacuum generators on Dreyer's vessels and doom them to staying on this side of The Void. As the arrangement now stood, the bulk of the natural wealth taken from the new world was going to Dreyer anyway. What did he care if those ships never got back to the Republics?

14 | Nuzalu's Killer

The party of Dahaians consisted of Nuzalu (or Udta, as his family still called him), his father, two of his uncles, and the old man, all but the boy armed with spears, bows, and long, curved knives. Following behind were Kellan, dressed in his own clothes and wearing sandals to replace the boots he lost in the flood; Stoney, who carried a borrowed bow and arrow, and complained often about the humidity of the steamy afternoon; and Bellycold. They were trekking through the forest toward Nuzalu's village, going up yet another steep incline, and the android struggled clumsily, pulling himself by the vines and tree limbs strong enough to support him, and occasionally getting down on hands and knees to manage a particularly difficult slope. The android looked awkward at the moment, but he was mastering the Dahaian language, which was beyond both Kellan and Stoney.

When the terrain leveled out again, the old one paused, hand on his chin, trying to determine which way to go. Then he began to speak, and Bellycold translated for the benefit of the other two Asturians. "None of the others have ever been to this village," explained the android. "And the old one has not been there in many, many years. So he is uncertain of the way."

Stoney, who was now complaining that he was providing a meal for all the gnats in the jungle, wondered how far away this village was; the answer, not far. Kellan then asked why, if the village was close by, none of the others had ever been there. The old man smiled, turned toward Kellan, and spoke in a very animated style. When he was finished, Bellycold translated, "It is not easy to get there even though it is close. And they have nothing that we do not already have ourselves. In fact, there is no lake near their village with great crabs." The old one added a final thought: "Besides, the two villages have not always gotten along in the past."

Later in the afternoon, the boy began to help lead the way, which caused Kellan to believe that there might be some truth to his strange story. Stoney, on the other hand, merely called the story "spooky."

The sun was low in the lavender sky of Dahai when they came across a forest path, and one of the boy's uncles said that he could smell the smoke of a cooking fire. A short time later they found themselves approaching a village, not unlike the one they left that morning except that it appeared to be somewhat larger. And other than their dark olive skin, the inhabitants of this village, tall, long-nosed, and cleft-chinned, looked the same as the Dahaians in their own party. As the olive-skinned villagers began to slowly approach their visitors, Nuzalu began to speak rapidly. According to Bellycold, he was affirming that this was, indeed, his village. He said his father was the village chief, and his family owned the biggest house. He also spoke about his mother and an infant sister.

A crowd gathered around them, the women and children remaining a cautious distance away while several of the men stepped forward to speak to them. In very cordial tones the old one explained the nature of their visit, but the news did not go over well. The Dahaians of this village wanted no more to believe that the pink-skinned boy claiming to be Nuzalu was a member of their tribe than Udta's family wanted to believe that he was not their child.

While the adults spoke, the boy looked beyond them to where a group of women in silk robes stood almost shoulder to shoulder, and he anxiously searched the faces among them. He noticed a woman with her hair pulled back in a knot, straining to pick up pieces of the conversation between the two groups of villagers, and the instant the boy saw her, his face lit up. Before his father could grab his arm, he dashed off, threaded his way through the crowd, and went straight to the woman, wrapping his arms around her legs as she tried to back away. The woman appeared confused, but when the boy said the name "Nuzalu," it struck her with great force.

"Nuzalu," she whispered.

Both groups broke into animated discussions, which appeared to Kellan to be debates or even arguments. Kellan now knew one thing for certain, that in this village there lived—or once lived—a boy named Nuzalu, but apparently no one wanted to accept that this particular boy, this stranger, was actually the woman's son—except the boy himself and possibly the woman he thought was his mother. One of the men of Nuzalu's village finally stepped forward to challenge the boy. As Bellycold translated, the man said, "It was only luck that this crab-eater picked the mother of the real Nuzalu. Why does he not speak to his own sister?"

Upon hearing this, the boy stepped back and looked all about him. "She is not here," he said, then spread his hands to indicate that his sister was only a baby.

The man claimed this was proof that boy was lying and pointed to a girl seven or eight years of age who was standing with other children on the fringe of the crowd. Nuzalu looked at the girl a long moment, then rushed to her, and embraced her. She seemed to accept him. The mother, her eyes moist with tears, explained that when Nuzalu died, the little girl was indeed an infant, and that she had grown enough it was no wonder that the boy did not recognize her immediately.

Stoney leaned toward Kellan. "You don't believe any of this crap, do you?"

"Haven't you seen enough amazing things on this planet, Stoney, to, at least, have an open mind about it?"

"Yeah, we've seen some amazing things, but I'm not certain God himself can die and be reborn. Maybe all these people have been drinking too much hooch."

"Yes," said Kellan sarcastically, "I forgot about the hooch factor. But this is a completely different world. Maybe everything from the hooch to the gods are different." Kellan's attention was drawn back to the conversation among the two groups of villagers. The woman had taken Nuzalu by the hand, and while some of the men continued to object, she announced that she was taking the boy home.

The entire crowd followed as Nuzalu, without taking a misstep, led the way to the family's house. Nuzalu's mother did not want the entire crowd to enter the home and asked only the boy and his escort inside. While virtually the entire village waited outside, Nuzalu went into the house, straight to a room on the second floor that had been the dead Nuzalu's bedchamber. While the mother watched, choked with emotion, the boy knelt down, reached under the bed, and withdrew the box of treasures that had remained hidden there since the day Nuzalu died, since the day he was murdered. The boy withdrew a flute, a miniature hunting bow, a handful of carved animals, and a small silk robe. A smile on her face and tears in her eyes, the woman was now certain that her son Nuzalu was in the body of the boy from the village of the crab-eaters. The father of Udta, observing all this, began reconciling himself to sharing his son with the mother of Nuzalu.

Nuzalu played with his treasures for awhile, then asked where his father was. Once again tears came to the eyes of Nuzalu's mother. He had died not long after the boy was murdered. Nuzalu's uncle had been the village chief ever since.

Nuzalu's mother invited the boy and his party to spend the night in her home, and prepared them a large meal, consisting mainly of the foods that were Nuzalu's favorites. During dinner the boy recalled aspects of Nuzalu's life, hunting with his father, playing with his closest friends, the day his sister was born. The woman verified everything he said. After the meal other family members came to visit. The boy identified seven of them correctly by name but could not place the remaining two.

The visitors, including the Asturians and the android Bellycold, spent the night on the floor of the large wooden house while Nuzalu slept in his own bed. The next morning the relatives returned to the house for breakfast, and as they continued to test the boy's knowledge of his other life and he continued to answer almost all of their questions correctly, Kellan became convinced that the boy was authentic.

Later that day, they all took a stroll through the village until they finally came to a square, where three men were playing reed instruments. Nuzalu's sister could not resist running over to the musicians and dancing to their song. After a few moments, Nuzalu joined her. He knew the dance, every step, every hand movement.

As they danced, a group of olive-skinned men entered the village from the forest. From the look of what they carried—bows and arrows, lots of small game hanging on ropes from their shoulders, and silk backpacks—they must have been returning from a hunt of several days' duration. They noticed their pink-skinned visitors and attracted a good deal of attention themselves from Kellan and Stoney and the pink-skinned Dahaians.

The boy Nuzalu suddenly stopped dancing. He began to scream frantically and pointed to the band of returning hunters. Kellan hurried over to Bellycold, "What's the problem?"

Bellycold singled out a broad-shouldered hunter with an angry expression on his face. "He says that man is the killer of Nuzalu." The boy opened his silk robe and pointed to a large, dark birthmark in the center of his small chest. "He stabbed me right here with his spear, the boy says."

Nuzalu's mother hushed the boy as the nasty-looking hunter, who could clearly hear the boy's accusation, glared at them, and when the hunting party was gone from the village square, the woman explained to the old man: Nuzalu was murdered by a spear or knife thrust exactly where the boy indicated. And the hunter he was accusing of his own murder was his uncle, the man who succeeded Nuzalu's father as chief of the village. The chief's position was hereditary, passed from father to son, or brother to brother, and so Nuzalu's uncle was the one person who had a motive for killing the boy years ago. Now the woman said she feared that the "evil uncle," as she called the killer, would murder Nuzalu a second time to prevent him giving testimony about the first murder.

Hearing all this, the old man agreed that the boy's life was in danger and decided that his group should immediately take the boy away from this village, away from the reaches of the uncle. After the boy bid a short but emotional farewell to Nuzalu's mother and sister, the men from the village of the crab-eaters gathered up their bows and arrows, and left for home with Kellan, Stoney, and Bellycold.

Their small party, the Dahaians in the lead and the android bringing up the rear, hurried through the forest as the afternoon sun began to descend in the purple sky. As the forest grew denser, the large android fell farther behind. They had traveled only a short distance when an arrow thumped on the robot's back. He did not feel it, of course, but he heard the noise that it made. A second arrow flew by his head and stuck in a tree trunk a few feet ahead of him. "Hey," shouted Bellycold. "They are shooting at us. They've come to get the boy."

While the Dahaian members of their party turned to make a stand behind the cover of some trees, the surprisingly spry old man took the boy by the hand and disappeared into the jungle ahead. Joining in the defensive line were Kellan, his laser pistol drawn; Stoney, fretting that he was armed with a bow and arrow rather than a laser; and Bellycold. Kellan caught a glimpse of one of their pursuers and fired a warning shot that blasted off a tree limb just over his head. The man returned fire with his bow and arrow.

"You'd think a laser would scare the living hell out of these primitives," shouted Stoney.

"I don't know," said Kellan thoughtfully. "Maybe a laser pistol isn't much to fear after experiencing the kind of ball lightning that they have on this planet."

Stoney looked at Bellycold. "Can't you throw rocks at them or something?"

The android shook his head, "I'm programmed not to harm people."

"Then try to scare them."

"I could do that, I suppose," he said as he stood up to face their attackers. Bellycold beat his metal chest and roared like a lion. Three Dahaians appeared out of the jungle and fired arrows at the large robot, several of which found their mark, only to bounce harmlessly off. Whether it was because of Bellycold's apparent invulnerability, or the fact that Kellan fired several more laser shots close to their heads, the olive-skinned men fell back.

Kellan looked over his shoulder at the pink-skinned Dahaians, who were involved in an animated conversation. "Bellycold," called Kellan. "Can you tell us what they are saying?"

The android listened for a few moments, then said, "They want to lead the bad guys away from their village."

"I wish they could lead us back to our Float," Stoney mumbled.

"Hell, I can do that," said Bellycold. "My radar sensors are reading the Float beacon loud and clear." Before Stoney, an expression of surprise on his face, could say a word, the android added, "Because you never asked me, that's why."

With the android translating, a plan was agreed upon. To protect the boy and the old man, the rest of the party would head toward the Float and away from the village of the pink-skinned crab-eaters, but eventually, when it was safe, the Asturians and the Dahaians would go their separate ways.

They resumed their journey, frequently checking all around them in case the olive-skinned men were still pursuing, and occasionally they would stop in a thicket of bushes, while the men from the village of the crab-eaters listened. Each time they paused, one of the crab-eaters would claim to be able to hear the olive-skinned men tracking them.

They continued on, and as the sun began to set, the two groups decided it was time to separate. The old man and the boy were safely on their way home by now, and Bellycold said they were not a great distance away from the Float, although travel through the jungle was slow going and would be even more difficult if they attempted to continue the journey after nightfall. The crab-eaters left for their village. Kellan and Stoney, agreeing that it was too risky to try to sleep out in the open with men hunting them, and the possibility of an exotic animal lurking behind every bush, decided to push on through the forest even though the light was fading.

15 | Showdown

Caitlin stood in Kit Dreyer's sparsely furnished quarters while Dreyer sat behind her small desk, stuffing a small pile of electronic paper into a traveling case. "I need to get to The Nemesis to supervise everything first-hand," Dreyer mumbled to herself. "But go on, go on," she said in a louder voice. "I want to hear the rest of your report."

Caitlin, who spent much of her day meeting Dreyer's demands, would never understand how the woman could insist that she needed something immediately, then lose all interest in it almost the moment it was delivered. "As I said," continued Caitlin, trying not to sound annoyed, "the man who actually did the shooting has been locked up in a secure area. The other four Asturians have been technically freed but have been disarmed and are under watch."

"And our little package is on our way to our friend Carlo?"

Caitlin sighed. "It is."

"Good, and don't ask me again if I'm sure I want to go through with it," said Dreyer as she stood to leave. "My shuttle is ready, and I need to get to The Nemesis."

"You'll also be happy to know," Caitlin quickly added before Dreyer left the room, "that Simmons is going to be okay as will the young woman Vickie Webb, although she'll probably itch for a while longer."

Dreyer's expression went blank for an instant. She was not certain what Caitlin was talking about. "Oh yes, good," she said dismissively. And with that, she started for the door and for her shuttle. She then suddenly turned back to Caitlin and said with more than a trace of anger in her voice, "You know that bastard Asana thinks he is sneaking up on me to get this ship within range of his laser cannons. I never liked Julian Alfiri because I consider him arrogant, and I owe him for something he did a few years back. But at least he has some integrity. This Asana is a snake in the grass. As soon as my shuttle leaves, tell Captain McBrien to increase his speed and to take any evasive action necessary to keep Asana and his Defender a safe distance away from this ship."

* * *

"How's he taking it?" asked Prelate Asana as he leaned back in his command seat on the Defender's bridge. This had become Asana's usual position, in the pilot's chair at the center of the circular command center. From here he could look out at the stars through the Defender's front window, observe the ship's captain and navigator, and turn back to the radar and communications consoles directly behind him.

Harlan Knorr, who had not been invited by Asana to sit in one of the vacant chairs, stood awkwardly before his new commander-in-chief. "He's having trouble accepting it," said Harlan, swallowing his air with some difficulty. "He still thinks there is something he can do to-to. . ."

"Kick my ass out of this command chair," said Asana crudely.

"Well, yes," admitted Knorr, who would have phrased it more diplomatically. "But he is not focused on you. He thinks the key is for him to figure out how to neutralize Dreyer's laser satellites."

Asana smiled and shook his head. "He just doesn't understand that the deck was stacked against him from the beginning."

Although Knorr felt guilty that he had been unable to help his long-time patron, he had barely managed to save himself.

And while he had been saved this time, he was still not safe and needed to remain useful to the Prelate. "The good news," said Knorr, taking another large swallow of air, "is that, as time passes, I think Julian's most fundamental concern will be about his return home and how he will be perceived on Asturias. I told him that he will go back to a hero's welcome whatever happens from this point forward."

"And he will," added Asana with mock enthusiasm. In the Prelate's view, they were in a game that involved only power and its use, and Alfiri had lost, having made three fatal mistakes. The first was trying to outmaneuver and embarrass Bishop Baggio; the second, allowing an enemy, Asana, to become his deputy; and the third, having in Harlan Knorr a chief of staff who was not clever enough to see Alfiri's vulnerabilities and not loyal enough to sacrifice himself for his chief. The great Julian Alfiri would be given a more than generous pension but would return home quietly.

Asana planned to take credit for the successes of this voyage.

"So, in the long run," continued Knorr, "if you give him some new title that is befitting of his stature, and he can be assured that he will return to Asturias with dignity and appearing to have had some measure of success on this expedition, I think we can hold him in line. Because as you pointed out, Prelate, it doesn't help to have a man of Julian's reputation speaking out against us when we return." Asana let the use of the words "us" and "we" pass without comment as he looked over Knorr's shoulder to Captain Goldschmidt, who was approaching from the adjacent planning room. Goldschmidt started to turn back when he saw that the Prelate was occupied, but Asana shouted to him and beckoned with a hand gesture. "Come ahead, Captain. You stay here, too," he said to Harlan.

Goldschmidt joined them and gave his report. As Asana requested, the Captain of the Defender reviewed the radar tapes of when Dreyer's laser satellites fired, and he now had their general positions, although nothing so precise that would allow the Asturians to attempt to destroy them. Goldschmidt also reviewed all the radio transmissions that the ship had monitored during the five minutes prior to the satellites firing their lasers. "You are correct, Prelate Asana," he said. "We found transmissions from Dreyer's Starhawk to the three quadrants where her satellites are located."

Knorr, not knowing what these two were planning, was made nervous by this discussion. "What if she has more than three satellites?" he asked timidly.

"That's not the point," said Asana as though Knorr's question were contemptuously stupid. "The command to fire them must come from somewhere else. That's what I wanted to know. And now we know for certain what we could have guessed, that they are fired from her command ship." Asana's expression turned from angry to worried, although Harlan sometimes had difficulty distinguishing one mood from the other. "I must admit I don't like having those laser satellites out there. They could be aimed at us right now for all we know. In fact, they probably are. That's what I'd do in her place. If we could only disable her command ship somehow, we would disable the laser satellites as well."

"Or simply disabling her communications system would be enough," Harlan offered. "I think I have some more good news for you."

Asana looked at Knorr with great interest. "Well?"

"When we were installing the vacuum generators on Dreyer's command ship," he said, obviously pleased with himself, "I thought we should take extra precautions, and so took it upon myself to install two extra LEDDs within the vacuum generator console. These are focused-beam dispersion devices rather than the usual spherical dispersion type. I had one aimed at the weapon's control panel, and the second at the communication console. Both the weapons and communications systems can be taken out by the LEDDs without hurting any people or destroying the vacuum generator."

Asana clapped his hands together. "Perfect! The balance of power can be shifted back the other way. And Alfiri didn't know about this?" The Prelate tilted his head back and laughed when Harlan shook his head no.

"Julian left many details to me."

The radar officer was now approaching Asana, and he was so nervous that he bowed as though greeting a member of The Triumvirate itself. "I thought you would want to know that we have made radar contact with the shuttle from The Nemesis, and the five captured Rangers will be returned shortly."

"Good, good," Asana smiled. "We will soon have our men back." His expression quickly turned serious again. "You," he said, pointing at the radar officer, "back to your post and keep an eye on that shuttle. You, Captain, do whatever you have to do to be ready to disable the lasers and communications system on Dreyer's command ship at a moment's notice. And you." Now it was Harlan's turn. "Get on the radio to Dreyer or her aide and tell them that they have destroyed property on three water tankers owned by the Holy Asturian Empire, and we want them fixed and returned to full operation as soon as possible."

Harlan did as he was told. He put in a call to Dreyer's command ship and found himself again speaking to Caitlin Cormack, whom he considered far more reasonable than her boss. Harlan stated his case, but this time Caitlin, saying that Kit Dreyer was temporarily unavailable to authorize such an agreement, would not budge. Caitlin did not believe that repairing the suction hoses on three tanker ships was an urgent matter. Neither did Harlan. But when he reported his lack of progress to Asana, the Prelate erupted with anger. His face red and his hands shaking, Asana told Captain Goldschmidt to activate the focused-beam LEDDs on Dreyer's Starhawk command ship.

* * *

Somehow Bellycold managed to lead Kellan and Stoney through the night rainforest. They had been tangled in vines, scraped on thorn bushes, and eaten alive by small insects but fortunately nothing larger. And at one point they had to circumnavigate a ravine that was too steep to descend in the dark. At sunrise Kellan suggested they rest for a while. But Stoney wanted to push on, and Bellycold estimated that the Float was only a mile or two away. So they continued to walk, following the android, whose internal antenna was locked on the Float's homing device. Soon they found themselves in the swamp where Vickie encountered the goo-worm, and the idea of being just a short walk and a long Float ride from the safety and comfort of their land base gave them the energy to continue.

Bellycold sloshed ahead in the dark blue water, then stopped, and extended one of his long silver arms. "There it is," he shouted. "Old Bellycold will never let you down." There, indeed, was the Float just as they had left it, tied to a bush, bobbing gently in the water. The trio surrounded the vehicle and prepared to enter it. Although the plastic cover that protected the open cabin of the Float was intact, the inside was covered with green algae. They began scraping it out with their hands and trying to clean the seats and controls by splashing handfuls of blue water on them. They even attempted to wipe the algae away with leaves from nearby bushes, but it was hopeless.

Reconciling himself to having to coexist with the slime and moisture in the Float, Kellan climbed inside and rested his laser pistol on the seat beside him. Stoney also began to hoist himself into the Float when the swamp became alive with splashing sounds. At first Kellan thought there might be a handful of goo-worms moving through the water, but when he looked up, he saw a tall figure he recognized immediately as Nuzalu's uncle. The man's arm had just snapped back from unleashing an arrow, and although Kellan could not see it, he heard its whistle, then a loud groaning sound from Stoney, who fell into the Float behind him. While Stoney moaned and cursed, Kellan grabbed his laser pistol, aimed squarely between their attacker's broad shoulders, and fired a blast that caught the uncle in the chest and toppled him backwards into the swamp. Little Nuzalu has finally been avenged, thought Kellan, and Udta was now safe from this man. There were at least two other archers in the swamp. Kellan pointed his laser at one of them, but without their leader, the other two had no interest in fighting, and they retreated into the forest.

Kellan turned back to Stoney, who was lying on the floor of the Float moaning and writhing in pain, an arrow lodged in his left calf.

Fortunately Stoney's injury was far more painful than it was life threatening. Bellycold, who found a small medical kit in the storage compartment, pulled out the arrow, soaked the wound with an antiseptic, and wrapped it with a bandage. Then he gave Stoney a painkiller, and soon Stoney was sitting upright and feeling good enough to be asking for a drink.

Kellan tried to start the Float's engine, but it sputtered, and once it did start, the engine ran roughly. "I'll bet the insides are wet," said Kellan as he turned the vehicle toward the grass-covered plain. "Let's get out of here in case those archers change their minds and come back."

* * *

The Republican Starhawk command ship went dark, and its emergency lights flashed on. The navigation system was also acting up, its screens filled with distorted patterns of blue and white lines. Captain McBrien had just finished programming a controlled 24-second rocket burn to increase the ship's speed and now tried to abort the program. But one and only one engine lit and fired for a few seconds, jarring the ship enough to almost knock Caitlin to the floor and throwing the Starhawk off-course. Caitlin caught herself on the back of the Captain's chair and shouted, "What's happening?"

"Don't know," answered McBrien, frantically trying to stabilize the ship. "The computers have gone crazy. Some kind of electrical problem that is sending shorts through everything."

"Oh no," whispered Caitlin. Then she told the Captain, "The computers have probably been sabotaged."

McBrien looked up at Caitlin and saw from her expression that she was not simply making a wild guess. "We're in trouble," he said, looking at their new flight path. "That rocket burn altered our course. Unless I can do something within the next minute or so, we're going to hit the planet's atmosphere and burn to a cinder."

The Captain turned to the first officer and told him to prepare the ship's last remaining shuttle. He then unlocked a button on the control console and pressed it, sending a loud buzzer sounding throughout the ship.

Caitlin, at McBrien's direction, activated the ship's internal speaker system and announced that this was not a drill, and that all personnel should report to the shuttle bay immediately.

The Captain tried a second rocket burn to correct the ship's course, but the rockets would not fire. While Caitlin gathered together all the mission records she could find on the bridge, the entire crew, except for Caitlin and the Captain, assembled in the shuttlecraft.

"We're about out of time," said McBrien. "We'd better join the others and get out now."

Caitlin suddenly remembered that in her quarters she had a portable computer containing vital mission information. "Do I have another 30 seconds?" she asked McBrien.

The Captain paused for a moment, then said, "Thirty seconds but no more."

* * *

On the Defender a three-man Asturian security team, armed with laser rifles, stood near the airlock leading to the flight deck. From a small portal near the hatch, their team commander looked out at the just-landed shuttlecraft, which was framed against a background of stars. The shuttlecraft's door opened, and out walked the five Rangers who had been taken prisoner on The Nemesis.

They were dressed in environmental suits and slowly walked across the landing pad in magnetic boots. At this distance the commander could not see the faces of his five compatriots through their helmet visors, but they were unarmed and carried in the weightlessness only a military footlocker that must have contained their belongings.

The security team heard the outer hatch to the airlock open and then shut a minute later. The airlock pressurized, but the inner door remained closed. The three puzzled security men looked at one another; then the commander went to the control panel and opened the hatch door himself. To their surprise their five returning compatriots were not in the airlock, only the footlocker.

One of the security men was about to suggest that this was a trick of some kind, perhaps a bomb, but before he could say a word, a fist broke through the top of the footlocker. Then the entire wooden box was smashed open from the inside, and from the wreckage emerged Kit Dreyer's dark purple sentry robot, Otto, fully armed with laser pistols in both hands and six other laser weapons—thin gun barrels on small turrets—protruding from his shoulders, chest, and back. As two of the security men aimed their rifles at him, Otto fired his two hand lasers, and both men fell dead. The third man, the commander, raised his hands in surrender, and Otto held his fire. But from the robot's nose compartment an invisible, odorless gas hissed out, and in a few seconds the commander fell unconscious to the floor.

Otto dragged the unconscious man and his two dead companions into the airlock, closed the hatch door, and continued into the crew portion of the ship. The purple robot's artificial intelligence did not include an understanding of what good luck meant, but he was able to recognize that his mission was benefiting from not encountering any other Defender crewmembers all the way from the flight deck to the bridge.

On the bridge Carlo Asana and Harlan Knorr were watching the tape of a radar scan showing Kit Dreyer's Starhawk command vessel dropping from orbit and destroying itself against Dahai's atmosphere. A smaller craft left the vessel a few minutes before impact, and Asana wondered if Dreyer and her whole crew had gotten off alive. The Prelate guessed that the ornery Dreyer was dead, or she would be on the radio at this moment screaming at him. But if he did hear from her, Asana planned to blame Julian Alfiri for sabotaging Dreyer's computers.

"There is a laser aimed at each of you." The sound of the machine voice startled everyone on the bridge including Asana. "Anyone who moves or speaks without permission will be shot."

Asana, Knorr, Captain Goldschmidt, and two other officers on bridge duty looked at the dark purple robot and saw that a separate laser was pointed at each one of them. No one moved; no one spoke.

"The man standing closest to me," said the robot. That was Harlan, who gulped a large swallow of air. "Close the bridge door."

"Now?" asked Harlan cautiously.

"Yes," answered the robot, which could watch all of them through its wide eye band without moving its head.

Harlan slowly walked to the door and pushed the button that caused it to slide closed. He had only moved a foot away when the robot fired a laser blast from its back that melted the controls, sealing them inside the bridge. Harlan's knees buckled, and for an instant he thought he would faint, but he made it back to his original position next to Asana, who looked both shocked and frightened, his face flushed, his hands trembling noticeably.

Next the robot instructed Asana, himself, to call "Ms. Kit Dreyer" aboard The Nemesis. Asana dreaded doing this, but with a laser pointed directly at his head, he had no choice. The Nemesis' communications officer put him through to Dreyer, and the Prelate's color turned from light to dark red as she began her harangue.

"First of all, Asana, mind your manners, or I'll ask Otto to remove your tonsils with one of his lasers," was how she began. "You know, Asana, I have to tell you that I was feeling a little bad about pulling this trick on you. But that was before you destroyed my command ship," she said angrily. Then she added in a softer voice, "I lost a couple of my best people in that crash." This last part was a lie that Dreyer told impulsively because she thought it gave her additional justification for what she was doing now.

"It was Alfiri's fault," Asana nervously offered.

"Bullshit! Don't give me that. And you'd better listen carefully, Asana, to what I say next. Otto there is going to escort you back through The Void, all the way back to your precious Holy Asturian Empire. And you're going to be leaving very soon." This last remark caused anger to well up in Asana despite the robot behind him. "We intend to round up the Imperial Rangers that are concealed among your land crews on Dahai and elsewhere, and send them back with you. I want a full list of them so that we don't miss any. And I want you to order them not to resist. Understood?"

Asana hesitated, then answered, "Understood," knowing that he had no choice, at least, not at the moment.

"One other thing, Asana," she continued. "I want all my computers and vacuum generators freed of whatever the hell it was that Alfiri did to them. Because so help me, if I lose one more ship. . ." Dreyer did not complete the sentence, deciding she had better calm down before her blood pressure shot up. "I'm a fair person, Asana," she resumed in a more sociable tone of voice. "And I keep my bargains, most of them anyway. You'll get to take your water tankers home with you, and when this mission ends, you—the Church, the government, whatever you want to call yourself—will get the original 50% that Alfiri and I agreed on. That's 50% less the cost of my Starhawk. But I'll keep Dahai."

Carlo Asana felt totally outmaneuvered until he thought about the return journey. She was making a mistake in letting him return ahead of her. He would have Bishop Baggio assemble the Asturian Space Force on the other side of The Void, and they would simply take from her every gem, every leaf, every grain of metal ore that she acquired in the new world.

* * *

After their escape from their doomed command ship, Captain McBrien gave Caitlin a front seat on the shuttle, and she now had an excellent view of The Nemesis as their craft approached it. All the Republican crews had been given the message that the Asturians were, or would soon be, under control. The Imperial Rangers hidden among the land crews, including those on Dahai, were ordered by Prelate Asana to put down their weapons and to surrender themselves to Republican security units, which were rounding up the Asturians for the long voyage home.

With that task well under way, Caitlin could relax and begin thinking about what had to be done next. The first thing she would do was to start up her portable computer to search for Kellan's safety pulse beacon. Her screen lit up with a three-dimensional image of the planet Dahai, which she rotated until she got to the southern hemisphere. Through a series of clicks, she focused closer and closer until she had a map of an area only a few dozen square miles in size. Then she put a tracer on Kellan's safety beacon, but nothing appeared. She told herself she would not begin to worry until she again checked his Float beacon, which had been stationary for days. The small blue light appeared immediately. It was crossing the grassland, apparently returning to base. Caitlin, feeling relieved, immediately sent a computer message to Karina Hudson, giving her the coordinates of the Float, which she assumed contained Kellan and the rest of his party, and asking Hudson's security team to pick them up.

The Nemesis was just ahead, and the top of its first large cargo section was now slowly lifting up. Everyone on the shuttle leaned forward for a better look as a long cylindrical vessel rose out of the cargo hold, jetted away from the mother ship, then began its descent to the planet's surface. This vessel, like the others in the other seven cargo holds, was full of men, women, and children, settlers who had come to make Dahai their home.

Caitlin was not someone who generally thought poorly of Asturians, and she certainly was aware of Kit Dreyer's shortcomings, but the cranky old woman was right in what she had done. Dreyer had intended to keep her bargain with Alfiri, or so she said, until they received the hologram bearing Analeigh Dundane's image. If the Asturians were plotting against themselves, how could she trust them? In that regard Asana and his backers were the ones most responsible for the complete breakup of the alliance. Of course, Alfiri, with his hidden LEDDs and Rangers masquerading as scientists, had not been completely aboveboard either.

It was also true that the Asturians, under either Alfiri or Asana, would have drained all the natural resources they could squeeze out of this world to take back to the Empire, even if it meant leaving Dahai a dry husk. Dreyer's plan to settle the new world was far better, although her motives were not completely altruistic. Kit Dreyer was almost ready for retirement, and the idea of having a large estate on a warm, water planet appealed to her. Still, Caitlin had a difficult time visualizing the hard-driving Dreyer actually retired.

As for herself, Caitlin knew that she would play a major role in establishing the first settlement here and in developing Dreyer's business operations in the new world. After that, she expected to return to the Republics to help manage SED-Corp's central operation. She even allowed herself to dream of some day being Kit Dreyer's successor.

* * *

The nose of the Float slowly plowed through a sea of eight-foot-high, yellow grass. Because the engine was still sputtering, they were moving at 60% of the Float's normal cruising speed. Kellan was at the controls with Bellycold seated next to him and Stoney stretched out in the rear seat, complaining about the pain in his injured leg. They were less than half the distance back to base when Stoney said he could hear thunder. Kellan listened closely. He heard the sound too. It was a deep, continuous rumble, more like an earthquake than thunder, but the noise was not coming from beneath the ground.

Stoney suddenly sat upright. "I think it's coming closer."

"He's right," said Kellan as Bellycold stood up to take a look over the windshield.

"Hey!" said the android, pointing straight ahead. "Remember that big, red-eyed, grunting creature we came across the first time we crossed this grass? There are about a thousand of them coming straight at us."

Kellan had not been paying close attention to his microwave imaging screen, but now he saw that what he thought was just a dark shadow on the screen actually consisted of hundreds of individual black dots. "Hang on!" he shouted and started to take the Float in a wide arc. The creatures, whatever they were, seemed to stretch in a near solid line from one side of the plain to the other. Kellan thought their only chance was to turn completely around and outrun them.

Kellan opened the throttle, but the Float sputtered worse and actually lost speed. "Damn," he mumbled under his breath as he cut back on the throttle and gradually eased it forward again. They picked up a little speed, not much. And although they could not see the creatures hidden behind them in the tall grass, they could hear them gaining. It was as if they were running before a tidal wave of thundering hooves. One creature, the size of a large elephant, rumbled past them on the right, and Kellan swerved away from it. A second beast crossed a few feet in front of them, blurring the entire microwave screen and leaving a trail of parted grass in its wake.

"They're all around us," shouted Stoney. "Can't we get more speed?"

Kellan tried working the throttle again but without success. Instead of running ahead of the stampede, now they were actually in it.

"Maybe I should try my lion imitation," offered Bellycold.

"Lord help us!" said Stoney.

Kellan, hearing snorting sounds and catching a glimpse of a large shaggy head with horns just a few feet to the left, thought it was worth a try. "Go ahead, Bellycold. We've got nothing to lose."

The android let out a loud roar, and the creature on the left turned on them, butting the side of the Float hard enough to dent it. Stoney leaned forward and grabbed Kellan's laser pistol as the creature charged a second time. He fired without taking time to aim and caught the beast in the shoulder. It gave a bloodcurdling cry and collapsed to the ground, causing Stoney to freeze momentarily as he remembered that first hunting trip with his father and the sound the giant boar made when he killed it.

Some of the other creatures began to grunt and squeal, and Kellan felt certain they were reacting to the injury of one of their own.

They were jolted from behind. The Float fishtailed; Stoney lost his balance and nearly went overboard. "Somebody help me," he shouted, half of his body hanging over the edge of the Float and holding on with only one hand. Bellycold reached back, grabbed his foot, and pulled him back inside. Stoney, wincing in pain from aggravating his arrow wound, got down on all fours to find the laser pistol, which he had dropped. The creature charged them again from the rear, hitting them so hard that Kellan feared the Float would be tipped over. Stoney found the laser pistol, braced his arm on the seat back, and fired at the creature that was charging them yet again. The beast fell, and its death wail dispersed the other animals from immediately behind the Float. "I think I bought us some space," he shouted to Kellan.

"Good because I think we are going down." The Float was losing speed and unable to maintain its three-foot cruising height. Kellan worked the throttle desperately and slammed his hand against the dashboard in frustration. The Float continued to lose speed and height. It bounced off the ground, then skidded to a stop in the tall grass as the creatures continued to gallop past them.

"What the hell do we do now?" asked Stoney while he kept the laser aimed behind them.

At first Kellan thought that their situation was hopeless, that he and Stoney would be trampled to death, and the android broken into thousands of pieces. Then he had an idea. "Let's overturn the Float and get under it," he shouted. "Stoney keep the creatures away from us. Bellycold, help me out."

Following Kellan's lead, the heavy robot stood on one edge of the Float and rocked it back and forth. Meanwhile Stoney had to shoot another creature, which squealed and fell dead a few feet from them. The Float was rocking back and forth like a child's seesaw, and when it reached the point where it was about to tip over completely, Kellan shouted for Stoney to join them. Stoney's additional weight was enough to finally flip the vehicle, which came down over them, battering both Kellan and Stoney, and making a clanking sound when it hit the android's head. As they huddled in the hollow of the vehicle's passenger compartment, the strange horned beasts continued to run past them. One animal brushed up against the Float, then a second tried to cross over it, stumbled, and fell on top it. All they could do underneath was wait it out.

* * *

Karina Hudson could hardly believe her eyes. There on the plains below their shuttlecraft were thousands of what she thought were either gigantic beetles or roaches. They were peacefully grazing on the tall yellow grass while a few hundred yards beyond them the carcass of one of their number was being picked over by a pack of dogs. The Float beacon she was tracing was coming from down there somewhere, but exactly where she could not tell. As the shuttle began a slow circle over the area, she noticed a Float overturned on the plain. "There's been an accident," she said to the pilot, pointing down below to the wreckage.

The shuttle landed, and when Hudson exited with several members of her security team, she saw the Float being lifted up a few inches from the ground. Someone was underneath, trying to get out. With the help of Hudson's team, the Float was flipped over and onto its bottom, revealing Kellan and Stoney, battered and shabby looking but otherwise okay, and the robot Bellycold. As they stood up and dusted themselves off, Hudson made the mistake of asking the trio what happened. All three began talking at once, describing in animated fashion their harrowing experiences, repeating the basics of the story several times but each time adding additional details. Stoney pointed to his leg and talked about being shot with an arrow. Bellycold repeated his lion imitation.

Hudson allowed them to continue to unwind as they walked to the shuttle, and once on board, she gave Kellan and Stoney food and water. When they were settled down, she asked to speak to Kellan privately, and they walked to seats away from the others at the back of the craft. "Caitlin Cormack sends her regards," Hudson began.

Kellan raised his eyebrows at the mention of her name. He had been so absorbed in his adventures on Dahai that he had not even thought of Caitlin in days. "How is she?" he asked.

"Fine." Hudson hesitated. "There is no way to cushion what I'm about to say; so let me say it straight out. I'm afraid you are going to have to make a choice and don't have much time to do it in." Kellan listened with interest but could not have anticipated how big a choice it was. "The Asturians are—shall we say—withdrawing. They are returning home across The Void."

That seemed impossible. "When?"

"Almost immediately. But you'll have a few hours to decide. As an Asturian, you can go with them, or as a SED-Corp employee, you can choose to be part of the settlement we've started here. I'll make the same offer to Gordon Stoney."

Kellan could hardly believe what he was hearing and asked Hudson to repeat it all, which she did. As the shuttle prepared to take off, she left him alone to consider the two options; then Hudson explained the situation to Stoney, who said unequivocally that he was going home.

In some ways Kellan thought this would be an easy decision to make, but as he considered the pluses and minuses of staying and going, he realized that his decision would be a difficult one.

The fact that Caitlin, through Hudson, presented the choices so plainly and objectively without trying to persuade him to stay on Dahai confirmed what he already knew, that Caitlin's job was her life and that he should make his decision irrespective of her. And she was right. They were wonderful company for each other on Imrada and would always have great affection for each other, but their lives were not intertwined.

For three years, he had been trying to go home—when he was on the moon base, on Imrada, and during the voyage across The Void. That had been his goal for too long to suddenly change it in only an hour or two. This was not his world, and he wanted to see Asturias again, see his family and friends, sit on the front porch and drink beer with Miles, go back to the rundown amusement park, and find out whatever happened to Auburn.

Of course, home would not be the same, not after what he had seen and done and learned in the intervening years.

As for Dahai and the rest of this new world, despite the dangers he had encountered here, he loved it. He never tired of looking at its lavender sky and was fascinated by its strange animal life, even if some of it almost trampled him. He was also intrigued by the humans on Dahai, especially by the boy who said he was both Nuzalu and Udta, and he wondered if there were more stories like that. He would like to know more about the Dahaians he had met and to search for other civilizations on this world.

And he might never get another chance to do so.

He had signed on for another year with Dreyer. Why not see the contract to its end? There would be other flights home. There had to be, in a few months or a year. This new world was just beginning to be explored. Eventually it would be a routine commercial destination.

So he made a decision that only a few days before he would not have dreamed of making. He would stay rather than take the first available flight home—although he still had several hours to change his mind.

Bellycold walked back to the rear compartment of the shuttle and sat next to Kellan, who affectionately slapped the android on the shoulder.

"Thanks," said Kellan. "You saved my life. Without you we would never been able to flip over the Float."

Bellycold nodded his acceptance of Kellan's thanks. "We're even now," the android answered.

"Even?" asked Kellan, searching his memory for a service he might have performed for the android.

"Sure. You rescued me from a derelict ship. Remember?"

Kellan momentarily dropped into a reverie. "No wonder I forgot," he said, his eyes closed as though he were reliving the incident. "That was a lifetime ago."